No Game for a Dame

D0937484

M. Ruth Myers

Cover design by Alan Raney

Published by Tuesday House

ISBN-10:1467957976
ISBN-13: 978-1467957977

Printed in the United States of America

DEDICATION

For
JoAnn Hague, Lee Huntington and Sandra Love,
Fine writers and peerless friends

and in memory of
Mavourneen Cross Flynn Parsons
and Florence McCaslin Mullis,
rooming house "girls"
who went on to long careers as teachers

ACKNOWLEDGMENTS

Thanks to Jessica and Chris, without whose help this book
would never have come to fruition;
to Suzanne Clauser
for her insightful editorial comments;
to William J. (Bill) MacMillan
for sharing boyhood vignettes
of life in downtown Dayton
and of music and restaurant hot spots
during Maggie's era.

Lastly, thanks to Henry,
who has patiently and lovingly
endured the ups and downs of a writer wife
for lo these many years.

ONE

The guy with the bad toupee strolled into my office without bothering to knock. His mustard colored suit set off a barstool gut and a smirk that told his opinion of private eyes who wore skirts.

"Maggie Sullivan?"

I kept filing my nails. "Who's asking?"

"You're bothering a friend of mine."

My legs were crossed on my desk. I have great gams. Sometimes I don't mind displaying the merchandise, but Mr. Hair wasn't my cup of tea so I sat up. I blew some filings off my pinkie onto the afternoon edition of the *Dayton Daily News* where a column predicted the French and the Brits would likely let Hitler have the Sudetenland. The wrong step to take with a bully, I thought, but no one had asked me. I made a couple more swipes with the emery board before I acknowledged my visitor.

"Lose the stogie if you want me to listen."

I saw his jaw tighten. He didn't like being told what to do. He looked around, saw the ashtray on the file cabinet by the door, and stubbed out his smoke. A top-of-the-line Havana by its smell, so the guy had money. Or knew people who did.

"Who's the friend?" I asked.

"Elwood Beale." He stood with his legs spraddled trying to look tough. Maybe he was tough. "Says you've been sniffing around asking questions. Mr. Beale don't like that. Him being a businessman with a reputation to consider and all. Could give people the wrong idea."

"I thought businessmen liked to advertise."

The eyelids of the man in front of me lowered to half staff. "People who stick their noses in things get them busted. Even broads. Woody thought maybe you didn't know that." Leaning over he planted his hands on my desk and gave a grin as phoney as Houdini's chains. "Woody treats girls right. Furs. Favors. Might take a fancy to a cute little brunette like you, smart mouth and all."

I picked the emery up and started on my nails again. "Anything else?"

I knew one of his hands would move, and it did, smashing the emery onto the desktop.

"Who hired you to snoop?"

"Maybe you came in so fast you missed the 'private' part of Private Investigations."

He lunged for my wrist but I was too fast. I stood up, balancing on my toes. I wasn't particularly scared. It was barely four o'clock and there were a couple of other offices down the hall from me if things turned nasty. All the same, Mr. Hair looked like the kind who might use his fists if he couldn't bully you, and I liked my nose fine the way it was. He stood maybe five-eight so he had me by five inches and about seventy pounds, but a punch to the gut with all my weight behind it would probably topple him.

He yanked my phone from the desk and ripped the line out of the wall, cutting off that help.

"Smart girl, huh?" he said heaving it at a lamp and missing. The phone cradle hit the wall. The receiver bounced off a table and hit my umbrella stand. "WHO IS IT?"

Presumably he was asking about my client. He dodged around my desk. I dodged the other way. I grabbed the umbrella stand and swung, clipping him in the chin. He staggered back against the file cabinet. With a sloppy jig step he just managed to stay upright against it.

"Beat it!" I feinted with the umbrella stand. "I don't give out names of the people who hire me. Come around here again and you'll be sorry!"

I was counting on my raised voice to make him decide against staying. After several seconds it worked. He heaved himself straight, gave me a murderous look, and stabbed a finger at me. "You're gonna find out snooping ain't no game for a dame." As a parting shot he swept the dime store ashtray holding his squashed stogie off the cabinet. He watched it shatter. Then he turned and left.

His toupee had slipped.

*   *   *

For several minutes I sat on my desk surveying the mess and waiting for someone from one of the other offices to come check on the commotion. No one did.

Since no one else seemed inclined to commiserate with me, I decided to let a gin and tonic do it. The necessities were in the bottom drawer next to my handbag. I sat on the desk again sipping consolation and looking morosely at chunks of glass scattered everywhere, a broken phone, and dirt from a long dead plant that had gotten upended somewhere in the scuffle. I hated to clean. It was why I lived in Velma Zieman's rooming house instead of an apartment. The other reason being I couldn't afford both an office and an apartment if I also wanted to eat. I wondered how much it was going to cost me to fix the phone.

Mostly, though, I wondered why the case I was currently working had earned me this kind of visit. I finished my drink and swung my legs a few times and thought about it. Three weeks ago Lewis Throckmorton, owner of a company that sold business forms and office supplies, had hired me to check on his nephew who worked for the company and, as Throckmorton put it, had been "acting odd". The nephew, Peter Stowe, had too many new clothes lately, his uncle thought. He'd become distracted at work. Furtive, too, slipping out early a couple of times without telling anyone where he was going. Not that his absences were the problem. Peter had always worked many more hours than his paycheck merited. He was a good worker, understood the company bottom to top. Maybe it was nothing.

It didn't take a detective to figure out Throckmorton thought his nephew might be dipping into the till. Nor was it the first time a business had hired me to investigate one of their own. Naturally Throckmorton didn't want his nephew to know about his suspicions. That meant my end was to check what the nephew did after he left work.

In three weeks of surveillance, what I'd unearthed would fit in a thimble. He'd visited an engineering firm. He'd made a couple of trips down to the university. A couple of times he'd met a girl but I didn't know who she was. Then two days ago after work, as he was legging it uptown, a dark green Packard had pulled up beside him. Two men swung out, one from the front seat and one from the back. By the looks of it they didn't engage him in very friendly conversation. As soon as they pulled away, Peter Stowe dabbed his forehead with a handkerchief and turned and made straight for home. He'd looked over his shoulder a couple of times.

I knew a kid who sold newspapers a couple streets over and might have seen the Packard before, or could keep his eye out.

"Easy money, sis," he said snatching the quarter I offered. "Car belongs to Elwood Beale. Goes to Ollie the barber and gets the works a couple-a times a week. Has business over this way 'most every day."

So I'd talked to Ollie, asked about Peter Stowe. I'd played a hunch and mentioned Beale at the tailor where Peter Stowe had gotten his snappy new suit. For my money that wasn't enough to merit sending a goon to sweet-talk me. Not unless Stowe was mixed up in a lot more than his uncle suspected. Or unless the uncle was dodgy as a revivalist's offering plate and had lied about why he wanted my services.

I reckoned it might be smart to let what I knew and didn't know simmer. That left me with not much to do except get rid of the worst of the mess left by my caller. I got most of the glass from the ashtray and some of the dirt from the upended plant. I put the phone back on my desk with what was left of the cord wrapped around it. That would have to do until the Negro girls who cleaned all the offices came in tonight.

The warning from Mr. Hair had made me cautious. I locked up fifteen minutes early. Downstairs I slipped a note through the management's mail slot telling them an irate client had ripped out my phone. They'd probably think I'd told some guy his wife was cheating, imagine risqué details and maybe see about fixing the phone sometime this century.

I continued a few steps past the management office and slipped into the janitor's closet. Behind mops and buckets and ladders there was an old exit that nobody used but me. Since our building sat near a point where two streets angled together, the main lobby door and the one for deliveries both opened on Patterson. The one in the closet, if you opened it all the way, smacked the side of the neighboring building, which probably hadn't been there initially. The narrow gap between the structures went on to the alley, where an electric pole and couple of trash bins hid it from view.

I squeezed along sideways. The alley beyond was deserted. When I reached the street I made a couple of zig-zags to make sure Mr. Hair wasn't following, and headed for the two storey white rooming house where I hang my powderpuff.

TWO

Dirty laundry can land you in trouble when you least expect it.

Mrs. Z had swept, and her geraniums glistened from sprinkling when I set out for work the next morning. It was Thursday, so I had my usual bag of dirty clothes to leave at Spotts' Laundry. As I shifted the laundry bag I noticed Butterball, Mrs. Z's nasty orange tom, crouched behind a geranium pot, just waiting to sink his teeth in the next leg that came down the steps. His girth matched his name so he couldn't move fast except when he bit. I let my laundry bag plop down on his backside. While he tried to scramble I caught him by the scruff of the neck.

I'd gladly have booted him into the next county, but Mrs. Z thought the world of him. She worried whenever he sneaked out. The cat growled and kicked, trying to shred some part of me with his back claws, as I took him back to her downstairs apartment.

"You're the only one who ever brings him back," she said sadly as she thanked me.

Small wonder. The cat had left puncture marks in the calves of every girl in the house. I told Mrs. Z it was no trouble and went back out and picked up my bag of clothes.

I noticed the cop car down the street but didn't think anything of it. Patrols come and go in every neighborhood, even the quiet ones.

My DeSoto was parked three houses up and I'd just about reached it when I heard a screech and whirled. The prowler had come to a stop right behind me. Two boys in blue sprang out. One started yelling for me to drop the bag and put my hands up. My brain tried unsuccessfully even to grasp what was happening.

"Hands in the air!" he repeated. But I was staring at the cop with him, who had an undersized head like a pigeon.

"If this is your idea of a joke, Fuller, I'm not laughing."

"Better do what the officer says, Maggie. We're taking you in one way or another."

Fuller had made a pass at me once and I'd had to say no with a knee where it hurt him. He hadn't been a bit friendly since. Him I wasn't worried about, but his partner was young enough to be my kid brother, and getting twitchy. His fingers slid toward his billy club. I put down my laundry. My purse too.

What happened next made it personal.

The young cop grabbed the laundry bag. He looked inside the way someone had told him to. He did some half-embarrassed poking. He nodded at Fuller.

"Yeah. There's blood on some of them."

"It's there every month if you want another gander," I snapped.

He frowned. Got it. Almost dropped the bag as he blushed.

"She lies as easy as she breathes," Fuller said. "Let's get it to evidence."

Fuller shoved me toward the prowler. From the cocky way he walked, he thought he was scaring me. I played docile. When I found out what this was about, he was going to be eating his shoes.

The ride to HQ took under ten minutes. When we got out Fuller grabbed one of my arms and his partner the other. They marched me between them like a burlesque queen who'd stabbed a senator. A small crowd had gathered, more than you'd normally find on the station house steps. As the young cop reached for the station door a voice I recognized called, "Smile, Mags!" A flashbulb blinded me.

"Jenkins, you jerk!" I yelled over my shoulder.

Behind me the onlookers chuckled and hooted. Then we were inside where I recognized cops who'd worked with my dad. No one hurried over to say "hi". I was hustled into a windowless room with two chairs and a table. A matron came in to stand by the door and I saw the young cop hand my laundry bag to someone outside. This wasn't looking like something Fuller had brains enough to cook up, and I didn't think anyone was surprising me with an early birthday party. I wondered what I might have done to mash the toes of someone up the ladder.

Fuller stuck his head out the door and yapped at somebody. Then he closed it and leaned against the wall while he smirked at me. The matron stood with her hands crossed. The young cop shifted uncomfortably from foot to foot. By this time most mornings I was at McCrory's lunch counter into my first cup of coffee. I felt the lack of it. My head especially.

Several minutes passed. The door opened. Three men entered wearing cheap suits that screamed "detective". One, a lean guy with a perfect little nose girls would envy, spun the empty chair around, straddling it to face me.

"I'm Detective Freeze," he said in a tone that pretended cordiality. "Please tell us where you were last night, Miss Sullivan."

He was homicide. I knew his name from the papers.

"What's this about?"

"Your whereabouts?" he repeated. He'd put a folder on the table. It probably listed my age as twenty-four, my height as five-foot-two.

"What time last night?"

"Any time."

I'd been sitting erect in my best Catholic girl posture. Now I leaned back. I didn't like the feel of this. Freeze's eyes matched his name. They watched to see if I so much as blinked.

"Left work around four-forty. Walked home. A friend and I went down to The Oaks for the meatloaf special–"

"The friend's name?"

"Genevieve Tompkins. Ginny. She has the room next to me. Look, if Sgt. Hanlon or Sgt. Leary's in the station they can vouch–"

"I'm fully aware your father was a policeman, Miss Sullivan. What did you do after dinner?"

"A couple of guys we knew ran into us and bought us a drink. We got back to the place we stay around eight. The bathroom was free, so I had my bath."

Another uniform had entered the room and was taking notes. I began to wish I was chums with a shyster.

"And after that?"

"Palled around with some of the other girls. One has a radio and she invited some of us in to listen to Charlie McCarthy.

"Names?"

I gave them. The two other guys in suits slipped out and I knew they were going to check. Freeze took out his cigarettes, held the pack toward me, and stuck one in his own mouth when I shook my head. He scraped a match across the table and lighted up.

"Describe your relationship with Benny Norris," he said watching me though the smoke.

I shifted to avoid the smell, knowing damn well he'd mistake it for nervousness.

"Who?"

"Benjamin Norris."

"Doesn't ring any bells."

"Funny. He had one of your business cards in his pockets."

"I give out lots of cards. People pass them on, leave them on tables, in trash cans. Last year I ended up with a client who'd found one in a library book."

Freeze worked his jaw so he didn't have to take his cigarette out of his mouth. His eyes were stony.

"You were with him yesterday afternoon. We have witnesses. They say you two had quite a row and you threatened him."

I sat upright again, one hand lifting. "Whoa. Stop. Are you talking about a middle-aged guy in a mustard suit? Cheap toupee?"

"Hard to tell about the toupee with the back of his head blown off."

I let my breath out with unusual care. "Where? When?"

"Your relationship?" Freeze prompted.

Now that I was getting the picture I didn't like what I saw. It inspired me to be more cooperative.

"He came to see me yesterday. Never gave his name. Busted my office up pretty good."

"And you threatened him?"

"He threatened me. Said he'd bust my nose. When he started going nuts, I took a swing at him with an umbrella stand and told him to scram. I told him if he came around again he'd regret it. Something like that."

"Meaning?"

I sat back again, crossing my arms. "Officer Fuller could give you an idea." Fuller looked daggers at me.

"Someone called about a disturbance at your place yesterday," Freeze said sharply. "Officer Fuller noticed it in the reports."

"Officer Fuller check all the other disturbance calls that came in? Haul them in too?"

The detective's jaw tightened.

"Look. The boys you sent down to poke through my office will find a Smith and Wesson in a handy little pocket under the seat of my chair. If I'd wanted to plug this guy Norris I could have done it there. I'm guessing the dames at that sock wholesaler down the hall called it in. They didn't so much as stick their noses out before or after. I could have lain there wallowing in my own blood for all they knew."

Freeze stubbed out his cigarette. His pretty nose twitched.

"Why would a man you'd never met show up to threaten you and wreck your office?"

"He said a friend of his, guy named Elwood Beale, had a beef over me asking questions."

I thought the name had registered. I couldn't be sure.

"Questions about?"

"About Beale." I crossed my fingers mentally and hurried on. "His name came up in the course of a job I'm working."

I was breathing easier now. Alibis didn't come any tighter than mine for last night, which is when I gathered Mr. Hair, now identified as Benjamin Norris, had been killed.

"What's the job?"

I gave Freeze a polite little shrug.

"Nothing to concern the police. Family matter."

He wasn't too pleased. I had a feeling he was even less pleased with Fuller, though. Twice now he'd flicked an irritated glance in that direction.

"Anything else that you'd like to tell us?" he asked tightly.

"Norris said Beale spent big on dames he liked – furs and such. I know Beale goes around in a dark green Packard with a driver and a toughie." My client Throckmorton had landed me in a mess without so much as a hint, so I had no qualms mentioning the car. At best

I'd saved the cops some digging. My reward was seeing Fuller get another sharp look from his superior. "Oh, yeah," I added remembering. "He – Norris – was smoking a fancy Havana. What I saw of him makes me doubt he had cash for that kind of stogie."

"What else do you know about Beale?"

"Nothing. Never heard the name until a couple days ago."

Freeze drummed his fingers. He stood. "I'll be back."

Fuller and the young cop followed him out. My temples throbbed from lack of coffee. I'd had a meeting scheduled with Throckmorton first thing this morning. He wouldn't take kindly to my being late. After awhile I asked to use the Ladies and the matron took me. Fuller and partner were back in the swell little room contemplating their shoes when we returned.

I'd just about settled back in my chair when Freeze entered. No sitting this time; he tossed my purse on the table and paced.

"Your alibis check out. People saw you both places."

Fuller chimed in. "Those dames could have lied – you know how they stick together–"

Freeze cut him off with a look. A guy in plain clothes came in with my laundry bag held stiffly before him.

"Doc says there's no need checking. The, uh, stains are from female business."

"Gee, just what I told the geniuses who dragged me down here." I got up. "Can I go now?"

"We have to follow all leads, Miss Sullivan. I trust you'll be around in case we have more questions?"

"Yeah. Sure. How about having some of your boys drop me back where they Shanghaied me?" Freeze's expression told me I wasn't going to make his Christmas card list.

The crowd that had gathered to have a laugh at my expense when I got dragged in had melted away by the time I made my exit. Guys who knew me had thought it was all a joke until they learned I was actually being grilled. A few stragglers – probably Fuller's cronies – found they had urgent business elsewhere when they saw me come out.

I stalked down the walk from the station house ready to chew nails. I'd missed my appointment with Lewis Throckmorton. Even if he could still fit me into his schedule I'd have to put up with his pompous lecturing. And without my car I'd have to lug my laundry ten blocks to Spotts', which was inconveniently far from a streetcar line.

My head hurt. I wanted coffee. All because that s.o.b. Fuller had seen a chance to even scores.

I stepped into the intersection. A horn blared and a cop car rounded the corner, stopping smack in front of me.

"Fancy a ride somewhere, Maggie Liz?" asked a cheery voice.

Billy Leary and Seamus Hanlon were leftovers from my dad's era. Nearing retirement now, they'd been regular fixtures at our kitchen table.

"You guys drive like cops," I said leaning into the open window.

Seamus, who was nearest me, grinned. "Fuller's getting what-for up his backside and it's like to go on for a time. We figured no one would miss us if we ran you somewhere."

"You can put me top of the list of girls who want to marry you both if you'll run my laundry over to Spotts'. It weighs a ton. Make sure Sal gets it, will you? You're angels for sure."

With them solving that problem for me, I'd be free to walk a few blocks south and maybe solve a couple more.

THREE

Once a month and on special occasions I got my hair cut and set at Goldie's. That acquaintance plus two pennies got me use of her phone to call Throckmorton's office.

"Mr. Throckmorton waited as long as he could," his secretary told me primly. "He'll most likely be out the rest of the day."

Maybe it was true; maybe it was a brush off. Neither way improved my mood. The missed appointment made me look unreliable in running my business. On top of that, two incidents in as many days were making me curious why Throckmorton's job had landed me in the middle of a murder investigation. Five minutes after entering Goldie's I left and retraced my steps and went another block south to the *Daily News* building. I took the elevator up to the newsroom to corner Matt Jenkins, whom I usually count in my Friends column.

Photography was at one side toward the back of the newsroom. I knew some of the reporters bent over clattering typewriters, but I wasn't feeling chatty so I was glad none of them looked up. I went through the door to the outer room of the photogs' lair, the non-sacred part that held their desks topped with In and Out baskets and connected them via two windows to the newsroom beyond.

"Go tell Jenkins if he prints that picture I'll wring a part of him that hurts a whole lot more than his neck," I told a round-shouldered old guy named Stutzweiler.

The codger had seniority and a reputation for picking those assignments most likely to involve attractive women and plentiful skin. Word was he spent a lot of time in the darkroom when no one else was around and emerged with prints he didn't show. It led to speculation he scheduled private photo sessions that didn't involve a lot of clothing. He shuffled off through a heavy black curtain. It covered an inner door through which chemical smells from trays and dryers escaped. He hadn't uttered a word, which was standard for him. Made me wonder how he enticed girls to pose.

A few minutes later Matt Jenkins nudged the curtain aside and came out wiping his hands on a rag. He was just a year shy of thirty and already bald on top. His halo of frizz was more gold than red. Tossing the rag on a desk he put his fingers together to make a frame and pretended to squint at me through it.

"You oughta be in pictures, Mags. I mean it. What's Sam Goldwyn doing out in California when there's a looker right here?"

"If you pass that shot of me around to those hacks out there, I'll feed you your socks."

His wire-rimmed specs didn't hide the twinkle in his eyes. There was an altar boy sweetness about Jenkins which was mostly true. He didn't scare easy.

"I was hoping you'd be in handcuffs, though," he said.

"Gee, thanks. Getting grilled for an hour by a suit named Freeze was fun enough."

He straightened, his breeziness vanishing.

"Scout's honor? Jeez. Somebody called and said they were bringing you in. I thought it was some kind of joke."

"If you want to make amends, you can find out a couple things for me."

"Like what?" he asked cautiously. Friendship and work sleep in separate beds.

"A guy named Benjamin Norris turned up shot in the back of the head sometime last night. He'd come in yesterday threatening me. Wrecked my office. Find out who he was. All I know is he had some connection with a guy named Woody Beale."

As soon as I'd told him I wanted something, Jenkins had motioned me into the corner and moved to one side himself, out of line of the windows. Only someone passing directly by the open door and looking in would see the two of us talking together.

He was frowning now. "This connected to something you're working on?"

"Maybe. I'm not sure."

Jenkins had his arms crossed, which he did when he thought. He levered up from the desk he'd been leaning against. "Had breakfast?"

"No."

"Meet you at the Fox in fifteen minutes."

I stood up. When we got to the door Jenkins waved his arms in a shooing gesture and raised his voice.

"Maybe you should get a sense of humor, huh? But no – you'd rather march around with a chip on your shoulder demanding everyone kowtow to you!" he shouted.

I gave a flounce and stomped through the newsroom as heads rose and a couple of catcalls rang out. After the morning I'd had, the stomping part felt good.

*   *   *

The Red Fox Grill was long and narrow and dimly lighted. In front a grill and service area ran along one wall. A counter for eight or nine customers angled around it. That left just enough space to get past to some booths in back. The place had decent food at bargain prices. I was into my third cup of coffee and just starting scrambled eggs with buttered toast when Jenkins arrived.

"Figured chances were slim we'd see note pads or billy clubs this far past Main," he grinned sliding in across from me. He ditched his camera and gadget bag on the bench beside him. "Nice exit."

"Thanks. How's Ione?"

"Great. Had a scare a few weeks back when she thought she might be in a family way, but it was just bad fish. She just sold a story to *Harper's*."

His wife was as smart as they came. I was glad she wouldn't be knee deep in diapers.

"I'm supposed to be on my way to shoot bigwigs at the Engineers' Club, so we'd better get down to business," he said after ordering a banana muffin. "Didn't learn a whole lot more about your boy Norris than what you already knew. He was a small-time fixer. Ran errands for Woody Beale."

"Who is...?"

"We'll get to it. I didn't dare act too interested right after you'd been there, so on my way out I said to Parenteau, 'Hear you caught some big-time stiff last night'."

Parenteau was crime reporter for the early beat. I nodded. "And?"

"He snorted. Asked if I meant the darkie who got knifed out on West Fifth or the white sap who got popped in the back of the head. Told me if a low-life like Benny Norris was big-time we both worked for the *New York Herald*."

"And Beale?"

"After you left I groused to Stutz how you couldn't take a joke, that I'd happened to see you at the station and didn't know they'd stepped on your toes looking into a beef over someone named Woody Beale. Stutz did his usual decline-of-the-empire lecture on how young guys these days don't bother to learn who's who. I don't know what Beale's game is now – Stutz thinks he may own a couple of clubs – but back before repeal he was bookkeeper for a bootlegger."

"Book KEEPER?" I repeated.

"Yeah, accounts not bets." He began to shrug into his camera gear. "Got to run. I'll keep an ear open for more. But listen, Mags, be careful. It sounds like you may have stuck your foot in a mess. Stutz kept calling this Beale a gangster."

"Okay. Thanks. Say 'hi' to Ione."

"Will do. It's been too long since the three of us closed down a jazz joint."

"I'm game."

He popped the last of the muffin into his mouth, gave a nod and breezed out the door.

* * *

The cops had left my place midway between how it looked after Norris left yesterday and how it looked after I'd tidied it. At least the splinters of broken glass had been cleaned up, but that was only because they hadn't undone all the work of the cleaning girls.

The room felt stuffy so I opened a window and stood for a minute listening to the sounds that drifted over from the produce market on Fifth Street. Ordinarily the calls of vendors and the clatter of handcarts on brick lifted my spirits, but not today. Jenkins was right. I'd put my foot in something. But I didn't know what. Had my client lied about why he was hiring me? Was he as much in the dark as I was? Either way I didn't like it.

A train went by on the tracks that angled between my office and the market. I closed the window all but a crack and tackled the day.

The cops had found my .38. I wondered whether it was before or after I'd told Freeze where it was. I also wondered when I'd get it back. Just now I wouldn't mind having it where it ought to be.

Someone in the office around the corner from me, which turned out to be an employment firm for household help, had left a note inviting me to come use their phone if I needed one. I took them up on the offer at noon and three and again at half-past four. Throckmorton still wasn't back, at least according to his secretary.

Meantime I went over the notes I'd made on the Throckmorton job, jotted a few more thoughts, and shoved the file under my blotter. Some time ago I'd figured out that was the handiest place for my current case. Since I seldom had more than one at a time that necessitated more than a page or two, the blotter didn't object.

Just as I was opening the door to the street, I saw a dark green Packard glide past. At least I thought I did. In case it wasn't imagination, I decided to give it five minutes and see if a car like that came by again.

Five stretched into ten. I wedged the door open and leaned where I could watch through the crack. As I was about to give up, I saw a dark green car come past. A Packard. I waited until it turned the corner, then lit out for the trolley.

FOUR

The advantage to being a dame in my game is not many people expect you to be smart. I wore a good-looking hat the next day, pumpkin yellow felt with a couple of finger-length feathers. Good for giving someone the slip since all I had to do was duck in somewhere, roll the hat in my purse, and walk out unnoticed. Good for a meeting with Throckmorton if I got one, too.

No cops snatched me up as I walked to my car. I had oatmeal and coffee on time on my favorite stool at McCrory's. I picked up my laundry at Spotts' only half a day later than usual. As a nod to caution I left my almost new gray DeSoto in a different lot than the one I normally used when I drove. I was optimistic as I walked to my office.

In the lobby, which was just about large enough for a kitchen table, the woman from the employment agency on my floor was waiting by a roll-around chair with a carton on the seat.

"If you need to use the phone again, we'll be up in five or ten minutes," she said. "Willard's bringing in a couple more cartons."

Willard was her husband.

When I got off the elevator I made sure to sneer as I passed the open door of the sock wholesaler. The middle-aged priss who'd most likely blabbed to the cops about me threatening Norris screwed up her mouth and got very interested in the newspaper spread on the counter before her.

21

I went half a dozen steps more and nearly stumbled as I stopped to stare at the door to my office. The glass with neat black letters advertising 'Private Investigations' had been broken out. I moved toward it uttering words that would have won me a ruler across the mouth at Holy Trinity.

Even before I tried the knob I knew I'd find the door unlocked. Dreading what I'd see I pushed it open. For several moments I just stood looking. Then I kicked the umbrella stand. The wreckage facing me made the aftermath of Benny Norris' visit look like a butler's tidying. File drawers out. Folders dumped and contents scattered. Books pulled out of the bookcase. One drawer was completely gone from my desk; contents of the other two littered the floor. Even the picture of my dad in his uniform, my diploma from Julienne, and a framed certificate of commendation from my days as a Rike's floorwalker had been yanked off the walls.

Either someone was desperate to find something or they meant to scare me. Underscoring it with a silent raspberry, the snapped wire that two days ago had connected my telephone still stuck from the wall. I spun and stormed back toward the sock wholesaler. A pretty young woman working an adding machine on the counter blushed and dropped her eyes in embarrassment when I came in. The priss – still reading her paper and apparently in charge – took a quick step back.

"May we help you?" she asked warily.

"Yeah. Since you run to the cops with gossip faster than you report a break-in, you can let me use your phone."

She dodged sideways toward where it sat between her and the younger woman.

"It's not for public–"

Before she could fling herself on it, the younger woman snatched the phone away by the cord and shoved it toward me. She bit her lip nervously.

The older woman glared at us both. I dialed.

"Let me speak to Hanlon or Leary. Tell them it's Sullivan."

The adding machine clicked and ka-chunked a couple of times.

"Maggie Liz. Something wrong, is it?" asked Billy's voice.

"Someone broke in at my place. Turned everything upside down. If Freeze isn't curious enough to send one of his boys, can you get whoever's on the beat to pay me a visit?"

"Your house or your office?" asked Billy.

"Office."

"On the way."

* * *

Back in the office I turned my chair right side up. I eased myself into it, planted my hands on my desk and tried to focus on what was still the same. The desk was still upright. So was the file cabinet. So was the umbrella stand, although it had two dents in it now, one from where I'd beaned Benjamin Norris and one from kicking it a few minutes ago. In the four years since I'd hung out my shingle there'd been only one other time when someone snooped through my office. He at least had been polite enough to pick the lock. Now, in just three days, the cops had turned the place over, persons unknown had turned the place over, and a guy whose name I hadn't known at the time had torn the place up.

The couple who ran the employment agency noticed the broken glass and stopped to offer neighborly sympathy. It was better than nothing.

I went back to my inventory of things that were still okay. My typewriter was where I'd left it. Whoever had done the decorating last night must not have wanted a hernia from hefting a Remington. Which meant the blotter was still in place beneath it. Which meant . . . .

For the first time since opening my unlocked door my thoughts began to sharpen. Only half expecting reward, I slid my fingers under the blotter. The folder on my job for Lewis Throckmorton was still there. Since it held only two typed sheets, it was hard to tell if it had been disturbed. Still, I'd bet a quarter whoever dug through my stuff hadn't found it.

I was frowning over it, tapping my fingers, when I heard an explosive "Jesus, Mary and Joseph!"

The cops had arrived.

Billy Leary let out a slow whistle as he came through the door and surveyed my office. He wasn't much taller than me with a robust head of hair that was mostly white now. It looked good with his merry eyes and ruddy cheeks.

"Looks like someone must've wanted something bad," he said planting his fists at his waist and turning for a fuller look.

"Yeah. Maybe this." I tapped the folder in front of me.

"Which is?"

"Client file." The hand I was resting on it spread protectively. Billy frowned, but he got the message.

"Have to do with that business Freeze was chasing yesterday?"

"I'm guessing so."

I cast a questioning glance toward the cop who was with him, who looked maybe six years older than me. His rusty red hair was just short of brown

"Oh, this is my partner, Mick Connelly," Billy said interpreting my look. "He's only been over a couple of years, so don't treat him too harsh. Mick, meet Maggie Sullivan."

"Miss Sullivan." He nodded politely.

"What happened to Seamus? He was with you just yesterday." Billy and Seamus had been a team as long as I could remember, which meant before I started school.

"Seamus has a knee giving out. Been doing mostly desk duty for the past eight months while I showed boy-o here some of the tricks. Yesterday Mick was in court."

Connelly had begun a slow circuit of my room, hands clasped behind him, inspecting everything. He wasn't a large man, five-ten or eleven, medium build, yet something about his presence made the room feel small. He moved soundlessly, a cat alert for prey. I tried to ignore his prowling.

"Freeze fill you in on anything?" I asked Billy.

He shook his head. "Saw him on the way out, told him you'd had a break-in. He said let him know if we found anything. His lads have other fish frying this morning. Had another big ticket burglary at a business last night."

I nodded. There had been a string of break-ins at businesses in the last month or so. Times were still hard even though FDR's New Deal was putting people back to work.

"Okay. I'll start with what I didn't tell Freeze."

Connelly paused and turned his head to listen. Billy straightened my overturned client chair and sat down.

"You ever hear of a fellow named Peter Stowe? Works for a place on Zeigler that sells stationery, paper goods, business forms. Seems clean as a whistle."

Billy shook his head and looked at his partner who gave a negative, then bent to study the books tossed onto the floor. Was he reading the damn titles? It felt almost like I was standing there in a swim suit. I forced my attention back to Billy's familiar face.

I told them I'd been hired to do a background check without telling who hired me; that the name Elwood Beale had come up without telling how; that I'd asked some questions and Norris had turned up warning me to keep my nose out.

"I got the idea Norris worked for Beale," I concluded. "But I know zero about who Beale is or what he does." I looked carefully at Billy. He looked back. I wouldn't ask him to find out for me just as he hadn't asked to see the folder on my investigation. We both knew it.

Connelly looked up from perusing my books. "Squad's not likely to send anyone to check these for fingerprints, seeing as how there's no murder or major theft involved. Want me to put these back on the shelves?"

My defenses started to raise. This was my place. Nobody touched things but me. Then my brain reminded me how long straightening up was likely to take.

"Suit yourself." My dad's voice chided me for not being more gracious.

"Any way to guess when your visitors might have been here? Anyone work late?" Billy asked tugging his lip and eyeing me curiously.

"Only one I've known to be here at night is the salesman with the locked office nearest the elevator. But that's only been Fridays, and only if he got off the road late."

"Night watchman?"

"Comes on at eleven. Spends most of his time downstairs in the back room playing cards. Two Negro girls come in to clean around seven. They'd go nervous with you just because you're cops, but they like me. I did one a favor. Let me talk to them. I'll fill you in if there's anything interesting."

Billy looked at his partner, who shrugged. "We can write it up that they'll be questioned when available."

26

"My money's on the watchman being too deep in his card game to hear anything," I said.

"And you're sure nothing's missing?" Connelly shelved the last of the books with a hand that hefted four at once.

"Only a pint of gin that was two-thirds full." Did he take me for a bimbo who wouldn't know if something was missing from her own office?

Billy pulled a face, standing and preparing to leave. "We'll ask around, pay a visit to the night watchman. But I don't like you getting mixed up in something like this, Maggie Liz. Your dad wouldn't either. Smart as you are, you'd make a fine teacher–"

"If you're worried about me, how about telling Freeze to give my piece back," I interrupted.

He sniffed and jammed his hat on his head. "And it's welcome you are."

Connelly followed him out, pausing to give the mere suggestion of a bow. His face was impassive.

"Ravishing hat, Miss Sullivan."

I reached up to discover I'd never removed it.

Ravishing?

What the hell did he mean by that?

FIVE

The prospect of putting my office together again so soon after I'd cleaned up from Norris stuck in my craw. So did bobbing around like a cork tossed into a barrel of something I couldn't identify. It was almost mid-morning and phoning to see if Throckmorton was in would give him a chance to duck if there was something he wasn't telling me. That made a good argument for legging it over instead.

The office supply company he now ran had been started by his grandfather. It was big enough to have its own building, three stories of brick and on a corner with the business entrance on one street and a freight loading door on the other. Throckmorton's office was on the second floor. His secretary looked up from a stack of letters she was sealing and stamping as I came in.

"I need to see Throckmorton ," I told her skipping the chit-chat.

"He's in a meeting–"

I was past her and through his half-open door before she could finish. I planted myself in front of his desk with my fist on my hip.

"We need to talk."

Throckmorton was a blinker when you caught him off guard, which I had. His eyes worked a couple of times. Then they glared. A girl with a pencil behind her ear sat next to his desk, and they'd been pouring over some papers. His secretary was right on my heels.

"I tried to stop her, Mr. Throckmorton. She pushed past–"

"Yes, yes, Helène." He turned to the girl with the pencil behind her ear. "Leave these. I'll come up after I've looked at the rest of them. Helène – close the door as you leave and see that we're not interrupted."

The women scurried. Throckmorton was a short little guy but he'd puffed up like a banty rooster.

"Our appointment was yesterday, Miss Sullivan. I don't take kindly–"

"How's your nephew mixed up with Benny Norris?"

He blinked. Hard to tell whether it was the name or me cutting him off that had startled him.

"What? Who–?"

"No bells ringing? How about Elwood Beale?"

"I've never heard of these people, and this intrusion–"

"Any idea why people you've never heard of would threaten your nephew?"

He sank back. All the air went out of him. There was a chair in front of his desk I sat down uninvited.

"Threaten!" He repeated it so softly the outrush of air disturbed his tidy gray mustache. "Oh dear. Oh my. "

His distress seemed genuine enough. Yet from the beginning there'd been something briskly guarded about him. He told me what he wanted to but not a lot more.

Nudging someone when they were worried was a fine way to get them to spill. I sat back and crossed my legs.

"Beale and one of his bodyguards stopped your nephew on the street the other day. It was clear they were having words and it wasn't too friendly. Peter looked pretty shook up when they left. I found out Beale's name and asked about him a couple of places. Next thing I know, a guy named Benny Norris, who's Beale's errand boy, shows up to warn me away. He rips my phone out, among other not-so-nice moves. That night he winds up with a couple of slugs in the back of his head. The cops haul me in to grill me about it – which is where I was yesterday. Don't worry. I didn't mention your name. Peter's either."

Throckmorton stroked nervously at his mustache. He stared at the desktop.

"It's not possible. Peter's not that sort."

"Somebody broke into my office last night, turned everything inside out. Hunting something to do with this unless I miss my guess. You sure there's nothing you forgot to tell me when you hired me?"

He straightened indignantly. "That's preposterous!" Behind his wide desk with its leather blotter and polished brass fixtures he looked scared as a lost child. He avoided my eyes.

"I – just knew Peter was acting strangely. As I said. He seemed to have something on his mind. And the fancy clothes...." As his voice dwindled he bestowed a stiff nod. "Very well. It did occur to me he might be involved with, well, the wrong kind of woman."

"Or have his hand in the till?"

He swallowed. I leaned forward, trying to make sure he grasped the seriousness of whatever was going on. He understood bookkeeping forms and carbon paper; orders and deliveries. Most likely he had no inkling of a world where greed made even good people stupid, and men killed each other.

"We're talking about murder, and something crooked enough and worth enough to commit murder. No matter how your nephew got involved, he's in the middle now, and it could get him killed. You hired me to find out what he's been up to. This is just the first whiff–"

A couple of quick raps sounded on his office door almost as it opened.

"Here are those order inventories– Oh! Excuse me!" A flaxen haired girl with wide blue eyes gestured awkwardly with the ledger she held. The blues swung toward me for a couple of seconds, staring, and then back to Throckmorton. She was biting her lip so hard I expected to see blood. "I'm sorry, sir! You said you wanted these right away. And Miss Abbott was in the hall showing a delivery—"

"Just put them there, Miss Taylor." Throckmorton gestured irritably toward a basket on his desk.

The girl's hand shook as she obeyed. Giving me another once-over she hurried out. Poor kid. Throckmorton would probably rake her over the coals. After the door closed we both were silent a moment.

"I'm game to keep looking into this," I resumed. "But there's no telling where it could lead and you may not like what I learn."

"I have to know."

"The cops might find out faster—"

"No. Not unless it becomes absolutely necessary. Peter's...." His chin lifted. "He was only nine when his parents died and he came to live with us. He's more than a nephew. I ... think of him more as a son, I suppose."

The words sounded stuffy. Either that or Throckmorton was laying it on pretty thick. "So this is hard," I said.

"It is."

"What exactly does he do in the business?"

Throckmorton spread his hands. "Everything. Technically he's supervisor of business maintenance. He's in charge of making sure everyone's satisfied with our service as well as our products. He makes regular contact with a number of our customers and suppliers, keeps his eyes and ears open for areas where we might improve; pays attention to trends, new products, things people wish they had that no one's come up with yet. He even rides along with our delivery people twice a week or so just to make sure everything's running smoothly. It also allows him to note any changes by regular customers that suggest adjustments we might want to make – for their sake or ours."

Throckmorton sounded proud as he reeled it off. For the first time since we'd met he seemed to relax.

"He sits in on meetings with sales, advertising, purchasing, even maintenance. I value his comments, though he's always reluctant to make them." He ran his fingers down some of the paperwork he'd been looking at when I came in. "Since I have no son to step into my shoes, I'm hoping he'll take over the business one day. Keep it in the family."

"He get involved in accounting?"

"No, that's my daughter's department." He squirmed in his chair. "She wanted a role in the business, and until she marries I see no harm in it. She's quite good, actually."

* * *

I left Throckmorton's office with new possibilities skipping around in my brain. His own daughter – only daughter, I was guessing – was interested in the business, involved in it, yet he planned to turn it over to his nephew. I wondered how she felt about that.

Odds were it had never occurred to Throckmorton his daughter and nephew could be on the fiddle together. They'd grown up together. They could be involved romantically. Or one could be using the other. Or they could have formed a partnership strictly for money. Or maybe one was crooked and the other, having learned about it, was trying to cover it up. Any one of those possibilities could come served with a side of blackmail.

I came out the front door of Throckmorton's office so deep in thought I'd have been easy prey for anyone wanting to jump me. As I passed an arch sheltering the door of the neighboring building the corner of my eye caught a blur of motion.

"I need to talk to you. About - about Peter Stowe," said the nervous blue-eyed girl who'd blundered into Throckmorton's office. Her hands wanted pockets they could shove into. Instead they were tightly curled. As she fell into step with me she flung a look over her shoulder. "Not now. I have to get back."

"You know a place called Finn's?" I asked.

She shook her head.

"Respectable little joint. A girl can have a beer there without being bothered." I told her how to find it. "I'll be there when you get off work."

She swallowed and nodded. "Sometime after half past five." She spun and fled.

Skittish as she was, I wondered if she'd show.

SIX

The super in charge of our building had three-day old breath and a personality that matched. I got off the elevator and saw him heading toward it from the general vicinity of my office. He noticed me and stopped, crossing his arms to show his authority.

"You're going to pay to replace that glass," he announced.

"Hey, thanks for your concern about my losses," I said. "Maybe if your so-called watchman got up from his card game now and then and actually walked his rounds, you wouldn't have hooligans breaking in. Or doesn't the rent we pay here cover frills like security?"

His face turned red. It didn't make him any handsomer. Throckmorton had told me to put any costs for repairs on his bill, so I wasn't overly concerned about the door. It was true about the watchman, though, and since I'd put a few hundred miles on my own feet making rounds as a floorwalker, I didn't think much of shirkers.

"I'm thinking your rent needs to increase," the super said sourly. "This here's a respectable building. Never was any trouble before you moved in. Now we got police all over two days in a row. Brawls. Break-ins—"

"The rent in this dump's already overpriced. That's why you've had two spots sitting vacant the last six months. Tell that poor excuse for a night watchman you're docking him for the door repairs. Better still, give him his walking papers." I marched past him. "And I want my phone working again by the end of the day or I can see to it there are cops here every day of the week."

I opened my office door, which I'd made the grand gesture of locking in spite of its missing glass. The super was still standing with his arms crossed, but his glare was slipping.

While I'd been out, something new had appeared in my office. I noticed it in spite of the scattered files and a few things still lying upside down. A large manilla envelope lay part way off one corner of my desk. Either someone had jimmied my lock again, or they'd lobbed the envelope through the hole that currently constituted the top half of my door. Given its tenuous perch, I suspected the latter. I bent over it, recognized the tidy lettering scribbled across one corner, and skewed my mouth.

See you're finally redecorating.
Very modern.
This will add some pizzazz.

It didn't take the initials to tell me who it was from. When I opened it, I found exactly what I expected. There in a glossy eight-by-ten was me being muscled into police headquarters by Fuller and the younger cop. Some day I might even put it on my wall.

* * *

Finn's wasn't an old place, but it felt like it. The scarred wood tables shone with polishing, as did the chairs which mostly didn't match. An L-shaped bar ran along one wall. The only brass at the bar was the foot rail. The only decoration was a few framed photographs here and there on the walls, old people in front of thatched cottages mostly, although one was of three barefoot kids and another showed a flock of sheep filling an unpaved lane as they came toward the camera. Somebody had said that sitting here was like sitting in County Clare, but I hadn't been there, or any place outside of Ohio, and maybe whoever said it hadn't either.

I sat at a table halfway back, facing the door so the girl I was meeting could see me. My guess was she'd never walked into a joint by herself, but there weren't many tearooms open this time of day. Finn's was far enough from her building that no one she worked with was likely to turn up, yet an easy walk to the streetcar line. I came here a lot at the end of the week. After the one I'd had, I was glad to sit in friendly surroundings and sip some good dark stout while I wondered if the girl would show and if I'd learn anything worth knowing if she did.

My stout was halfway gone when she finally came in. I noticed her standing just inside the door. She was clutching her pocketbook in front of her for support. Raising one hand I tootled my fingers.

"Sit down," I invited when she came over. "Any trouble finding the place?"

She perched nervously on the edge of the chair and shook her head. Her hands continued to clutch the pocketbook, which she balanced on her knees now.

"I was counting on your hat to help me spot you, though, so I'm glad you waved. It's a wonderful hat," she added with a wistfulness that told me she meant it.

"Didn't think." I smiled. In the interest of playing it safe, I'd ditched the hat before leaving my office. "Could I buy you a beer?"

She looked down shyly. "I usually stick to lemonade, or ginger soda."

"They've got ginger. This time of year they have cider mixed with fizzy water, too. It's pretty good."

The novelty of it took her mind off her nervousness. "That does sound nice. I'll try that."

I went to the bar and brought it back. While she took a sip I got a better look at her. She had the soft-edged prettiness of a watercolor. Cheeks and lips uncommonly pink for a blonde. A sweetness about her that just about invited a man to break her heart.

"My name's Maggie," I said. "Maggie Sullivan."

"I'm Thelma." She swallowed, and it wasn't from the cider. At least her pocketbook had found its way onto the table. "I – I overheard what you were saying about Peter – about Mr. Stowe. I didn't mean to, but Mr. Throckmorton had asked for the inventories and Helène was busy out in the hall and when I saw the door was closed, I started to knock, but then –"

"It's okay."

"I heard you saying things about murder and Pe– Mr. Stowe being part of something crooked and it's not–"

"Hey, take it easy," I said. Her blue eyes were filling with tears.

"You don't understand! He wouldn't do things like you're saying. He's not like that. He's honest. He's good and he thinks about other people. He does! And when I heard you say Mr. Throckmorton had hired you to - to find out things about Peter – and that he could be in danger – Peter, I mean, I – well, I had to see what you looked like. So I came in."

Her tears spilled over. I reached in my pocket and offered her a fresh white hanky. She shook her head and scrabbled in her purse until she found her own. It was edged in lace. Delicate. Like her.

I waited until the downpour ended and she'd dabbed at her eyes. "Have a drink of cider," I encouraged. "You wanted to know what I looked like so you could wait for me outside?"

She took a couple of hiccuping little sips. When she looked at me the unhappiness on her face was laced with bewilderment. "I don't know what I intended. I just knew right then – when I heard – that's what I had to do."

I sat back and studied her. The kid had been scared to death when she blundered into that office but she'd done it anyway. Only one thing likely to make her do something like that.

"Are you and Peter Stowe an item?" I asked.

Her blush was all the answer I needed.

"Nobody knows ... and that's not why I said he'd never do things like the ones you were talking about. Anybody who knows him would tell you the same thing. He *is* good, and he cares about the business, even if–" She broke off and took a quick drink of cider in hopes of erasing her last words.

"Even if?" I prompted.

"It's just, well, I don't think he's as crazy about the business as Mr. Throckmorton and Miss Flora are. But he'd never do anything to hurt the business – or his uncle."

I nodded, which would let her think what she wanted, which was that I believed her. She wouldn't be the first girl to think the rat she was crazy about was a saint. I was guessing 'Miss Flora' was Throckmorton's daughter, but I'd delay the side trips until Thelma had spilled all she had to spill.

"That all you wanted to let me know about Peter? That he's a good fellow?"

Her teeth crept out on her lip, but they didn't bite down the way they had in Throckmorton's office. She was only worried now, not scared.

"He - he might be in some kind of trouble. But I don't know what – and maybe I'm wrong."

"Okay."

She frowned, still reluctant to be what she probably considered disloyal. "You're some kind of detective, aren't you?"

"Private. No connections with the police. Peter's uncle came to me because he thinks Peter might be in some kind of trouble too. Says he's been acting strange lately. Distracted. Jumpy." I made the last one up and I didn't mention the nephew's new clothes. It worked.

"Yes. That's it exactly ." She let her breath out and drank some cider. I gave her a minute. "We've been seeing each other since March. It's kind of steady now. We - we really get on." She blushed again looking shyly at the rim of her glass. "Like I said, nobody knows. It might not look right at work.

"Peter's kind of quiet, but a couple months back – not long after the Fourth of July – he picked me up one night and he was in such a good mood. When I asked why, he just laughed and said because we lived in a city filled with possibilities. He took me to a really nice restaurant – fancier than we usually go to, I mean. I said we oughtn't go someplace that expensive, but he said not to worry.

"After that he was like his old self for a while, only ... happier."

"Then what happened?"

"I don't know when it started." She frowned. "I just began to realize he was quieter than usual. Like he had something on his mind. Then one day – it was maybe three or four weeks ago – we'd met to have a sandwich after work. We were leaving the restaurant and Peter had started to open the door. All of a sudden he let it close and spun around, said he'd left something on the table. Then he patted his pocket and said he guessed he'd been wrong. But it looked, well, phoney. Like he'd been avoiding somebody he didn't want to meet."

"Someone from work?"

"I don't think so, because that weekend we went to a play at the Vic. After it let out we were bumping along with the rest of the crowd when a big car started to roll along next to us, quite slowly. Peter shoved some change into my hand and told me to walk on ahead to the corner and take a cab home."

"Did he get in the car?"

"I don't know. When I looked back I didn't see him. Next day he apologized, said he'd seen someone he'd been trying to get in touch with. After that, he always seemed to look around a lot. He never relaxed."

She was into her story now. Relieved to be telling someone. She gulped some cider.

"Monday ..." Her teeth scraped lightly across her lip. "Monday he was going to pick me up after he got out of this class he's been taking. Sometimes we do that. Just have coffee or maybe take a walk. But he didn't show up when he was supposed to. It was almost two hours before he called. He said he had a terrible headache. The next day when I saw him at work, his lip was all cut and puffy. There was a cut by his eye, too."

Monday. The day I'd seen the goons from the green Packard muscle him. But they hadn't roughed him up. A few hours later I'd followed him to the university and back and nothing had happened. When had someone gotten to him without my seeing? And why?

"Did you ask him what happened?"

"Yes. He said he got up in the night to take more aspirin and banged his head on the medicine cabinet."

Thelma didn't believe it. Neither did I. Her blue eyes were large with frightened pleading.

"Please – I know Mr. Throckmorton hired you to find out what Peter's been doing. But can't you help him somehow? Please. Don't let him get hurt."

SEVEN

My stout was flat by the time Thelma left. I got another one which I savored slowly as I walked my mind back through what she'd told me to see if I'd missed anything. Stowe lived in a respectable apartment building, so I couldn't keep tabs on him in the evening unless he went out. That meant the roughing up he'd gotten on Monday must have happened in his own apartment and whoever gave it had known where he lived.

For the price of a cider for Thelma I now knew a good deal more than I had when I'd left Throckmorton's office. I knew Peter Stowe had a girlfriend. She was a nice kid, not the floozie his uncle suggested as the cause of his behavior. If Stowe really was sweet on her it might explain his new clothes, even his distracted manner. But Thelma's account of his split lip confirmed he was in serious trouble.

Could be he gambled and owed someone money. Thelma had denied it, but I wondered how well she knew him. When I'd asked about his friends, she couldn't name any except Flora, his cousin. Thelma claimed he read a lot, mentioned his class again. In the end, I told her the best way to help Peter was to tell him to come to his uncle or me and level about whatever was happening.

It was going on six and Finn's was getting noisy. Comfortable noise. Customers who knew each other exchanging greetings, kidding and laughing. It wound around me like a friendly cat, soothing me after a week I'd like to forget. Sitting here was the closest I felt to being at

41

home. A month before my father died, I'd sold the house I'd grown up in to pay for his medical needs. Mercifully, he hadn't known. Four days after his wake I'd had to clear out to make way for strangers.

I was contemplating a bowl of Irish stew – the real thing except without lamb since it was Friday. All at once I sensed someone had stopped by my table. Expecting to see one of the regulars at Finn's I looked up. It was Billy's new partner, the one with rusty hair.

"Billy told me I'd like as not find you here. Okay if I sit?"

Before I could answer he dropped onto a chair and slid a squarish parcel discreetly toward me. "Billy thought you might be glad to have this back."

The shape was disguised but I knew without even lifting it my .38 was inside.

"Thanks. I appreciate it."

He was still in uniform. Tossing his hat aside he swept a glance at the surroundings. It reminded me of Jenkins' camera clicking, capturing details. Connelly – was that his name? Mick Connelly.

"I have information, too, the price of which is a pint."

"Tell Billy I'll buy him the pint."

"Ah, now." He had a fine mouth and one corner lifted. "Trouble is, Billy wasn't inclined to let you know whatever it was he learned about your admirer Beale. To my mind, though, if somebody picks a fight with you, you've a right to know who they are. So I did a bit of digging myself. It's me you'd be owing the pint."

Did I only imagine a challenge as clear as a finger reaching out to twirl a wisp of my hair?

"Yeah, okay." I didn't mind challenges. And I wanted the info. "What are you drinking?"

"Guinney if they have it."

"They do."

"I'll go," he said as I started to rise.

Finn, the pub owner, looked at me in surprise when Connelly spoke to him. I nodded to add the pint to my bill. Now Finn was going to read too much into that single pint and speculate about it with some of the regulars. I gritted my teeth. A party of four arrived and pulled out chairs at the neighboring table. Not the best situation for discussing crooks. Gathering my things I caught Connelly's eye and signaled I was going to move.

A few minutes later he joined me at one of the seldom-used tables for two against the back wall. As soon as he sat down the table felt small. He undid the top two buttons of his uniform jacket, the mark of a cop off duty. Taking a pull of stout through foam he nodded satisfaction and stretched out his legs. He took a minute to look me over. I ignored it.

"There's a file on Beale, as you might guess," he began. "I may still be one of the new boys down at the station, but I've made a few connections with some not-quite-upstanding citizens here and there who filled in more details.

"First off, Beale has a record, but nothing major and well in the past. During Prohibition he worked for a bootlegger named Tuffy Langstrom. Was his accountant, if you can believe it. Apparently Beale's a whiz with numbers."

So far, it matched what Jenkins had told me. Langstrom had run a big operation, Connelly continued. Trucks bringing booze down from Canada; connections in Detroit.

"A fellow who grew up with Beale says he was a mean little s.o.b. even in knee pants. Claims he wasn't just the outfit's accountant, he was a button boy. The one Langstrom sent to charm somebody and follow it up with a bullet."

Swell. Benny Norris had made it clear Beale wasn't happy with me. I was guessing Peter Stowe was in the same boat. And so far I hadn't heard anything that told me why.

"Word is he's got a friend or two at City Hall."

I looked up. Did that mean friends in the cops as well? If so I might have put my foot in it mentioning Beale's name to Freeze. Was Connelly warning me? I didn't think so.

"This bootlegger – Langstrom – ever get caught?" I asked.

Connelly took a pull at his beer before nodding. "Walked into some bullets when they raided the bakery he used as a front for his operation. Saved your fair city the price of a trial. Some of his boys got stiff sentences, but Beale claimed he thought the accounts he kept were for pies and cookies. He wasn't much more than a kid, so he got off with two years. Been clean ever since. Owns a nightspot called The Owl up on Main. Another place named Fanny's. Has one on West Third, Jimmy Joe's, that accommodates Negroes. Model spots all – or at least as good as joints like that are likely to be."

Owners of legit joints might make enough to ride around in flashy cars like Beale's, I reflected, but they didn't take along muscle. Legit guys wouldn't mind people asking about their acquaintances. They wouldn't send goons to warn people off, or rough them up. But I had no proof. Just speculation.

"Anything else?" I asked.

"Not that I learned. Any of this shed light on things?"

Forgetting how tough I was I propped my chin on my hand. "Nothing socks me in the nose. But thanks all the same."

Lacing his hands behind his head he tipped back in his chair. "Why a gumshoe? Why not a cop like your dad? The force has hired women a while now, Billy says."

I wasn't about to tell him about my brother taking off. I shrugged.

"Girl in our neighborhood had her husband run out on her. Then she heard rumors he might have another wife down in Cincinnati. It weighed on her, how she might have committed adultery. She... went mad. Killed herself. My dad said it might have been different if she'd had a private detective to help her."

"Jesus." His glass was empty. He got up. "Think I'll start a tab. They serve any food here?"

I hesitated. This was my place. Special. If I told the truth he might muscle in. Still, he'd done me a favor.

"On Fridays if you're in the know and early enough you usually can get stew," I admitted.

"Any good?"

"I was just about ready to have a bowl when you walked in."

"I'll get two then, shall I?"

That small twist of syntax and lift to his voice was the only hint he came from the shamrock shore. As I watched him make his way to the bar I wondered what part it had been to sound that smooth. At the bar he spoke to Finn's wife, who lit up with the sort of smile young girls got over matinee idols. She moved to the two-burner hotplate she'd set up. Finn threw me a grin, noting the two bowls and no doubt adding to the story he was concocting.

Connelly returned with our bowls and took his first spoonful. "Just as I like it, more turnip than carrot," he sighed. "So Billy and Seamus used to change your nappies, did they?"

I snorted. "The day Irish cops change nappies, the turnips in that bowl will talk."

Chuckling softly he wolfed down more stew. I buttered a slice of the sturdy brown soda bread that could be had almost daily at Finn's.

"So what county?" I asked.

"Monaghan. Little village between Carricktoe and Ballynowhere." He looked into the distance, face softening even as he made the joke. "Grand place, barely rubbing along. I'd had some training knocking heads. Figured I might be able to find work over here, send a bit home to my ma and the younger ones."

"And not a hint of brogue?"

"English school master. Beat it out of us." He took a longer than previous draught of Guinness. When he lowered his glass he grinned. "Where are the freckles, then?"

"What?"

"Fair as you are, you must have them."

"Well I don't."

His gaze wandered over my shoulders, dipping low across my throat. "Bet you're covered with them where they don't show."

"You'll have to wonder."

He cocked an eye while I bit my tongue knowing this time he was the one who imagined a challenge.

"You think Beale could be running numbers given his accounting background?" I asked briskly.

"Or craps. Or cards. Things I've heard about him, I'd guess he's got something going in the back room of those joints of his. Your office supply guy have a gambling problem, do you think?"

I shrugged. "No idea what his problem is, and that's the honest truth. I just know Beale's got a beef with him. Does Beale have an office at one of the clubs?"

Connelly leaned back from his now-empty bowl and surveyed me through narrowed eyes. "And why would you want to know that?"

"Might be useful. No reason."

"I've told you all I know."

I wasn't sure I believed him.

"What about the guy who got killed? Benny Norris?"

"Current theory is he pissed someone off. No shortage of suspects."

"Anyone report him missing?"

"Not so far. No family. Liked the ladies; changed them often."

"Dames don't usually pop a guy in the back of the head."

"Nope. Fuller would have saved himself a world of grief if he'd had brains enough to know that. And while you have a gun – and word is, better aim than half the boys on the force – you'd have needed to stand on a crate to pump the bullets in at the angle they entered. Not that anyone considered that." He drained his glass. "I'm going to get another. Care for one?"

I declined. His change of subject told me Connelly was through sharing information. But without intending to, he'd given me an idea.

EIGHT

Sometimes when you go fishing, you catch a duck.

On Monday I decided to fish.

The weekend had been uneventful. The girls who roomed at Mrs. Z's had been chatted up by cops to determine if I had an alibi for when Norris was murdered and were splitting to ask me questions. But the day I'd been hauled in I'd managed to make it home ahead of everyone else. On Friday I left Finn's late enough that most of them had gone out on dates, which meant I was able to sneak up the stairs to my room in stocking feet. Saturday morning I made sure the hallway was empty when I went to and from the bathroom. By that afternoon, just as I'd anticipated, much of their initial excitement had given way to other things like last night's movies and swains. Vague answers on my part satisfied their remaining curiosity.

Monday it occurred to me the same trick that put Beale on my trail in the first place might work again to my advantage. After noting with satisfaction that I once more had a working telephone I opened some mail and told a man who wanted me to keep tabs on his wife that I didn't do divorce work. Then I walked over to Ollie's Barber Shop and peeked through the window. No guys with bulges under their jackets appeared to be cooling their heels there, so I marched in letting the door bang behind me.

"Which one of you ratted to Beale that I was asking about Peter Stowe?" I demanded. I reared back with fists on hips in my best one-foot-forward-bristling-to-punch-someone stance. Ollie and a junior barber, the shave guy and the manicurist looked up and stared, along with some customers.

"I thought we lived in a democracy," I ranted. "Freedom of speech and that. But I guess not, huh? Guess we have some sort of bolshie police state where I ask a question and somebody runs to a guy I don't know so he can send over a goon to bust up my office."

The bleached head of the manicurist bent quickly over her work. The others except for Ollie, who had a button nose and a beard that pranced along his chin in the shape of a W, looked here and there and lowered their eyes with various degrees of nervousness. Ollie tried to look tough but wasn't so hot at it.

"You're bothering my customers. Get out before I throw you out."

I snorted. "Rats run both directions. I got half a fin for anybody wants to tell me about Pete Stowe – or his pal Beale. Here's my card. You can phone or stop in."

Taking a step that made Ollie fall back several, I pitched a few of my business cards in a semi-circle. Most landed on the floor, one in the soapy manicure water and one on the belly of a customer who'd retreated under a hot face towel prior to his shave. No one made a move to grab one up. No one moved at all. That was okay. I'd cast the bait.

* * *

Heading back to the office I bought a pitiful excuse for a morning paper from the scrawny straw-haired newsboy at Fifth and Jefferson, the same kid who'd told me the name of Elwood Beale.

"Lookin' swell today, sis," he said flashing his dimples. "Fine as Ginger Rogers."

Smart talk from a kid not old enough to shave. I gave him my usual tip and the dimples widened. At a coffee shop a few doors down from my office I picked up a cake donut rolled in cinnamon sugar along with a mug of joe which the owner let me take to my place since I always returned the mug.

Before settling in to enjoy my treats, I took some precautions. Since plywood hid where the glass ought to be in my door, I left it open enough to see anyone coming down the hall. Putting my .38 in my lap I read the paper and enjoyed the luxury of my coffee and donut. Then I sat back and thought about something that had been nagging at me.

Why had Benny Norris been killed?

I didn't care that he had been, since he hadn't exactly gone out of his way to be my pal. Nor did I much care who'd pulled the trigger. But if I knew why he'd been popped it might shed some light on the business with Peter Stowe.

There'd been nothing in the papers so far on services for Benny Norris. Maybe the cops hadn't even released the body, though that seemed unlikely. I steepled my fingers and tapped them against my teeth. Calling Billy or Seamus wasn't likely to get me what I wanted to know, and it wouldn't be right. I doubted I could worm it out of Mick Connelly. I'd have to go with the idea I'd hatched after he'd referred to Norris as a ladies' man.

I got my pencil out and dialed. When someone picked up at Headquarters I pinched my nose together.

"Yeah, my name's Flo Norris," I said. "Someone sent me a note up here in Chicago said my jerk of a husband might be takin' up space in your meat cooler. If he had cash in his pocket I got first claim on it. The s.o.b. took every cent we had when he skipped out on me."

On the other end I could hear the scramble through papers.

"I'm sorry, ma'am. What did you say the name was?"

"Norris. Benjamin Norris. You got him or not?"

A brief pause. "I'm sorry. His body was released Saturday–"

"To who?"

"Let me get one of the officers who investigated–"

"How about just tell me where they took him, huh? Which cemetery? My boss just got out of his car. He'll kill me if he finds me talking long distance."

"If you'll give me your name–"

"I'll call back, okay?" I broke the connection. Fooling Freeze or one of his boys might not be so easy.

Half of what I wanted was better than nothing. It didn't seem likely that Woody Beale would want his name connected with a murder victim. If I could find out who'd claimed Norris, it might lead me somewhere, so I gave that some thought. Norris didn't strike me as a likely church member, and he wasn't in the echelon of society that got planted down at Woodland with bluestockings like Wilbur Wright and the Deeds clan. Since no one seemed in a hurry to take the bait I'd tossed out that morning, I decided to call a few cemeteries that had potter's fields and inexpensive plots. At the fourth place I hit pay dirt.

"Oh, hello," I said when someone picked up. "I just came in on the train from Minneapolis because someone called and told us my uncle had died, but they didn't say what time the funeral was, and I need to know how to get to your – your memorial gardens. Oh – Norris is his name. Benjamin Norris. I should have said...."

Apparently I sounded flustered enough to be convincing. The guy on the other end gave a grunt. "Norris. Yes. I'm sorry, Miss. The interment was yesterday."

"Oh, gee. My mother will be awful disappointed. She isn't up to traveling herself, so I came down to, well, represent the family, only now I've gone and missed it. I feel just terrible. I guess if I come out you could show me the grave though, right? I could maybe put some flowers on it?"

"That would be very thoughtful. My condolences to your family."

Now I'd have to gamble. I was betting Norris, with his cheap toupee and sleepy eyes, had been a ladies' man.

"Uncle Benny wasn't much on staying in touch. We didn't even know he was married 'til we got that call. And Ma didn't even think to write down her name – his widow's, I mean. She was that upset."

I paused to see if my gamble was good. The sound at the other end could have been a sniff or a snicker.

"I don't believe the lady who made his arrangements was, ah ... I don't think they were actually married. If you get my drift."

"Oh. Well, if she cared enough to bury him, maybe I should meet her anyway. Don't you think? Hey, maybe I could go and see her and the two of us could come out together. That is if you wouldn't mind telling me her name again. And her address. You've been such a peach."

* * *

I was sitting on the corner of my desk, congratulating myself on the name and address I'd just gotten and thinking it was too bad I'd never had a chance to go someplace like Las Vegas where gambling would pay better, when the call I'd been hoping for all morning finally came. The voice at the other end was female and muffled. Maybe by a handkerchief.

"I got a friend wants to know will you really pay half a fin to find out about that Peter What's-his-name and Mr. Beale," it said quickly.

I straightened up giving my full attention. "Yeah, cash in their pocket for something worth hearing. You need my address?"

"Nix on where you work. Mr. Beale's got eyes and ears."

"Okay there's a haberdasher on St. Clair three or four doors north of Fifth–"

"What's a haberdasher?"

"Place that sells gents' hats."

"Oh yeah."

"Apollo Hats, it's called. Faces west." I hoped she was writing it down. She didn't sound like a genius. "How's five-thirty today?"

"Make it six. My friend needs to make sure nobody's following."

"Six, then. I'll pin a red silk flower on my pocket."

NINE

The Great Miami River wound around the city of Dayton like a feather boa. I decided to walk up toward it to clear my head and think about what I'd learned that morning. Stuffing my coat pockets with a couple of Jonathans I'd picked up on my way through the produce market that morning I strolled out into a fine September day.

My gut told me I was finally getting somewhere on this job. Or at least I was following crumbs that could lead me somewhere. Now I needed to think about how to approach Benny Norris's lady friend. From the one time I'd seen him, I couldn't imagine Norris attracting women with money. That meant Mae Johnson, whose name I'd gotten from the cemetery guy, was probably working now and I didn't know where. At mid-afternoon I'd head over to her address. That would give me time to look around her neighborhood, maybe find out something about her, talk to her when she got home and still get back to Mr. Seferis' haberdashery to meet whoever had information to sell.

The air had just enough crispness to freshen my cheeks, but there was no wind to speak of. I cut over to Jefferson and followed it north until it hit Monument. In front of the Engineer's Club I waited a minute for traffic to clear. They said Orv Wright had a barber's chair in the building because he was so shy he found it easier to talk through new ideas with his fellow inventors while he trimmed their hair.

On the other side of Monument a grassy levee overlooked the river, protecting the city from floods like the big one they'd had two years before I was born. An old man and a little boy too young for school were barely managing to get a kite up. Not very high; it wasn't the best day for kites. It was high enough for the little boy to shriek with delight, though. I sat down on a bench watching them and remembering times I'd flown kites here with my dad. For several seconds I could almost hear his laugh. The sound of him playing his pipes. *Paidin O'Rafferty*. I polished an apple roughly on my sleeve and took a bite. It was hard to swallow, I stilled missed him so.

"Would you mind company?"

Startled, I looked up to see the girl who'd grabbed the phone and let me use it at the sock wholesaler's.

"Sure. I mean, no. Sit down." Lucky for me it hadn't been one of Woody Beale's boys who caught me daydreaming.

"I didn't mean to sneak up. I was getting ready to come down to your place when I saw you go out so, well, I followed you. I thought you might enjoy this." She handed me a paper wrapped sandwich and took another from the small cloth bag she carried.

"Gee, thanks," I said in surprise. "I'm starved, but I didn't think to go by the Arcade and buy something on my way here."

"It's just cold pork," she said modestly.

"I haven't had cold pork since I was a kid, and I'm crazy about it." I took a bite. "Delicious."

"I wanted to say I'm sorry about – about not doing anything when that awful man was shouting at you and throwing things. I wanted to call the police, but Maxine wouldn't let me. She said it would only make trouble for us."

"It's okay." I reached in my pocket and offered her the other apple. "How about one of these with the sandwich?"

"Oh ... thank you. I think this officially makes it a picnic, don't you?" She laughed, then put out her hand. "I'm Evelyn, by the way."

"Maggie. Maggie Sullivan. Does Maxine suck on lemons or what? She looks like a real pill to work with."

Evelyn made a face. "She's even worse as a mother-in-law. She and her husband own the business. Simpson's Socks. I married their son."

She was attractive. Dark hair swept into twin rolls at the top of her head. Cold cream skin. It was the wry intelligence in her eyes which set her apart, though.

"Lousy fate, falling for someone with a mother like her," I said.

She laughed again. "Well, yes. At noon I get away for a bit whenever I can, until it gets so cold I absolutely can't stand it outside." She was quiet a moment. "That ... man who was shouting at you. Why did the police come asking about him?"

"Someone shot him." I figured that was just about all the detail she could handle. She studied her hands and gave a nod.

"I thought it must have been something not very pleasant. I expect he brought in on himself, the way he sounded." We sat for a moment. "I have to get back," she said standing. "I'm suppose to pick up some carbon paper on the way. I hope we get a chance to talk again."

"Maybe when it gets too cold for you to escape you can bring your lunch down to my place now and then."

I didn't intend to say it. Somehow it just slipped out. Her face brightened.

* * *

Even though Mae Johnson had paid to have Norris buried she might be guilty of nothing worse than bad taste in men. Woody Beale could have someone watching me. I'd noticed a car parked by my place with a guy inside reading a paper. If Beale had someone on me I didn't want to lead him to Mae and get her in hot water. When I left my office that afternoon, instead of heading toward her place I drove south on Jeff, then cut over to Brown. I was pretty sure a blue Ford followed me. A few blocks later I pulled into Wheeler's Garage and pecked on the horn. Almost immediately Eli Wheeler emerged from his service area wiping his hands on a rag.

"'Afternoon, Miss Sullivan. That clutch getting balky again?"

"Still working smooth as butter, thanks to you. Could I borrow Calvin for twenty minutes? Pay for his time?"

Eli grinned and rubbed the edge of his ear. "Well, now, I expect he'd pay to ride around with you, especially on this nice day. You can have him for nothing." He gave his cheery laugh. "Eli!" he yelled over his shoulder. "Bring one of them sheets."

A beanpole kid with freckles ambled out. He was nutty for cars. A good worker, too.

"Calvin, I need you to drive me back to my office and drop me off," I said as Eli opened my door for me. Calvin nodded and put the much-laundered sheet on the driver's seat to keep it clean while I went around and hopped in the passenger side.

By the time we got to my building I'd explained what he was to do. He pulled to the curb and let me out as he usually did whenever the DeSoto needed work. I made a show of leaning in the window to tell him one last thing. He drove off. I sniffed the air and stretched and took no notice of the blue car that cruised by and parked half a block away. As if consulting my watch I went inside. I waited in the lobby a minute for good measure before heading to the janitor's closet with its unused door that for the agile of foot and not too portly led to the alley. Calvin was waiting exactly where I'd told him to.

"Haven't seen any cars go by out there more than once," he reported indicating the street.

"Good. Keep an eye out." I clambered into the back seat and lay down out of sight and we pulled out of the alley's far mouth.

TEN

Eli still wouldn't take any money when we returned. Making a mental note to stop back with a wedge of the cheese he and Calvin both liked and some fruit from the market, I headed back toward Union Station.

Mae Johnson's address was in a pocket sized area wedged between the tracks and the river. The neighborhood was down on its luck but holding its head up. Starched curtains hung at windows. Mums and coneflowers bloomed in front of houses that needed paint and mostly had been divided into apartments. Vacant lots here and there gave testimony to structures swept away in the Great Flood. Just west across the river was another neighborhood exactly like it except the residents over there would be Negro.

I parked half a block down from Mae's place and across the street. It was half-past three. For the better part of five minutes I studied the street and kept an eye peeled in case anyone had managed to follow me. By all appearances I was alone except for a young woman who came past pushing a baby carriage and leading a toddler. When they got the carriage onto the porch of a house down the way and went inside, I got out and made my way to the stoop of the house next door to the one I wanted. It was a single with no bell. I knocked at the door.

Driving over I'd stopped and bought an African violet in a pretty pot with a bow around it. When the door opened I extended the plant demurely.

"Miss Johnson? The boss asked me to stop by with this and tell you how sorry we are for your loss and see how you're getting along."

"You're looking for Mae Johnson? Next door. One twenty-seven." The house dress on the middle-aged woman was as worn as she was. "Didn't know she had family. Who died?"

"Mr. Norris."

"Her gentleman friend? Not much of a loss. Came around when he was broke, mostly. 'Least that's how it seemed to me." She was looking wistfully at the violet. I felt like a rat. "She's at work. Gets home around four-fifteen. Want me to take that for her? I might have to pinch a leaf off." She gave a tired smile. "You can start 'em that way, you know. Grow a whole plant. I have a couple I got that way. Back when I could get out and walk through a store. Now I can't leave my dad."

"I got another errand to run," I said. "I'll stop back. Looks to me like this plant could use some pruning, though. Why don't you take a couple?"

She took the pot with joy spreading over her tired face and removed two leaves.

"Thank you," she said shyly. "That's a real pretty one. Double blossoms. If Mae's not home and you need anything, stop back."

* * *

I killed time in a diner which gave me a clear view of Mae's place. Coffee and red raspberry cobbler bathed with cream helped. A little past four a woman with fading blonde hair went up the steps to the house and opened the door. Fifteen minutes seemed about right for a woman just home from work to take off her girdle and get comfortable. I waited, then walked to my car and got the African violet.

Mae's place had one apartment upstairs, two down, with a bell for each. I turned the bell marked Johnson and waited. After a couple of minutes I heard footsteps.

"Mae Johnson?" I asked the woman who opened the door. When she nodded I repeated the line I'd used next door: My boss had sent me, sorry for her loss, etc. She blinked as though bewildered, looked down at the plant I was holding out to her, and blinked again.

Mae had shed her working garb for a blue flowered house dress and satin mules with feather trim. She was no femme fatale, but she'd been pretty once. The years had caught up to her and her frame was better upholstered than it needed to be. Still, she'd taken some pains with her hair and had on a dab of lipstick that brightened her face.

"That's ... real nice. Thoughtful. Thanks." She took the plant and held it awkwardly. "It's – it's nice of you," she said again. "Would you like to come in?"

"I won't stay long," I promised.

She lived downstairs on the right. Her living room was tidy and kept up like she was. A couple of pillows brightened the sofa. An archway gave a glimpse of a small kitchen with an icebox. She put the pot of violets down and gestured me to a seat as a shaky laugh escaped her.

"Kind of knocked me for a loop, you bringing me this. Didn't think Benny had many friends, to tell the truth. I like flowers, though. No one's brought me any since I can't remember when. Who'd you say sent them? Your boss?"

I nodded and waited, hoping she'd jump to conclusions and mention Woody Beale. She didn't. I decided I'd better not chance it either.

"Down at the lunch place. Mr. Norris was a good customer. Came in two, three times a week." I tried not to think what a thug he'd been in my office and laid it on. "Nice guy."

Mae traced a doily on the back of the armchair where she was standing. "Yeah, he could be real good company." She looked up. "I just got off work. Have water going for tea. Would you like a cup?"

"I don't want to put you to any trouble...."

Waving off my feeble protest she went into the kitchen. She clattered around and returned with a tray displaying a five-and-dime tea set.

"How'd you know about me?" she asked when we were settled with our cups.

"Lefty – my boss – said Mr. Norris mentioned what street you lived on once when he was talking about you."

"Benny talked about me?" For a moment her eyes got moist. She shook her head to banish sentiment. "Surprised to hear it. He spent more time chasing floozies and propping up the bar at The Ace than he did coming here. Still, he turned up pretty regular. Sometimes we'd just have a drink here. Sometimes he'd take me out. Woman my age, that doesn't happen a lot. He – well, like I said, he was company."

"My granny always claimed we need to make the best of what we have," I fibbed. I'd never met my grannies. I was wondering about the joint she'd mentioned. It wasn't one Mick Connelly had connected to Beale. "Anyway, I just came over and asked around. Is how I found you."

Mae looked up from her thoughts and gave a wry smile. "I guess that's a good way to put it. Benny and I made the best of each other. Tell you the truth, though, I wouldn't have paid to bury him if somebody hadn't slipped the money for it under my door."

I managed to swallow my tea without choking. I looked at her with the curiosity I figured anyone would show. She laughed.

"It's crazy, isn't it? Could have knocked me over with a feather when I came home and found that envelope." She sighed and stretched out her feet in their fancy mules, contemplating the toes. Her voice grew dull. "It's how I found out Benny was dead."

"Jeez. That's tough."

"Yeah. Just some fifty-dollar bills and a typed note saying Benny was at the morgue, here was money to bury him. I didn't know he'd been shot 'til I went to see about him. Next thing I knew a pair of cops were standing there asking me questions." She hesitated; sent me a glance. "I didn't tell them about the note – just said someone at the grocery, I didn't remember who, had mentioned they'd heard Benny was dead."

Now I was in a bind. One I'd think about some other time. Right now I wanted to keep Mae rolling.

"Probably best," I agreed. "There'd have been all kinds of bother for you, them wanting the money and asking you who you thought sent it. Maybe even coming over and questioning your neighbors."

She nodded. "That's how I thought. And I honestly don't have a clue who sent me that envelope. Like I said, I never thought from the way he talked that Benny had many friends."

"Maybe it was the guy he worked for," I ventured. "Mr. Norris always let on how his boss was important."

Mae's smile grew skeptical. "Benny liked to make everything sound big, you know? I think the guy owned a couple of nightclubs. But all Benny did was run errands for him, and now and then tend bar. Maybe he did have friends. I mean if your boss sent a plant...."

"Or maybe somebody owed him money," I suggested.

She shook her head ruefully. "More likely Benny'd owe it. Got gulled a couple of times 'cause he didn't think things through as well as he should. Too sure of himself, if you know what I mean. But it's wrong speaking ill of the dead when here a month or so back he turned up and took me out for a real nice evening. Steaks and pie a-lamode and some dancing after. I could count on one hand the number of times he'd bought me dinner."

My ears were ready to fall off, but Mae was lonely. Since her chatter had already yielded one good-sized nugget I made encouraging sounds while she talked on.

"He was in the finest mood. Said some of the contacts he had were paying off and there were good times to come." She gave a small sigh. "That's how it was with Benny. Things were always big – good or bad. Last time I saw him he was mad as spit, snarling how he wasn't going to be made a patsy just because some muckety-muck in a fancy office building in Kettering was getting cold feet.

"He scared me some when he got mad like that. I told him to come back when he cooled off. Almost turned him down when he asked could he have a glass of water before he left. But I got it for him and that was that, and next time I saw him...." She looked at her hands.

"Life's funny," I commiserated. "Gee, I have to be going. Thanks for the tea."

"Sure thing. Thanks for the plant." She got up with me and we went to the door. Just before she opened it, I turned back.

"He usually came for our hash on Wednesday. We wondered where he was. Guess maybe that was the day he was upset, huh?"

"Not likely he'd stay mad that long. It was Monday night he came here. Just a week ago. Like you said, life's funny."

She watched from the front door as I walked up the street to my car. An ordinary woman who craved company, even company like Benny Norris. Because of her loneliness Lewis Throckmorton had gotten a lot for the price of the African violet I'd be putting on his expense account.

I hoped the two-fifty I'd dangled as bait for my next meeting would yield half as much.

ELEVEN

Rain blew in half-hearted raspberries onto my windscreen as I drove back across town. People were already lining up outside soup kitchens, as eager for half an hour of shelter on a night like this as they were for food. There was plenty of time before I met the "friend" with information to sell about Woody Beale and his connection to Peter Stowe. I parked next door to Mrs. Z's in the spot where Calvin left the car when they took it for servicing, got the umbrella I kept in the back seat and walked to the trolley stop.

Even though the ride wasn't long, by the time I got off I could feel the temperature starting to creep down. The rain had decided to fall in earnest. Fortified with the evening paper I took the back way into my building. The warmth of a gin and tonic seemed prudent to keep away sniffles, so I mixed one and put my feet on the desk, nestled my Smith & Wesson in my lap and read for a while. A previous client had sent me a check, so I typed a receipt to drop in the mail. At a quarter to six I left my lights blazing and paced back and forth in front of my window so anyone checking on me would think I was working late. A few minutes later I was in the alley again, this time following it a couple doors down and across to the back door of Apollo Hats.

The haberdashery sat on the opposite side of the block from my own building. Mr. Seferis, the owner, let me in with a smile.

"No customers," he reported. "I give my wife's uncle the bum rush, but him I glad to be rid of anyway." He chuckled.

It wasn't the first time I'd come in the back way at Mr. Seferis'. I'd helped him out once, and I'd ordered hats there for my dad. Right now I was having a cap made for Seamus' birthday. We chatted about it while I watched the street. I hadn't pinned on the red flower I'd told my unknown caller I'd wear. I had a pretty good idea who was coming to meet me.

The rain made watching easier. Customers weren't likely to shop for hats after work on a day like this. At five 'til six a man crossed the street and hurried past, his shoulders hunched. Two minutes later a woman with an umbrella walked slowly up the opposite side of the street and stopped in a doorway. She pretended to look in a shop window but the movements of her head said she was checking her surroundings. Six o'clock came and went. Just as I began to think I'd been wrong she left the doorway and walked quickly toward the haberdashery. Beneath her umbrella there was a flash of platinum blonde.

By the time the bell on the shop door jingled I had my back toward the entrance. As her heels clicked uncertainly past displays of hats, I picked up a felt fedora and pivoted back toward the window as if to examine it in better light. The woman's caution before she came in suggested her nervousness at talking to me was real. To make sure she hadn't been followed I watched the street a few more minutes while she gave Mr. Seferis malarkey about looking for a hat for her boyfriend.

When I finally turned, even though she knew who she was meeting, the manicure girl from Ollie's barber shop seemed startled.

"Figured you'd remember me well enough without the flower," I said.

Her tongue ran nervously around perfectly painted lips. "I got on the trolley like always, but halfway to my stop I got off and took another one back. As a precaution, like. Figured you'd pay me back the extra fare."

Her brashness was unbelievable. She stood to make a nice little wad just talking to me and she wanted a nickel for a trolley transfer on top of it.

"Smart thinking," I said drily. "Let's talk in back in case someone comes in."

We sat in a corner where we couldn't be seen through the open doorway to the shop, her in a dilapidated chair and me on a three legged stool. She undid her coat. I took two bills from my pocket, smoothed them out on an overturned crate and anchored them down with a fifty-cent piece. After fishing around I found a nickel and set it down separately. Noting the arrangement the blonde frowned.

"Woody Beale. Peter Stowe. What do you know about them?"

The tip of her tongue wet her lips again. Her hands clasped her knees.

"It was Ollie told Mr. Beale about you. Right after you were in the first time. I heard him call. Couldn't hear much of what Ollie told him except that some dame – that's what he called you – had come in asking about Mr. Stowe. And that you had showgirl legs." She giggled nervously.

"Why did Ollie think Beale would be interested?"

She furrowed her brows. I had a hunch thinking didn't come naturally to her.

"Well, it was a guy who works for Mr. Beale brought Mr. Stowe in the first time. And Ollie does that now and then – tells Mr. Beale about people. Things he's heard. Mr. Beale's a real big customer – gets the works three times a week. No great tipper." Her nose curled fractionally. "Ollie falls all over himself to please him."

"Tell me about Peter Stowe coming in that first time."

"Oh. Gee. Well, you could see right off that he was a gent. Nice manners. Kinda shy. The fella that brought him in–"

"The one who works for Beale?"

"Yeah, I forget his name. He brought Mr. Stowe in, introduced him, told Ollie they were pals and to give him the works, that he'd pick up the tab. I think it embarrassed Mr. Stowe, all that fuss. Like I said, he was real classy. Always thanked me when I finished his nails. Not many do. They just keep on talking to Ollie or somebody else like I'm just a door stop."

Now I was stumped. If Stowe was pals with someone who worked for Beale, what had gone wrong?

"How long ago was all this?"

She thought some. "Couple of months. He came in maybe half a dozen times. Then just like that–" She snapped her fingers. "– he quit showing up."

"Any idea why?"

She shook her head. "So there. I've told you all I know. Can I have my money?"

"In a minute."

"Hey, I've kept my part of the bargain!"

I slid one of the bills toward her. "What you've told me so far earns that. Maybe you need to think some more. Beale? Stowe?"

Snagging the bill with a polished red fingertip she began to pout. I let her. About a minute was all it took.

"There's nothing else to tell you," she wailed. "Mr. Beale and some guy he knows had words a week or two back, but that wasn't about Mr. Stowe."

"What was it about?"

She shrugged. "All I know is I was outside having a smoke – Ollie lets me take a break now and then if we're not busy. Anyway, I was leaning against the side of the building, having my cigarette, when this rich guy I'd never seen stormed in. A minute later him and Mr. Beale came out. They were arguing that way people do when they're really sore but they're too upper crust to swing at each other. Not shouting but you can tell anyway.

"The guy who'd stormed in kept saying something about an errand boy and how could they be sure the idiot wouldn't talk? Mr. Beale told him not to worry, but the other guy kept saying 'He knows too much ... he knows too much.' I couldn't hear what Mr. Beale answered, but it made the other guy more upset. Leastways he got louder. He said first the pigeon Al picked blew up in his face and now–" Her fingers snapped. "Al. That's it. That's the name of the guy who brought Mr. Stowe in that first time. So anyway this guy who was mad at Mr. Beale said two blunders was two too many, or something like that, and Mr. Beale told him he'd take care of it."

In the other room the shop bell jangled startling both of us. A woman's voice spoke. Then a child's. Very young footsteps pattered across the wood floor. The blonde across from me let out her breath but this sudden reminder of other people spooked her.

"I gotta go," she said standing abruptly. "You going to pay me all you owe me or welsh?"

Thoughts twirling with what she'd just told me I started to hand her the rest of the money then paused. "One more question. This Al who works for Mr. Beale, does he wear a rug?"

"A toupee?" She pronounced it as two equal words, 'two pay'. Her nervousness receded enough for her to giggle. "Nah, he's got a nice head of hair. Good looking, except for the scar on his pinkie. Dresses almost as nice as Mr. Beale, but the way he looks at people gives me the willies."

The shop bell jingled again and the pattering footsteps skipped out. I held out the rest of the money, including the nickel. She snatched it greedily.

"If Ollie finds out I talked to you, he'll fire me. If Mr. Beale ever did...." She creased the bills lengthwise and pulled them between her fingers a couple of times. Her gaze veered back toward the front of the shop.

"I didn't come in from the street," I reassured. "No one will known you saw me."

"Yeah, okay." She picked up her umbrella and turned toward the front of the shop. "If you come to Ollie's again, don't let on you know me."

"I don't even know your name," I said to her back.

Over her shoulder she flashed me a smirk at her own cleverness.

TWELVE

Izzy had been bringing me my morning oatmeal and my noontime sandwiches for four years or better. From eight in the morning 'til four in the afternoon she stood behind the McCrory's lunch counter taking orders and refilling coffee. If she got tired, neither her friendly expression nor the efficiency of her movements betrayed it. Her given name was Isabel.

"Did your gentleman friend get up courage enough to say hello?" she asked scribbling my ticket and putting it in without waiting for me to say what I wanted. On the rare occasions I got the urge for an egg and sausage I told her fast as I sat down.

"Gentleman friend?" I looked up from unfolding that morning's *Journal*.

"He came in yesterday and asked if a pretty little brunette named Maggie ate here." Sliding coffee to me she moved along to take the orders of two new arrivals just settling onto stools.

I frowned at her snippet of information and let the coffee knead my brain. Whoever was asking could be someone I'd met. Mick Connelly, maybe, though I doubted that one. More likely, it had been one of Beale's boys, which didn't strike me as good for my health. Or maybe the cops were still sniffing at me over the Norris murder. Or because I'd mentioned Beale and he was supposed to be off limits. That possibility didn't hold much more appeal.

"What time yesterday?" I asked when Izzy returned with my oatmeal and a large glass of milk.

"Right at four. End of my shift. Looked like he had a bank account." She gave an approving nod as she turned away to grab another order.

I drank some milk and added some cream to my bowl to keep the butter and brown sugar company. Having exhausted my cooking skills I mulled her information. A guy whose appearance suggested money wasn't likely to be a cop or anyone I knew. That left Beale himself, or one of his boys. But why?

Right now Izzy was swimming for her life in breakfast orders which wouldn't let up until shops and offices opened. I'd stop back later; see what else she could tell me.

Last night's chill had lingered. As I cut through the produce market it sharpened the sound of hand carts on brick. When I got upstairs a glazier was unpacking his tools, preparing to fit the pane of glass beside him into my door. His unexpected presence suggested I'd won my latest round with the building super, so we exchanged pleasantries and I left him to his work.

I hung my coat and hat on the rack and settled in at my desk with a nice blank tablet. Then for the better part of ten minutes, I sat clicking my teeth with a pencil. Unless I was missing something the size of an elephant, everything that had happened the last six days kept looping back to Peter Stowe. I asked questions about him; Ollie the barber called Beale to report it. Beale sent Benny Norris to warn me off and wreck my office. Norris ended up dead and someone broke into my office. It was at that point that things turned murky.

Presumably whoever broke in was hunting something they thought I had. But what? And why had Norris been murdered? Did it have to do with his visit to me, or to something else? His girlfriend Mae said he'd been flush a month or so back. And two days before he'd played tough with me he'd been mad because he thought someone wanted to make him a patsy.

Something about that burst of prosperity followed by anger began to wink at me from the edges of my mind, available but playing hard to get.

I switched to trying to fit the bits and pieces I already knew with what I'd learned from the manicurist. Judging from her reaction to my question about the toupee, Benny Norris wasn't someone she'd seen in the barbershop. He wasn't the one named Al, anyway. Turning my tablet sideways to give me more room, I began to jot down names in my cast of characters for this little play: Peter Stowe. Beale. Norris. Al. The "rich guy" the manicurist had overheard having words with Beale. I sat back and studied the names. Under each I wrote things that might be relevant.

Norris got a dollar sign, since he'd apparently had more money than usual, and under that the word *patsy*? He'd maybe known Peter, or known about him at least, so I drew a line between them to show a connection, and another line from Norris to Beale. There surely should be a line between Peter and Beale, but until I had confirmation I wouldn't draw it. Al worked for Beale and had also brought Peter into the barbershop, so there were two lines. Most likely he knew Norris as well, but again I'd wait for proof. Finally there was the "rich guy", who definitely knew Beale, and knew Al at least by name, which I decided merited a dotted line.

The glazier knocked politely, bringing me out of my concentration. He wanted to know what lettering went on the door. I wrote it out for him and came back to my list. There was something useful in it I felt certain, but like those tidbits I'd gleaned from Mae, it eluded me. I studied it and clicked my teeth some more.

The nameless "rich guy" was worried because someone knew too much and might talk. He'd also referred to Al's pigeon blowing up. I had a strong suspicion he wasn't discussing birds.

Beale had promised he'd take care of the matter. Was Benny Norris what got taken care of? Was a pigeon the same as a patsy? I didn't think so. And why send Norris to threaten me and then turn around and kill him? Why break into my office? What did any of it have to do with Peter Stowe?

I groaned. At the speed I was going, I'd lose a race with a turtle.

The glazier finished. I decided to go have some lunch. Then I'd track down a codger I knew who managed to stay about one step shy of being an alkie while frequenting most of the not-so-posh beer joints in town. With luck he'd be able to tell me how to find the one where Mae said Norris had been a regular.

* * *

The Ace of Clubs was the sort of joint that made you want to wash it off you as soon as you stepped inside. A years-old stink of tobacco juice missing spittoons and mingling with spilt beer oozed from corners where dreams had died. What few rays of sun fought their way through a dirty transom over the door met their death on the gummy floor before reaching the bar. I waited a minute so my eyes could adjust before I approached it. No brass here, polished or otherwise. Just a stretch of scarred wood lighted by two chintzy lamps, one at either end of a shelf that held liquor.

A bartender built like an elevator eyed me with more wariness than curiosity.

"You lost, sis?"

Anticipating I might come here today, I'd worn my brown tweed jacket. After parking I'd buttoned my blouse up like a church matron running for president of the altar guild. I'd fastened my best dime store cameo at the collar. My shoes were sensible lace ups.

"I'm looking for Benny," I said. "Benny Norris. He told me I could always get hold of him here. Has he been in?"

The bartender gave a mean-spirited grin displaying a gold tooth next to a gap where one was missing. "Try the cemetery."

I waited a second, then widened my eyes. "You mean he's dead? Oh, gee. My goodness. He wasn't that old."

Shrugging indifference he slapped a gray rag onto the bar with a hand the size of a phone book. His burst of helpfulness past, he began to work his way down the bar's length.

"Um, could I have a ginger?" I hadn't gone to the effort of finding this place to hear what I already knew.

"Beer, whisky, gin, seltzer, tonic," he intoned.

"Oh ... tonic then, if you please." Booze might stand half a chance of sterilizing a glass, which in this place would need it, but tonic seemed more in keeping with the role I was playing. I didn't intend to drink whatever I got.

He stomped around in what was possibly better humor and slid the tonic toward me. I paid, then toyed with the glass. I'd timed it to come in during the dead time that follows the last of the lunchtime drinkers. The only other customers were two men on stools about as far apart as they could get. By their looks they'd probably made a beeline in at noontime or a little before and would stay where they were till they slid off the stools. A woman with too much rouge on her cheeks sat at the only table. None of them took any notice of me.

"Dead, huh. When did he die?"

"Wednesday, Thursday. Somebody shot him."

"No kidding? Gee. He wasn't a crook or anything, was he? He'd said he could get my brother a job – said he had real good connections."

The bartender snorted. "Not good enough to keep his bill paid half the time. Good thing for me he got bumped off in the half when it was."

"What about Al? You know, good looking, nice dresser, has a scar on his pinkie?"

He showed me his gold tooth again. "Nice dresser, huh? You come to the wrong place."

I cupped my chin in my hand, damsel in distress.

"What about that pal of his? Has he been in?"

"Pal?"

The goodwill my untouched tonic had bought me was just about gone. I knew so damned little about Norris that anything out of my mouth would be a gamble.

"The big guy."

He looked at me blankly.

"Well, not as big as you, of course." I slid four-bits across the bar to him. "Come on, mister. My brother really needs that job. Maybe Benny's pal could tell me about it."

He rested a fingertip on the coin. "Big, huh? Mighta been Muley. He's kind of big. Two of 'em used to sit together sometimes. Have to come at night if you want to catch Muley."

I made a big deal out of sighing.

"I don't suppose you know where he lives?"

The bartender raised his voice and inquired. His three customers raised their heads and shook them. I wasn't sure they really saw anything or heard the question. Could be they were like plants, just turning automatically.

"Next time he's in, ask him to give Mavis a call." I scribbled my office number on a scrap of paper. "Oh, and tell him Benny asked me to keep something that I guess he might as well take. Them being friends and all."

I slid the phone number to him with another two bits. Maybe he'd give the message to Muley and maybe not.

THIRTEEN

I was getting tired of sneaking in and out of my own building. When I got back I went in the back door and brazenly out the front one down to the market. Some of the vendors already were packing up. Good housewives shopped early. So did restaurants that wanted to offer first-rate fare at suppertime. The wind bit hard. Pretty soon the offerings here would be largely cabbage and turnips, parsnips and sprouts, maybe some kale. I bought a Gravenstein and added a Winesap to keep it company. Back in my office I nibbled them both to the core while I worked on my columns of names.

When my telephone rang I was startled to see it was half past five

"Hello?" I said keeping my fingers crossed it was Muley hunting for "Mavis".

"I can tell you about Peter Stowe," said a pleasant male voice. "In fifteen, maybe twenty minutes I'll be walking my dog along Stewart between St. Mary's and the cemetery. A brown and white terrier."

The line went dead.

I shrugged into my jacket and grabbed my coat. Fifteen minutes. I could just about make it. Somewhere in my brain an alarm bell jingled. I stopped with my coat halfway up one arm and dragging the floor.

What if it was a trap?

Call and dangle meeting I'd have to rush to make and maybe I wouldn't take time to think. Was that the plan? Okay, I'd think as I walked. The spot the caller had named was public. This time of day there'd be plenty of people. What once had been St. Mary's College was now the University of Dayton. Students would be going to Mass, or maybe just coming out. Some would be leaving the library. Those who stayed in dormitories would be going to dinner. Those who lived at home would be walking to trolleys. People who lived in the neighborhood would be coming home from work, taking out garbage ... and walking dogs.

By the time I'd weighed the odds I'd almost reached my car. I quick-stepped the last half block, slid into the driver's seat and started the engine. Everything pointed to the meeting being safe, and I was about due a break in this case. I pulled into traffic, went half a block and cut through an alley to double around and check for a tail. Satisfied, I made my way through after-work traffic and headed south on Brown.

North of Apple the street was closed. Flares and saw horses marked an open manhole. I detoured into a warren of side streets, then turned south again. A youth with a parcel under his arm who'd hopped on a bike somewhere near the detour whizzed past me, causing me to hit the brakes and curse the superior speed of two wheels as he shot in front of the car ahead of me and wove through traffic to disappear a block ahead. I hoped my caller wasn't the impatient type. The detour had delayed me.

Just ahead of me, a furniture van pulled into the intersection, swung and began to back in my direction. I hit my horn and my brakes at the same time. Unfazed, the van continued to back while one of the men inside jumped out on the passenger side and made hand signals guiding the driver. The truck was too far into the street to squeeze past it. I glanced in my mirror to see two cars and maybe a third had come to a stop behind me.

Another blast from my horn won a cheery wave from the helper who was opening the back of the van. Fuming at the driver's failure to pull to the curb so traffic could keep flowing I cranked down my window.

"Hey!" I shouted sticking my head out and catching a glimpse of a sofa upholstered Coke bottle green. "Hey, pal!" I leaned farther. "Pull over closer so folks can get–"

A hand came from behind to cover my mouth and a sickly sweet smell overpowered me.

FOURTEEN

It was the cold that finally woke me. A body I didn't recognize as my own was shivering. After a time the shaking penetrated my consciousness. I made vague, useless movements trying to pull up something for warmth. Unable to find it I forced open reluctant eyes.

My reward was darkness.

Silence.

And primal panic.

Everything seemed to be spinning. My head ached. Something had happened. I moved and my elbow struck something hard. Like a single bit of colored glass falling in a kaleidoscope and launching a pattern I remembered. The phone call ... the furniture van ... the handkerchief over my nose.

My stomach heaved. Blindly, weakly, my fumbling fingers caught at a handle and wrenched open the car door, pulling me part way out into crisp, fresh air. I clung to the handle while the contents of my gut spilled out, mostly missing the running board. For several minutes afterward I clung and hung, too shaky to do anything else and feebly aware I should wait to make sure the nausea was past. Finally, crooking my free arm through the steering wheel for leverage, I managed to tug the door closed. Trembling and cold I rested my head on the steering wheel.

I was in my own car. But I didn't know where. I was alive. At least I thought I was. What I had to do now was start my car, get away.

Instead, I dozed off a couple of times. When I finally woke my head still spun like a merry-go-round but was mostly clear – and I was even colder than before. Moving carefully I sat upright and waited for the worst of the dizziness to pass. It took a while.

Next order: start the engine and put on my headlamps. First, though, I reached under my seat, glad to find my small automatic was still there. Fumbling, I made sure it still had its clip. Then I set about finding the ignition key, which had been pulled out and tossed on the floor. By the time the engine finally purred to life and I pulled the knob for my headlights I'd have signed on a dotted line to be a housewife. The wash of the DeSoto's lights brought more bad news. I was off the road and a dozen yards down an embankment. Getting out would require rocking the car, spinning the wheels – and maybe a tow truck.

Cutting the engine I sat again and listened to silence so undisturbed I knew I must be in the country, or at least the outskirts of town. I hoped that town was Dayton, but for all I could tell from my surroundings I could be outside Osborne or clear up to Troy. In the glovebox I found my flashlight still present and in working order. My watch showed almost eleven. With that much time gone I could be all the way to Cincinnati.

Rather than think about it I got out and opened the trunk and put on a sweater I kept there. Unless I wanted to spend the night in my car I'd have to walk somewhere. With my coat buttoned over the sweater I turned in a slow circle looking for lights or the shape of a building to guide me. Far off in one direction I saw a high, steady light that might be the railroad tower on West Fifth. Since Dayton was the only area where I knew landmarks, I might as well assume that's where I was. I didn't know if I was north or south or east or west of the dot of light. No matter, if it was the railroad light, walking toward it would bring me closer to town. I'd use the first Gamewell box I saw to call for help.

Weak as I felt, I'd have to choose between toting the flashlight or my automatic. If someone wanted me dead they could have finished me off when they dumped me here, so I chose the flashlight.

By the time I'd climbed the embankment through thigh-high weeds I felt weak as a kitten and dizzy again. I sat down and rested and muttered a few Hail Marys while I listened to a cow somewhere in the distance. I got up and began to follow the narrow paved road. Ten minutes passed without meeting a car. Decent folks were in bed now. Occasionally the beam of my flash touched the shape of a house or barn set back at the end of a dirt track or a dog bayed as I passed.

A time or two my stomach went queasy again but I gulped breaths of air until it passed. I kept myself going with thoughts of evening scores with Woody Beale. He was the only one miffed enough and with clout enough to set up that play with the furniture truck. It was meant to show me his power. To scare me. But why?

Lights from a car appeared, raising my spirits until it turned and vanished down some unseen crossroad. After forever the pavement beneath my feet widened. Other paved streets started to cross it but all the houses were dark. So far I hadn't seen a single blue light marking a police call box. Maybe I was still outside the city limits.

The merry-go-round in my head began to return. Whisps of scenes, real or imagined, bobbled in and out. Did I remember voices? Struggling as a cloth was pressed to my nose for a second time?

Focus. Why would Woody Beale go to this much trouble to warn me off? He wouldn't swat at gnats. Either I had something that jeopardized him and his operations or he thought I did.

I zig-zagged a few streets over in hopes of spotting a Gamewell box. My passing caused a dog somewhere to start sounding a shrill, high-pitched warning. Unlike the deep bay of the farm dogs it pierced my already aching head. Something about the sound caused a memory to flirt and vanish as I tried to retrieve it. As the dog continued his frenzy I stood hoping a light would go on, a door open. Nothing happened. Whoever lived with the vile little mutt must be stone deaf.

As I started on, the memory that had been teasing me dropped into place. Spinning drunkenly I looked back the way I had come. There. A few houses down. It was too far away for my flashlight beam, but on either side of a porch I could see the pyramid shapes of two spruce trees. With all the speed exhaustion allowed I returned to the corner where I could make out a dark, spreading mass that spring before last had been an explosion of yellow forsythia. It had made a swell, half-hidden place to wait in the car I'd had at the time as I tailed a guy who turned out to be an embezzler. In the half a dozen times I'd sat there I'd often had to endure the tantrums of that yappy dog.

An imposing Victorian house just beyond where I stood was the one I'd been watching back then. I opened the gate in an iron fence and went up the walk on unsteady legs.

Like its neighbors, the house was dark, or appeared to be from the street. But along the edge of one handsome front window a line of light no wider than a hatpin was barely visible around tightly drawn draperies. The fabric must be thick. Maybe velvet. Maybe I'd get to see.

On legs as bendable as a Slinky, I climbed the steps and for the first time in my life rang the bell at a cathouse.

FIFTEEN

No porch light went on, but after a minute I thought I heard a whisper of sound. I was leaning hard on the door frame, supporting myself by one arm. The door opened.

I expected a hard looking dame in too much rouge and a tight dress. Instead I found myself looking up at a tallish man in an honest-to-God butler's outfit.

"I'm not here to make trouble," I said before he could speak. "I got chloroformed and dumped in a ditch somewhere out in the country. I need to use your phone to call a cab."

"I'm sorry. My employer is out for the night."

I tried to stick my foot in the door, but he'd seen the move before. Deflecting it with a tight, quick kick that almost sent me sprawling, he closed the door. For several seconds I clung to the frame. Hard to tell if my muscles were shivering or going to rubber. Before I could summon enough strength to think, the door opened again, this time to reveal not a gaudy madam but an impeccably coiffed and turned out middle-aged socialite.

Her gaze swept over me, as penetrating as a nun's.

"Go to the side door," she said. The one between us clicked shut.

Processing thoughts was becoming an effort, but my eyes made out a narrow walk for tradesmen. It hugged one side of the house and was five or six feet from the driveway. Dredging up the last of my strength I followed the walk to a door near the back. Before I could knock the door opened. I peered wearily into the face of the woman

I'd seen at the front. I think she took my arm. Maybe I floated along on the warmth of the place. I ended up in a chair at an oversized table and realized I was in the kitchen. My coat slid off and something warm settled around my shoulders. A mulatto girl wearing a starched white apron over a black dress brought a cup of steaming tea and set it in front of me.

"Drink up," said the socialite.

Except I knew she really wasn't a socialite in spite of the gleaming copper hair done up in a twist and the clusters of garnets winking on her ears and the rope of garnets knotted around her neck like she was headed to dinner at Hawthorne Hill. Inside, this house was alive with voices. Men and women. Laughing and spirited. Not the anemic chat of society parties. My memory hadn't played tricks. I was sitting in the kitchen of a cathouse and unless I missed my guess, the madam herself had just let me in.

"Drink up," she said again.

I thought of Woody Beale and the web of contacts he probably had. I hesitated.

The madam noticed. Annoyance started to shade her face. All at once her head darted down, close enough to kiss me. Straightening, she glanced at the other end of the table where a goodly amount of polished silver lay on a towel. She seized a gravy ladle, dipped it into my cup and swallowed its contents.

"Guess I'd be cautious too if I'd been chloroformed. You reek of it."

Feeling foolish, I raised the cup and swallowed greedily. I was shaking so I could hardly keep the cup to my lips

"You looking to be taken in?" the madam asked. "Work for me?"

Her voice was crisp, authoritative – and surprisingly cultured. Startled by her question I shook my head. A lift of her finger brought the girl in the white apron to refill my cup.

"Leave it," she said indicating the teapot.

With a curtsy the girl scurried back to the sink. The madam sat down in the chair facing mine. Her russet silk dress showed a fine pair of shoulders and a throat betraying no hint of age. A pair of shrewd hazel eyes examined me. Leaning forward she gave her knuckles a sharp rap on the table, demanding truth.

"Why did you come to this particular house? We're as dark as all the others on the street; no noise, nothing to call attention."

Fumbling in my jacket pocket produced one of my business cards, which I slid toward her. Anger tightened her face as she read.

"Spring before last I was following a guy who turned out to be an embezzler," I said. "He liked your place—"

"That little s.o.b. I had to let one of my best girls go for giving him a free romp. I guess you could say he embezzled here too. But sugar lump, I wasn't born yesterday. You want me to swallow some story that you remembered my address after a year and a half? Or maybe recognized my house in the dark?"

"It was a dog," I said weakly. "That little yappy one. He used to drive me nuts. I heard him tonight and it made me remember and then things looked familiar.... Look. I don't care what you do here. I just want to call a cab. I have money for the fare —"

She held up a hand. I shut up. She wasn't looking quite so angry.

"I wish to Christ someone would shoot that mutt," she said darkly. "You need more warmth inside you before you're fit for a cab. If you start to be sick, try and make it to the convenience there." She pointed to a small room next to the pantry. "I'm Mrs. Salmon if you didn't know that. Now let me take a look at your noggin. I've seen a few cracked heads in my time."

"My head?"

One of the will-o-the-wisps that had fluttered inside it while I was walking started to jell into memory. I'd been roused by voices. Started to struggle. A hand with a cotton pad had darted toward me. I'd fought harder, felt a blow....

Mrs. Salmon pushed away my hand as I raised it. She probed gently. She had the maid bring her a warm cloth and wiped, while I uttered several words I was glad to think she'd heard before.

"I've seen worse, but it's nasty enough," she said at length and sat down again. "What day is it?"

"Tuesday. Maybe Wednesday depending which side of midnight we're on." I was too tired to look at my watch, but my starch was returning.

"Half after. You have any idea who it was who gave you that lump?"

"My guess is someone working for Woody Beale."

I wanted to see if the name would make her react. It did. She leaned back slowly and patted her fingertips on the table.

"Your boyfriend?"

"No."

"Good thing. The guy's nutsy."

"He got wind of something I'm working on and he's been trying to scare me off."

She nodded without comment.

"What did you mean about him being nuts?" I asked.

Her gaze dropped to my business card, which still lay where she'd dropped it. She picked it up and thumbed one corner. Deciding.

"He came here half a dozen times, back when he was legging for Tuffy Langstrom. I threw him out."

"Why?"

"Second time he visited he started giving orders like he owned the place – and him just a punk with money, hardly dry behind the ears. Then one night upstairs he went nutsy; started shooting. I don't allow guns. When gentlemen arrive, they go into my study and Winston asks them to take off their jacket. If they have a firearm, Winston locks it in the safe. He gives it back when they're ready to leave.

"That bastard Beale always gave his over okay. Trouble is, he had another little one strapped to his ankle. The girl who entertained him should have told me." Her mouth hardened at the memory. "Apparently he's terrified of rats – goes crazy if he sees one. One of the girls had a little gray kitten. He saw something gray scuttle out and blasted away. I threw him out and his pants after. Told him if he ever came back, he'd be singing soprano."

She gave my card another flick with her thumb as she studied me. "Can anyone with cash in the bank hire you?"

"You could, if that's what you're asking."

She tapped the card on the table and got up. "You never know." All at once she smiled. "My chauffeur will take you home when you're ready. I'll send him in."

SIXTEEN

Mrs. Z. locked her door at 11:30. Any girl who hadn't come home by then was out for the night, and come morning would be hunting somewhere else to rent a room. Luckily Mrs. Z. understood my work sometimes required me to bend that rule. It didn't happen often, but that night it had, so I threw some pebbles at her bedroom window and she let me in, the way we'd worked out.

Once she saw how I looked and I'd mumbled a half-truth about my car getting run off the road and hitting my head, she insisted on helping me up the stairs to my room. I collapsed on my bed fully clothed, though I had the vague recollection of someone at some point helping me into my nightie. The ache in my head, or maybe the after-effects of the chloroform, interrupted my sleep with dreams of gangsters shining lights in my eyes and someone asking my name. Then, like the heavy velvet draperies at Mrs. Salmon's house, sleep blotted out everything.

When I finally woke there was daylight. The silence in the hallway, more than the sun streaming in, told me I'd slept past the time I usually set on my Big Ben. The other girls had all left for work. I rolled over to look at the clock and a landslide in my head brought back what had happened. It was half-past ten. Someone was tapping at my door.

"Are you awake yet?" Genevieve poked a mop of curls the color of hickory nuts around the door. My scowl brought a smile to her face. "Oh, good. You're feeling well enough to be a pill. You must be okay."

She came in as she said it, setting a tray on a straight-backed chair beside my bed. "Mrs. Z. let me make you some tea and toast. Can you sit up?"

I didn't have much choice. She was already lifting my shoulder, sliding my extra pillow behind me and fluffing the one I'd slept on so they made a backrest. Ginny probably fell a few years shy of being old enough to be my mother but we'd hit it off from the day we met. She had the room next to mine and income from somewhere so she didn't go out to a job. She was the only one at the rooming house I'd have let fuss over me like this.

"Thanks," I croaked as she set the tray on my knees. My throat felt like it needed oiling.

"You had the heaves the first time I checked on you, so I didn't butter the toast. Better safe than sorry."

I took two or three swigs of tea and squinted at her. "You come in with a flashlight? Ask my name?"

Her squarish face turned somber as she nodded. "When you get a hard bang on the head it can make your brain swell. Doctors tell you to wake the person, make sure they're just sleeping."

I wondered how she knew, but I don't press Ginny about her past just as she doesn't press me about my work. It's why we're friends. While I drank the tea and tried to keep from gobbling the toast I told her highlights of what had happened. She laid out clean underwear and my robe and helped me down the hall to the bathroom. While the tub filled she went to call Eli at the garage and convey my request for him and Calvin to get my car. They'd have to find it first, but at least I'd been able to tell them the general direction.

A soak in hot water made most of my body feel better. A couple of aspirin gave encouragement of better days for my head. I put on my tan flannel suit, with a soft sweater instead of a blouse, and let Ginny mother hen me onto the trolley. I wasn't ready for a footrace, but at least I wasn't wobbly. When I got off downtown I turned into the first diner I passed and drank a mug of coffee so hot it scalded the back of my throat. It left me perkier, and too mad for a refill. I had things to do.

* * *

Chances were good the flowers that arrived for me hadn't come from the barkeeper at the Ace of Clubs. They were tea roses, pink ones, spilling over the sides of a china basket. Some greenery kept them company and a florist's card peeped from the arrangement. A kid in his teens with a big Adam's apple was turning away from my door with it as I got off the elevator.

"This your place?" he asked as he saw me coming in his direction.

An inner alarm that had been on the fritz the day before began to sound. I stopped a few yards shy of reaching him. "Who sent you?"

He stared at me, edgy. "What do you mean?"

"What shop do you work for?"

"Meadows. Meadows' Flowers. Up on Main. 'Freshest flowers in the Miami Valley'," he recited, puffing his chest out. "Harold says half of that's fast delivery. He chews me out good if he has to drive around the block more than once. So can you take 'em, please?"

It sounded like stuff a boss drilled into employees. I took the roses, unlocked my office and cleared a corner of my desk for them.. The whole place looked classier.

In the time it took me to hang up my coat, I ran through a short list of who could have sent them. The architect I'd dated for a couple of months in the spring until we'd argued over something I couldn't remember. Some satisfied client who found himself in a new jam. It

93

was even possible Mick Connelly was trying to make amends for his cocky comment about my freckles. I doubted it, given what I'd seen of him. Not on a cop's salary. In any case, I wasn't interested.

I snipped the ribbon that tied the envelope to one of the rose stems. Inside was a plain white card with a raised border.

Don't take a turn for the worse.

Neat penmanship. No signature.

I stared at it for a minute, then ripped it in half and hurled it into the trash. A warning, that's what it was. A smug, victorious jab from Woody Beale flaunting his cleverness and rubbing my nose in his power to do worse. But I couldn't prove he was the one behind my abduction. If I went to the cops about it, the only thing likely to happen was Billy and Seamus would learn I'd been roughed up and start fussing over me. The flowers' taunt set my head off again, which made me so furious I didn't immediately register the tap at my door.

When I did, my hand shot to the sling beneath my chair where I kept my .38. The flowers and the previous night's events had turned me into such a hen brain that I'd left the door ajar. But even as my fingers reached for the gun I recognized Evelyn from the sock place down the hall.

"May I interrupt?" she called, making sure I wasn't with a client.

I wasn't keen to see anyone, but she was a nice girl.

"Sure," I said. "Come on in."

She glanced around her, taking in my office for the first time. "No holes in the wall." A small smile played at her mouth. "I'm a bit surprised after that ruckus." She had a slip of paper in one hand. "I thought you should know – Oh, my!" She'd noticed the roses. "Aren't they lovely! Either you have an admirer or I work in the wrong office."

I waved at them in dismissal. Becoming businesslike she pried her eyes away and cleared her throat.

"Well, anyway. I thought you might like to know someone followed you yesterday when you left for the day. I'd picked up some office supplies Maxine ordered so I wouldn't have to catch an earlier trolley to do it this morning. I was bringing them back when I saw you dash up the street and get into your car. Just as you whizzed past me another car pulled away from the curb, so fast he almost hit an old woman. Not that he stopped."

"What kind of car?"

She sighed. "My husband despairs that I can't tell one from another. It was smallish, navy, quite ordinary looking, I'm afraid. The only thing I can tell you about it is the license number." With that she handed me the slip of paper.

My mouth opened several seconds before I managed words. "You got the license number? You're a gem!"

Evelyn looked embarrassed. "Well I work with numbers all day. My brain sees five or six of them as a unit, I suppose. It's just easier that way, don't you think? Besides, I only had to remember it long enough to get upstairs and write it down."

Evelyn and I were definitely in different leagues when it came to numbers. "Thanks," I said. "For telling me and for being so fast on your feet."

She looked pleased at the compliment. "I have to get back. I told Maxine I was going to powder my nose."

"Hey." Beale wouldn't send anyone up to check on the flowers. There'd be no harm. I stuck the number she'd given me under my blotter and grabbed the china basket of roses. "Take these. I don't think much of the guy who sent them, so why don't you enjoy them?"

Her eyes widened. "Are you sure? They're beautiful
– and frightfully expensive."

"Someone ought to enjoy them. Tell Maxine I sent
them to thank her for letting me use the phone."

Her eyes shone with mischief. "It will drive her crazy
wondering if you mean it or you're up to something."

She closed the door on her way out and I looked at the
paper bearing the license number with satisfaction. I was
starting to learn things. And I was done waiting. Time to
nudge things along.

I dialed Throckmorton Stationery and Business
Supply and asked for Peter Stowe. Apparently no one
except his uncle rated a private secretary as Stowe himself
answered a minute later.

"This is Mr. Stowe. How may I help you?"

Baritone voice, on the soft side. I hadn't heard it
before. I said my piece quickly.

"Woody Beale's boys drugged me and left me in a
ditch last night because of you. Unless you want to risk
having that sweet little blonde of yours get the same
treatment, get up to the Arcade and wait at the giant pickle
place. You've got ten minutes."

My finger came down on the hook before he could
speak. If he cared anything about Thelma, he'd do what I
said. Even if he didn't, he was probably scared enough to
show.

I grabbed my coat and headed out. To conserve my
depleted energy, I hailed a taxi and rode the few short
blocks to Daphne's, a hole-in-the-wall hat shop on Fourth
Street. The shop was popular and on the pricey side for
my budget, which didn't keep me from frequent browsing
and an occasional splurge. Today my mind wasn't on hats,
though. Today I'd come to Daphne's in case I was
followed. It wasn't a spot a man was likely to enter, and
Daphne's, though it didn't look like much from the
outside, was many times deeper than it was wide. Half a

dozen display cases and stands showing creations that made my mouth water led the way back to a second entrance into the elegant, enclosed Arcade. Not far from where I expected to meet Peter Stowe.

SEVENTEEN

The glass-domed Arcade sat just south of the courthouse and beckoned shoppers through entrances on Main Street, Fourth Street, Ludlow and Fifth. It was lunchtime when I arrived, past the peak but still early enough for the place to be crowded. Ringing the ground floor and running around the second floor gallery with its iron railing were shops and a handful of offices where people came and went. At this time of day more activity focused on the stalls and counters that sold food.

Clerks and secretaries and plenty of others milled around the stalls with housewives who were doing their marketing. The downtown workers were after a bite of lunch they could carry. A roll from one of the bakery stalls with something from the cheese counter or one of the sausage sellers. Or maybe they'd choose a couple of pickled eggs and an apple turnover. Meanwhile housewives roamed the various butcher stands looking at chops and roasts and pale pink veal. If they didn't make their own noodles they could purchase those at another stand. High above them all, the glass dome admitted soft light and reflected back their mingling voices.

After my rough night I stayed well away from the smell of the fish sellers. Instead I sat on a bench where I could inhale the fragrance of Spanish peanuts roasted in oil and have a good view of the four main entrances. I'd spot Peter Stowe as soon as he came in, plus maybe have an edge if anyone had managed to follow me.

If Stowe walked, he'd be here in about five minutes. Less if he took a cab, but they weren't as easy to come by from his place as they were from mine. I watched a gray-haired woman buy a bar of fancy soap, a man buy chocolates – and here came Peter Stowe. He was slender with light brown hair and shoulders that already showed signs of rounding. The levelness of his gray fedora made me wonder if he was too much like his fussy uncle. His jerky steps betrayed his tension.

Across from me and a few yards up was a pickle seller commonly referred to as Giant Pickles, though the owner probably gave his stand a different name. Other merchants sold dills and sweets and pickle relishes, but this one had a specialty, dills so enormous a single pickle could feed a family. Peter Stowe halted a good fifteen feet away from the stand, looked tensely around, then began what he probably thought passed for a casual circuit around it. At the end of the circuit, his nervousness more apparent, he glanced around again, probably fearing a gun in his ribs from one of Woody Beale's goons. I waited until he moved uncertainly to the end of a line of customers waiting at the pickle stand and his back was toward me. A couple of quick steps put me at his elbow.

"It's me you're looking for," I said sliding my arm through his. "Let's walk."

It startled him so that he obeyed for a step or two before pulling away.

"Who are you?" At least he didn't blink like his uncle.

"Maggie Sullivan. I'm a private investigator. Your uncle hired me."

"My uncle?" He looked as though he'd been punched in the gut.

"That's right." I gave him a card. "And I meant what I said on the phone. Unless you're prepared to see your girl roughed up – maybe roughed up bad – you better let me help you. The man you're mixed up with gets what he wants and doesn't like people who get in his way. He'd beat up a sweet girl like Thelma as easily as he'd kick a kitten."

Oblivious to the throngs moving past us, Peter Stowe slid both hands up his face and pressed the heels to his forehead. His hat slid back, but he didn't notice that either. His face was gaunt with despair.

"I've already tried to see to it Thelma's not hurt," he said in hollow tones. "I broke up with her over the weekend."

Typically male solution. I wanted to kick him. Dimes to donuts poor Thelma had been crying her eyes out with no idea what had gone wrong. Clumsy as his attempt was, however, it made me think Stowe might be okay.

"Let's go get some lunch. You may not be hungry, but thanks to your pal Beale I haven't had anything but a piece of toast in twenty-four hours. Anyway, we have talking to do."

He shook his head with surprising stubbornness. "You can't help me. It's too big a mess."

"Woody Beale underestimated me too."

Color washed across his unnatural pallor. "I didn't mean to be insulting...."

As the manicurist had told me, a real gentleman.

"It's okay," I said taking his arm again. "And I've handled messes before."

* * *

The Embassy Grill was just across Ludlow next to ex-Governor Cox's news mill. Going there meant a chance someone from the evening paper would come in for a ham on rye and see us together. But that same chance of news hounds almost guaranteed Woody Beale's boys would steer clear of the place.

The lunchtime crowd had thinned and we were able to get a booth at the back with the next booth empty. Peter Stowe didn't speak as he glanced at the menu. Or when he set it aside to stare at his hands. I didn't press him. When the waitress came he ordered a toasted cheese sandwich, his enthusiasm just about equal to that of a dress shop mannequin. In consideration of my not-yet-quite-sturdy system, I went for chicken and noodles.

I waited until the waitress returned with a glass of Dr. Pepper for him and coffee for me. I cut the coffee with milk and sugar, which I didn't usually do but figured was good for regaining strength.

"What did you mean, my uncle hired you?" Stowe asked at last. "Why? When?"

"Three weeks ago. Four now. He said he was worried about you – that you'd been acting odd, flashing new clothes. When I learned Beale was leaning on you, and a guy who came to see me ended up dead that same night, your uncle claimed he didn't recognize either name. So." I crossed my arms on the edge of the table and leaned across them, eyeing him steadily. "Is Uncle Throckmorton into something crooked or are you?"

Stowe's head jerked as the trance that had held him let go.

"My uncle doesn't have a dishonest bone in his body!" he said angrily. "He's a fine, decent man who's never turned his back on anyone in need. He worked without taking a penny of salary so he could pay the people who worked for him when the stock market crashed–"

"Funny, he sang your praises too."

The words deflated him as abruptly as my bait about his uncle had set him off.

"I don't deserve them," he said looking down at the edge of the table. "I-I suspect I'm not worthy of all the things he's done for me. But the only thing I'm guilty of is being stupid. I swear. Stupid and gullible and maybe having dreams that are ... impractical." He frowned at the table edge. "Impractical," he repeated softly. He was talking to himself now, and the way he sounded made me feel sorry for him.

"Why don't you tell me about it?"

He nodded.

"Start from the beginning. How did you meet Al?"

He looked up in surprise. "You know about Al?" A rueful smile pushed its way through his wretchedness. "But then, you are a detective. I apologize for being surprised."

"Not necessary, but thanks."

We waited while the waitress set our plates in front of us. Peter broke one corner off his sandwich; stared at it; dropped it back on the plate. My chicken and noodles came with rolls and a side of peas. I decided the peas might slow my recovery so I set them aside and buttered a roll.

"Okay, here's part of what I know about your pal Beale," I prompted after I'd had a nice chunk of chicken, which was so tender that the only point in chewing it was to savor the taste. "I know he owns three night spots and has a lot more money than those bring in. "The cops figure there's gambling in the back rooms, but they don't have proof yet." That was stretching the truth, but Stowe needed some nudging. I watched for his reaction about the gambling. There wasn't any. Which meant I could maybe eliminate him or his cousin having unpaid debts from the gaming tables.

"I know Beale's right-hand man is Al," I continued. "And I know when Beale gives the order, people can wind up dead."

Peter had taken a small bite of grilled cheese. He swallowed with difficulty.

"I've never been to his clubs! I don't know anything about the gambling. There's no reason you should believe that, but–." He put the corner of sandwich down and gave it a nudge. "I'd never heard of Beale. I'd never laid eyes on him until his car pulled up beside me one night and two of his musclemen got out and dragged me to him. In the beginning it was just Al, and I realize now that I was an idiot, but it all seemed so harmless. Now it's a nightmare!"

"Then maybe you'd better tell me about it," I said gently.

EIGHTEEN

Peter Stowe gulped some of his Dr. Pepper.

"My uncle's an excellent businessman. He says it's more productive to satisfy the customers you already have than to chase after new ones. At least once a week I drive one of our delivery routes to keep up with customers. Occasionally I see how we can alter a route or do something else to be more efficient. Mostly I listen for little complaints. Or maybe someone mentions they wish there was a product that did such-and-such. I might have read about something new that would do the trick. Useful stuff, I suppose, but not very exciting."

He glanced at me shyly. So far it matched what his uncle had told me.

"That's how you met Al? Doing deliveries?"

He'd made another stab at eating some sandwich. He was relaxing some, but his manner was grave. He nodded.

"It was, oh, two months ago, I guess. I was doing the south route. I'd made a couple of stops and was coming out of a place in Oakwood. He was standing there on the sidewalk. Hands in the pockets of a suit that probably cost more than I make in two weeks, a cigarette in his mouth, looking at my delivery truck. He said something like 'That was some armload of cartons you carried in there.' I said 'All in a day's work.' I figured he'd come out of the tony little restaurant that's across the street.

"Then he asked did I deliver things all over the city and I said yes. He said boy, the things I must see, like a cowboy riding the range. We both laughed, it was so outlandish. He was – he was pleasant."

I nodded encouragement.

"Then he said 'Hey, I'm a writer and I've got a million questions I'd like to ask you. Any chance I could ride along with you? I'd treat you to lunch.' I thought, what's the harm?"

Bitterness hardened the voice of the slender young man facing me. He managed a rueful smile and pinched the bridge of his nose.

"It's awfully dull, my job. And–" He spread his hands. "I suppose I was flattered."

"So what did he ask you to do?"

"Nothing. Nothing at all." Peter shook his head in bewilderment. "He just took it all in like a carnival ride. Said how great it was. I was such a damned fool – excuse me–"

"I've used worse myself. And I've had some experience being a fool."

That seemed to encourage him, or maybe now that he'd started unburdening he couldn't stop.

"At lunch he told me he'd been hired to do a movie script, and he'd been hunting a job like mine that took the hero all over the city. He didn't go on about it, which somehow made it all sound believable. At the end of the route he asked could he ride with me again. He said the studio would pay me an advisor's fee, but I said that wasn't necessary, that I enjoyed his company. Which was true. He was likeable. Then."

Peter swallowed. "So he rode with me several more times, asking questions about the places we went – how often I delivered and such, helping me carry in cartons sometimes, taking notes –"

"Taking notes?"

"To make him seem like a writer, I guess."

Or maybe not. I began to get a bad feeling as several things nudged me at once: Someone telling Beale the pigeon Al picked had blown up in his face. Peter going into businesses all over the city. A rash of burglaries.

But words were pouring out of Peter now. The dam of fear inside him had burst.

"He gave me twenty-five dollars, cash, every time after the first. Said he'd talked long distance to the producer who was crazy about the idea and insisted I be paid. Then, a week or so later, he called and asked me to have a drink with him after work. When we did, Al said the producer was coming to town and wanted to meet me, that he'd seen my snapshot. Did I mention he'd brought his Kodak one day? Al said the producer thought I'd be perfect for a small part. Only a couple of lines, but 'a nice chunk of money' as he put it."

A blush replaced the pallor on his face. "I'd – I'd been saving up so I could propose to Thelma. And I wanted to take more engineering courses down at the university. I've had some already. It's what I want to do. Electrical circuits. Antennas. My uncle, though, expects me to take over his business someday, and he's raised me, given me everything. I feel like a traitor even thinking of anything else, but–. Anyway. Al's rubbish seemed like a dream come true. I suppose I wanted to believe it. So I did."

A noisy trio entered the restaurant, ribbing each other. One was Matt Jenkins. His specs hid his eyes at a distance, but as his companions slid into a booth near the front he said something and began ambling toward me.

"Grab my hand and look lovey-dovey," I said.

It took Peter several seconds before he reacted. He grabbed my hand so clumsily it maybe looked like passion. Another second or two and he added his other hand, squeezing mine between both of his. Jenkins raised his eyebrows at me, gave a wicked grin, and did an about face to rejoin his friends.

"Problem solved," I said retrieving my hand. "Don't look around – it was a friend from the paper you didn't need to meet. So you spent the money Al paid you on a new suit to impress the producer?"

"Only one trip's worth. I was keen to save as much as I could, but I wanted to make a good impression on the producer."

"And Ollie's barber shop?"

Once again Peter looked startled by my knowledge. "It was Al's idea, his treat the first time. To get me looking just right and wish me luck, he said." Bitterness returned to his voice. "When the non-existent producer got delayed, and then delayed again, I went to the place several times on my own. I wanted to look right when he finally came since he was giving me a chance."

I'd polished off most of my chicken and noodles. I waited while the waitress refilled my coffee.

"How did it turn ugly?"

"One day, oh, maybe six weeks from the time the whole thing started, I got home from a lecture on regenerative circuits one night and there was a car in front. Al got out. He said he'd misplaced some notes he needed. We'd been out that day and he thought they might have fallen out in the delivery truck. He wanted me to let him in where we keep our trucks so he could check.

"I said I couldn't, that I'd look first thing the next morning and call if I found them. He said he had to have them that night. All at once it felt queer. I'd never told him where I lived. And I remembered reading about a burglary up at Holtz Brothers not long before. Maybe – maybe deep down I'd always known it was all too good to be true, his hooey about a movie. I told him again I'd check the next morning.

"Then, well, once it didn't feel right, I guess I needed to test it. So I told him I wouldn't be able to let him ride with me for a while, either, that a customer had complained about him wandering around in the warehouse while I finished paperwork on a delivery.

"What happened?"

Peter drew a deep breath. "He went all quiet and lighted a cigarette. He took a couple of puffs leaning there against his car, all calm and casual. Then he looked at the tip like I wasn't worth the bother, and his voice was pleasant, and he said 'Don't get cute, Pete. The people you're crossing will swat you with no more thought than they swat a fly.'"

NINETEEN

The remainder of Peter's story went fast compared to the first. Al laughed at his offer to repay the so-called 'advisor's fee'. He never saw Al again. Soon afterward, two thugs hustled Peter to a car where a man in the passenger seat said he wanted his property back or Peter would get hurt. Peter's response that he'd tell the police if they didn't leave him alone won him a gut punch along with a warning that he was the one who'd end up in jail. They kept turning up, their persuasion getting rougher. He didn't know which way to turn.

"When I realized they were watching me, and that they'd seen me with Thelma several times, I worried they might - they might hurt her. I felt awful giving her the brush off, but it was the only way I could think of to keep her out of it."

My urge to kick him wasn't quite as strong as before. He was a decent fellow. Like his uncle, he just hadn't seen much of the bad side of life. He and Thelma seemed about right for each other. Assuming I got him out of the fix he was in.

"The night you missed your date with Thelma and wound up with a split lip – I was following you, but I didn't see anyone rough you up."

"They were waiting for me. Inside my apartment." His shoulders sagged. "The hell of it is, I still can't figure out what it's about or what they want." We slid from our booth preparing to leave the restaurant. "Will you be able to, now that I've told you?"

"Yeah, once I fit a few pieces together." I had a hunch, but if I was right, Peter Stowe was in a far bigger mess than he realized.

The restaurant was almost empty now, just us, two other tables and the booth full of newshounds.

"You head on back, and watch you're not followed," I said. "I need to say 'hi' to these jokers."

Jenkins had looked up the moment we stirred. Eyes crackling with interest behind his specs he flashed a lascivious grin as we neared where he sat.

"You guys get a lot of hot scoops eating ham sandwiches?" I asked as Peter continued out the door with a small backward nod.

"Just the one about you," Jenkins said, grin widening.

"Sorry to deny you bits for whatever peek-through-the-keyhole fantasy you're slobbering over, but he was just a prospective client begging me to help him."

"I've begged a few girls to help me," cracked a freckle faced guy across from him that I'd seen before.

"Yeah, but I charge more per hour and keep my clothes on," I said.

To the sound of their hoots as the freckled guy turned beet red, I walked on out. On the other side of the street Peter was getting into a taxi. I watched for a minute. No one pulled out to follow. I crossed Ludlow and reentered the Arcade. Meandering through, and watchful of people around me, I emerged onto Main and turned right for half a dozen breaths of air before entering McCrory's. It wasn't near quitting time yet, but maybe things were slow enough for Izzy to give me a quick description of the guy who'd been asking about me. But Izzy wasn't there; she was sick.

That left me two choices. I could head back to the office, call the florist and maybe get proof about who'd sent the roses. Or I could settle in somewhere for several of hours of serious reading and note taking that might persuade me I was on the wrong track. More likely it was going to give me a worse picture of the trouble Peter Stowe was in.

The good lunch had put me back on my pins. My brain, though, didn't feel as sharp as I wanted for poring over columns of print where details that seemed unimportant could sometimes yield gold if you caught the glint. So I picked Choice Three: go back to Mrs. Z's. One of the girls there could maybe answer some questions if I could catch her before she left for work.

* * *

"I wish you could see my outfit. It's cute as they come," Jolene said giving her fingers a lick and smoothing her stockings expertly. She giggled. "Of course Mrs. Z might throw me out if she caught me in it, so I guess it's just as well we have to leave them in the dressing room."

Jolene was a cigarette girl. She came from a farm out near Xenia and was crazy about what she referred to as 'the big city'.

"I'll bet you look swell," I said. I'd never been in her room before. Her bed held a pair of lounge trousers, a magazine, a crumpled candy wrapper, and strips of rag she'd used to curl her long blonde hair. "Hey, listen, did you ever work at a place called Fanny's? Or The Owl up on Main?"

She shook her newly freed curls, dropped her robe on the bed and began wiggling into a blouse.

"The Mademoiselle and Parker's and three years where I am now. Harry, the manager, just offered to switch me to selling roses instead of cigarettes, pay me fifty cents more a week. I said thanks all the same, but you make more tips selling cigarettes. Everybody buys those. I think one of the hat girls used to work at The Owl though. You going there?"

"No. I need to find out if the guy who owns it has an office there." It would save me tossing a coin to decided which of Beale's places east of the river I wanted to watch. Wherever he kept his office was where I'd be most likely to get a look at Al and his other boys.

Jolene's eyes grew large. She stopped halfway thought checking her reflection in the oval mirror on her dresser.

"Is this about something you're working on?" she whispered.

I thought half a second, decided to chance it.

"Yes."

"Want me to find out about the office? I can be real slick about it."

Jolene wasn't dumb. She'd come to Dayton not knowing a soul and found a job and kept it. She couldn't be blamed if the job didn't make much use of her brain.

"Okay," I said. "I'll treat you to the picture show some Sunday when you don't have a date. But listen, Jolene, don't let anyone hear you asking about it, understand? The man who owns those two places I mentioned is bad with a capital B. He hurts people."

"Okay." She was still half whispering. "How about if I say I heard he's a real ladies man and keeps stacks of money all over his office and did he ever spend any on her?"

I laughed. "Jolene, you ought to be writing for magazines."

* * *

When the downtown library opened the next morning, I was waiting. Over the last few years one of the librarians, a matronly sort with a pigeon-toed walk and cantaloupe bosoms that rested on a surprisingly tidy belly, had taken a shine to me. Tucking wisps of white hair into an untidy bun that always held a couple of pencils she trotted off to fetch the first of the armloads of newspapers I'd requested.

At one of the tables I set out my tablet and three sharpened pencils for note taking. Then I began to read. First I went through the wooden rods that held the current week's papers, one morning, one evening. Then I worked backwards. Three months' worth. Then, to be safe, I went back another two weeks.

By the time I finished my eyes were dry enough for kindling and it was almost noon. I squinted and opened until my peepers revived. I stood up and walked around the table a time or two and flexed my shoulders. Then I sat down again and looked at the list I'd compiled. Nine burglaries at good sized businesses in the past six weeks, plus the usual number of run-of-the-mill ones which I didn't think were related.

I walked back to the office and called Throckmorton.

"I'm making some headway," I said. "I need to talk to you. Somewhere private."

I could almost hear him working up a head of steam preparing to object. He was used to being the one in charge.

"I suppose you could stop by the house," he said reluctantly. "Tonight at eight?"

"Fine."

He gave me the address. I hung up and called his nephew.

TWENTY

Lewis Throckmorton lived on the tony part of Harvard Boulevard five miles or so north of downtown. It wasn't a mansion, but it was old-money substantial with plenty of elbow room between it and its neighbors. Two stories of dressed stone and timber, with a garret above to accommodate a couple of servants, opened onto a porticoed verandah running the length of one side. Lights glowed in downstairs windows, spilling out enough for me to make out the thick trunks and graceful branches of mature trees on the gently sloped lawn.

I doused my headlights and parked at the curb to wait for Peter. My own neighborhood wasn't one where an unfamiliar car with someone at the wheel could wait around unnoticed, so I was reasonably certain I hadn't been followed. No harm in watching some, though. Besides, I wanted to make sure no one had followed Peter, and to give him a little moral support. He was likely to need it.

His uncle didn't know I'd invited him. It might get unpleasant and Throckmorton might not like it, but the time had come to toss the two of them together and see if anything came to light that I hadn't gotten from either individually. Peter was feeling bad enough as it was. If Throckmorton popped his cork I wanted to make sure it didn't hit Peter too hard. Unwitting as they'd been, Peter's actions had put his uncle's business in a very sticky spot.

A modest little gray Ford turned onto Harvard, coming from the direction of Salem. It was Peter. I cranked down my window and told him to park and sit. After eight minutes passed without anyone else showing up, I got out. We went up a curving walk together and climbed a few steps. I rang the bell.

A slightly built man in a gray suit opened the door. He was nowhere near as impressive as the butler at Mrs. Salmon's place.

"My name's Sullivan," I said. "Mr. Throckmorton is expecting me."

"Please come in. He's waiting for you in the study. 'Evening, Mr. Peter." He gave a curious look at Peter, who hadn't uttered a word. I bet Mrs. Salmon's butler never showed he was curious.

" 'Evening, Kimmel. How's the knee?"

"Much better, thank you."

A curved staircase rose from the hallway. Kimmel led us to the left of it and we followed a Persian runner woven in browns and gold. Oak floor gleamed at its edges. The walls were white. Kimmel stopped at the middle door of three and rapped lightly.

"Miss Sullivan is here, sir. Mr. Peter is with her." He stepped aside to let us enter.

"Peter!" Lewis Throckmorton wavered uncertainly in front of the dark blue wing chair from which he'd just risen. To the right of the wing chair a fire burned cheerily on a marble hearth.

"I asked Peter to join us," I said quickly.

"You *what?*" The corners of his mouth pushed down. Behind his spectacles his eyes were blinking.

"Did I hear voices?" A young woman with hair the color of dark honey materialized from an adjoining room. She was leggy, taller than Throckmorton, clad in a camelhair skirt and a frilly white blouse with a real cameo. "Well, look what the cat dragged in," she beamed at Peter. Noticing me she became self-conscious. "Oh, hello."

"Er, I thought you had a committee meeting of some sort." Throckmorton was blinking again, regarding her with near dismay.

"It was cancelled, Father. I told you yesterday," the young woman said patiently. Her hair was tucked back in a pageboy that cleared her collar.

"Oh, yes. Yes of course. Um ... perhaps you would ... excuse us, then, my dear?"

She looked startled, but managed a gracious smile. "Of course–"

"Actually, I'd like her to stay."

"Stay?" Throckmorton's eyelids would be exhausted before the evening was over, the way they were bouncing. His stuffy little mustache thrust forward. He was used to order. He was used to giving the orders. "Well. Perhaps Kimmel could bring us all a drink," he huffed.

Peter was by the fireplace, one hand clenched on the mantle, the other rigid at his side. Yesterday when he'd finished talking to me he'd been wrung out. Tonight, standing there, he displayed an abject determination, but his gaze didn't stray from the carpet. Throckmorton's daughter began to look puzzled.

"A gibson for me, please," she said when Kimmel appeared.

I said I'd have a gin and tonic. Apparently Kimmel knew what the men drank. As soon as he left an awkward silence filled our little tableau.

"I don't believe we've met." The honey haired woman extended her hand. "I'm Flora Throckmorton." She had a nice handshake, firmer than most women.

"Maggie Sullivan. Your father hired me."

Her eyebrows rose, but she didn't pursue it. "Why don't we sit down?" she suggested.

"Right," agreed her father without enthusiasm. Across from his chair was another one nearly identical. Between them a sofa of the same dark blue was flecked with tawny gold like that in the carpet. Flora Throckmorton settled herself on the end of the sofa nearest her father. I took the chair. Peter stayed at the fireplace.

"Perhaps you should be the one to explain," said Throckmorton, his equilibrium returning. "Since you've called us all together, as it were." His tone warned I'd better deliver.

I nodded. "What Peter and I have to say concerns all of you, I think." I broke off as Kimmel returned with the drinks. A toast didn't seem in order, so I had a nip of my gin and tonic while he served the others. When he'd gone out again and closed the door, I sat forward a little.

"I'm a private detective, Miss Throckmorton. Your father called me several weeks ago because he was worried your cousin might be in some kind of trouble."

Flora Throckmorton's fingers went to her cameo. She looked at Peter in alarm. It had been an impulse when I told her father she ought to stay. I'd all but decided she had nothing to do with the snare that had closed around Peter. Still, having her sit in gave me a chance to judge her reactions, which so far looked innocent.

"The behavior your father described to me – seeming distracted, unexplained absences – made me think Peter might have his hand in the cookie jar, or maybe was being blackmailed." Throckmorton squirmed uncomfortably. Peter looked at him in dismay. "It's nothing like that," I continued. "Peter's done nothing wrong. He has, unfortunately, landed himself on the bad side of some very tough characters." Flora's fingers flew to her lips. Her father muffled a groan. I nodded. "I think it would best if I let him tell you about it."

Peter took a quick slug of the whiskey he was drinking. He straightened and faced them. Red patches of self-consciousness spread across the wanness of his cheeks.

"I never meant any harm – and I certainly never meant to worry you, Uncle Lou. I was stupid, and there are consequences for that just as there are for everything we do. I'm afraid I may have somehow jeopardized the business by my lack of judgment. I certainly don't deserve your trust. So once you hear what I've done, if you want me gone – from the business and – and from your life as well, I'll understand."

Throckmorton looked ill. His daughter had locked her hands around her knees and was listening anxiously. Neither spoke. They scarcely seemed to breathe. And Peter told the story he'd told me the previous day.

* * *

When Peter's voice at last fell silent Throckmorton looked at his glass as if to find a starting place. The glass was empty. He tried to speak. His voice broke. He frowned.

"I don't know what to say to you, Peter. This is betrayal. A betrayal."

"Father –" His daughter moved to his side and place a hand on his shoulder. He ignored her.

"I've tried my best to be a parent to you. Tried to teach you the value of level-headedness and practicality. But rather than appreciate the trust I've place in you, you've succumbed to - to some absurd fantasy. You've jeopardized–"

Abruptly the starch went out of him. He tugged his glasses off, polished them savagely and settled them back in place.

"I'm paying you. Can you get him out of this?" he snapped at me.

Behind his bluster I heard the appeal. For the first time since he'd hired me, I decided Throckmorton was on the level.

"I can try," I said.

Throckmorton nodded. The reality of my answer possibly reassured him more than a flat promise. He took off his specs again, studying them.

"Could this – do you think it might have something to do with those burglaries we've been reading about?"

"That occurred to me. I expect it has to Peter as well."

"Uncle Lou, I am so abysmally sorry–"

"So you should be. Still mooning over Tom Swift engineering nonsense at your age."

"Don't make him feel worse, Father! Pete would no more do anything he thought might hurt the business – or you – than I would."

Throckmorton waved a hand at her words.

"The important thing now," he said eyeing me, "is what do we do?"

Tackling something the way he would a business problem was more comfortable ground for him than sorting out feelings. It was also just what was needed.

"To start with, you can take a gander at the list of places that have been hit and that the cops or the papers seem to think are big enough to be part of this rash." Opening my purse I took out the list I'd made at the library that morning. I'd typed it up minus my notes. "Let me know if these are all your customers."

Flora, who had settled herself on the sofa again, got up and handed it to him, moving behind the chair and leaning over his shoulder as he read.

"Yes ... yes ... yes...." His spirits sagged as his finger moved down the column. "Hang on. Miami Steamworks isn't ours."

Peter, after hesitating, had come to read over Throckmorton's other shoulder. "Neither is Gibbs Brothers."

"Ours ... ours..."

"MJ&J is ours, but they have another supplier as well," Flora said with excitement.

Throckmorton looked up blinking. "What do you mean?"

Peter looked at her too. She flushed under their gazes.

"Haven't you ever compared their orders with orders from other places their size? It's about half as large. I wondered why, and the only explanation I could come up with was that they also purchase supplies from someone else.

"I thought if I could confirm it, Pete could do his magic with someone there and get the whole account. There's a girl from my class at Miami Jacobs who works there, so I took her to lunch one day and asked her what we'd have to do to get all their office products business. She said we couldn't. One of the owners apparently made it a rule that they have to use two suppliers – his way of making sure they weren't left in the lurch a few years back when things were awful and places went broke every day and couldn't deliver their goods."

She'd come around to the front as she spoke. Both men stared at her for a very long moment.

"Well done!" exclaimed Peter.

Flora smiled at him.

"Aren't you a clever girl to figure that out," her father said tepidly. His eyes drifted back to the list I'd prepared. "Nine burglaries, then, and only six of them are our customers, plus one that appears to be shared."

"But that means seven *are* our customers," Peter said pacing.

"I'll bet the one behind this is that scallywag Morris Gibbons!" Throckmorton bristled. "It's just the sort of crooked scheme he'd pull. Try to make us look bad and then steal our customers!"

"Rival products company," Flora told me.

Somehow I didn't think someone like Woody Beale was throwing his muscle around to help a guy poach customers for office supplies. Even some of the robberies looked like small potatoes for Beale. But I didn't think we were likely to hit on the answer tonight.

"It's getting late," I said. Everyone, myself included, was likely to benefit from time to mull over the tidbits tossed up in the last few hours. "We need to sleep on this – see if anything new pops into anyone's head. First thing tomorrow I'd like to stop by your office to look at some of your delivery records. Peter, your part in ending this mess is going to start before then, bright and early."

TWENTY-ONE

The list of burglaries I'd given Throckmorton was out-of-date by the following morning. A story detailing a break-in at the warehouse of a cigar and cigarette distributor on South Dixie saluted me from page one. I read about it while I sipped my first cup of coffee at McCrory's lunch counter the following morning.

"Hear you've been sick," I said when Izzy brought my oatmeal.

"Kid. Couldn't tell,"she said under her breath.

It never had occurred to me she might have kids, but I got the picture. A first-rate waitress would still have a job if she called in sick, but not if she stayed home to care for a child who was. I liked Izzy. We didn't talk much but we said things with looks and grins. I guessed a lot of customers didn't even see a waitress, not any more than they did the salt shaker anyway.

"My admirer been back?" I asked when she refilled my coffee.

Izzy shook her head. Al or whoever it was had probably just wanted a close look at me. Wanted to make sure he tossed the right girl into the ditch.

After breakfast I headed on down to Throckmorton Stationery and Business Supplies to look over Peter's delivery schedules on dates Al had ridden with him. Peter had been eager to pull them and go over them with me. When I held firm on my plans for him, his cousin Flora said she'd be glad to do it. Her office was on the floor above her father's, one of four small rooms opening off a short corridor that set them apart from a large open space with clusters of desks. Men and a scattering of women sat at the desks, some talking on telephones, others clattering away on adding machines or typewriters. Others were surrounded by neat stacks of papers which looked like orders or billing forms. I recognized Thelma bent over a desk in one corner.

Apparently Throckmorton himself was the only one in the firm who rated an outer office and his own secretary. One of the girls at a typewriter pointed me to "Miss Flora's" office. The door stood open and Flora was typing away at a roomy little typewriter stand placed at right angles to her desk. The table and desk matched to a T. Suppressing a twinge of envy at the thought of how nice it would be not to heft my Remington out of the way every time I needed to spread papers out on my desk, I rapped on the door jamb.

The concentration on Flora's face gave way to a smile as she looked up and saw me.

"If you go any faster that thing will start to smoke," I said.

"Advantages of a business school education." Her mouth twisted. "Pull up a chair. That one's quite comfy. I thought it would be best if I was the one to type what you wanted. Keep anyone who works here from getting curious."

"Smart." I tried the chair she'd indicated. Leather covered the padding that cushioned its seat and back and part of the arms. Nice as it felt I wondered if it might make visitors stick around longer than they were welcome.

"Here, have a look at these while I finish," Flora suggested sliding me a manilla folder which held half a dozen or so typed sheets. Turning back to her machine she began to clatter away.

If her fingers ever missed a key I didn't see evidence on the pages before me. The top of each held a date when

Peter had let Al ride with him, followed by names and addresses of businesses who received a delivery that day. Counting the page she was working on, it looked as though the total came to eight trips in a little over five weeks. So few times to land Peter in so much hot water. I had time to compare the first page against my list of places burgled before I heard the zip of the final sheet leaving Flora's typewriter.

"If you like, I'll give you the carbon copies as well," she offered peeling them apart. "But you did mention that your office was searched–"

"Makes more sense to keep them somewhere else."

"Yes, I thought so."

"Why don't you keep them?"

"I hoped you might say that. We've a safe here and it's quite fierce. They'll be quick to get to if the others are lost."

I had a feeling most of Flora Throckmorton's abilities were being wasted in her current position.

"Peter get off okay?"

She nodded. "I drove him to the station myself so he couldn't turn stubborn. He thinks he's being a coward of course, leaving town. But I see your point wanting him out of the picture. You can get more done if you don't have to keep an eye on him as well, isn't that it?"

"Mostly. Also his disappearing will make Beale at least a little bit nervous. Beale won't expect it after the way Peter stood up to his goons. When crooks get nervous they sometimes get careless. They do stupid things. Whether that happens or not, at least Peter's safe. I expect his father's side of the family will be glad to see him."

"Yes. It's probably been six or seven years since he made the trip to St. Louis."

I'd been scanning the last page she'd typed. Nothing popped out that made me want to shout 'eureka!'.

"That place that got hit last night one of your customers?"

"Dawes Tobacco? Yes. And it's on this list, I'm afraid. Father had a conniption when he read about it. He's already beside himself at the realization Pete doesn't think working here is the be all and end all – and fretting about how to manage without him while Pete's out of town. The robbery at Dawes has started him worrying that customers will start to notice how many of the places hit do business with us.

"Last night he said some competitor might be trying to ruin his business. That sound likely to you?"

"Morris Gibbons?" She started to laugh but then grew thoughtful. "He's a horrible man. Loud and self-important. And greedy, I'd say. I'm sure he's underhanded enough. But he doesn't have guts enough, I don't think. Not to do it on his own, and certainly not to get mixed up with someone who's an out-and-out gangster like you say this man Beale is. Gibbons would love to steal our customers, but this seems too grand a scheme for that, don't you think?"

I did.

"Anything in this list of deliveries catch your eye?" I asked.

"One can't type well and think about what one's typing. Let me have a look."

Her chair had rollers. She pulled it around to the side of her desk and I slid the typed pages sideways so we could both see them.

"None of the places robbed were from their first trip together," she said after a minute.

I'd noticed it too. Could be a way to prevent a connection between the robberies and Al turning up. Or could be the first time was only a test run to see if Al could make contact; find a way in, get away with whatever it was they were planning. Flora rested her chin on her fist.

"But the first place robbed was a place they'd delivered to. The next one wasn't one of our customers. Then our customers five times in a row...." Her fingers skimmed the pages. I'd put a dot in front of the ones that were robbed. She hadn't needed a map to know what it meant.

"Do the ones that aren't your customers all use the same supplier?"

"Don't know. Sorry." Her brows were drawn in concentration.

"Any of them get their supplies from Morris Gibbons?"

"Fine Brothers used to three or four years ago. I can't say about now." Leaning back she tapped the last page. "What I *do* notice is that only one of the smaller accounts Pete made deliveries to on these particular dates has been robbed. And it was the first one hit."

Testing the waters, I thought again.

"After that they're all big accounts?"

"Speaking only for ours of course, the next one was. But then there was a medium one. After that they've all been big, except for the one where we only do half their supplies."

We looked at each other. I wasn't sure what it meant, but it meant something and she knew it too.

"How long would it take you to look up all these places, not just the ones that were robbed, and mark the big ones?"

"I don't need to look. I can tell you right now, except for a couple that sort of fall in the cracks between big and medium."

Ten minutes later Flora tapped the pages together and slid them toward me. The big accounts were marked with a red check, medium ones with blue. A few times she'd stopped and pursed her lips as if reviewing ledgers in her head. I began to wonder if she'd memorized the average monthly bill of every Throckmorton's customer. When she told me the dollar amounts she'd used as the basis for big and medium I whistled.

"They equate, more or less, to the size of the company," she explained. "The bigger the company, the greater their need for office supplies. There are exceptions, of course. Some places use more paper because they do lots of reports or contracts – insurance firms or big law offices for example. And some of the really big ones like The Cash use several suppliers. Wouldn't it be a plum to get all his business!"

'The Cash' was John Patterson's cash register company, one of the jewels in the city's crown. It had gotten deliveries twice in the period we were considering, but it hadn't been burglarized. Flora frowned, maybe thinking as I was that getting linked to a burglary there would just about ruin a company.

"You're a whiz to work with," I said neatening the typed pages in their folder and getting to my feet. "Thanks for helping on this."

Flora stood up too. We shook hands. She walked a few steps with me toward the open door through which I'd entered. Just before we got there, to my surprise, she stepped past me and closed it.

"There's something I thought I should mention, now that I know what's been going on. I didn't like to say anything around Father and Peter, but twice in the last week or so I'm pretty sure someone has followed me. A car, I mean, meandering along several cars back–"

"Watch out," I said bluntly. In a couple of sentences I told her about driving into the trap with the moving truck and waking up woozy down in a ditch. "I can give you the name of a good bodyguard," I offered.

"Thanks all the same, but I'm on good terms with the men on the loading dock." Her eyes danced. "There are two in particular, brothers who'd put Paul Bunyan to shame. I'm sure they'd be glad to pick me up and deliver me home in their truck every evening if I pay them a bit for their time."

"See if you can get your father to ride with them too."

"Easier said than done. I'll try."

She opened the door and we shook hands again. I hesitated. "Maybe with Peter away your father will start to notice how well you know this whole operation."

Her mouth gave its wry little twist again. "I shan't hold my breath – but thanks."

Thelma was on her way somewhere with a stack of papers when I came out. She nodded at me. Her eyes were red from crying, and I wanted to say something to her, but I didn't know what. That her boyfriend was an idiot but his heart was in the right place? The best I could do was to nod in return.

I had plenty to think about walking back to my office.

To top it off, I got there just in time for a phone call from Muley.

TWENTY-TWO

"This Mavis?" growled the voice at the end of the line.

My visit to the Ace of Clubs had nearly slipped from my memory, it seemed so long ago. In fact, not even three days had passed.

"That's right," I said, saved by remembering the name I'd used.

"Bartender down at the Ace said you got somethin' Benny Norris left for me."

It wasn't quite what I'd said, but I'd roll with it seeing as how it had led him to call.

"You must be Muley," I said. "I was just about giving up. Tell you what, why don't you meet me at the Arcade–"

"Ix-nay. I, uh, I gotta stick close to home. Look after a sick friend. You know where the Ace is. Why'nt you bring it over there tonight? Quarter of nine?"

I'd already been ambushed once this week and that was plenty.

"No thank you," I said. "It's bad enough going into that dreadful place in the daytime. I could leave work right on the dot; maybe make it there by a quarter past four –"

"It has to be after––. It has to be later!" His voice skidded up a couple of notes. Not the sound of someone setting me up. The sound of panic. I was almost certain he'd been about to say the meeting had to be after dark.

"Okay. Okay," he said hastily. "It's just that I gotta stick close ... and this friend don't sleep so good in the day."

He was scared. My gut and mind both revved anticipating I was finally onto something.

"How's this?" he was saying. "Landlady where I stay lets renters sit in this little piano room off the parlor. Ain't no piano there. That sound okay? Brown's Rooms. One block up from the Ace? Same street?"

The neighborhood was still lousy, but I could make it work. Park under a streetlight. Maybe find someone to ride along. Have my gun in my pocket.

"I bet it's that insurance he said he'd just got last time I saw him. Poor bugger. Said it would help him if ever he got in a tight spot. Turns out it's me it'll help." He paused for me to confirm it. I didn't. He gave me his address.

"Don't tell no one you're coming to meet me, though" he cautioned. "Can't always trust people, they find out some stiff left you something."

*   *   *

For several minutes after I hung up I continued to sit on the edge of my desk and swing my legs, increasingly satisfied about all the things I finally knew. I knew Al had used the deliveries with Peter to get inside businesses and look around. I knew what those businesses were and where they were located. I knew Al worked for Beale. I knew Benny Norris had worked for Beale too. I knew Benny had come into money but gotten upset that someone was trying to make him a scapegoat. And now I knew one of Benny's pals was scared enough he was lying low.

There were plenty of things I didn't know, too. Like what Al was looking for inside those businesses. Was he checking the merchandise? Hunting an easy or lucrative haul? And why was Muley scared? And why had Benny Norris thought insurance could help him?

At the moment, though, one thing I didn't know bothered me more than all the others: Beale's boys knew what I looked like, but I wouldn't recognize any of them.

I didn't like being at that disadvantage. I'd come back from meeting with Flora Throckmorton keen to drive past all the businesses on her list to see if anything in their locations caught my eye. I headed out again, but with an amended plan. As I passed the open door to Simpson's Socks, Maxine glanced furtively up at me, then glued her attention on the envelope she was sealing. The pot of roses sat on the counter.

Ten minutes' walking put me in the lobby of the *Daily News*. I asked one of the clerks at the counter to call upstairs and tell Matt Jenkins someone wanted to see him.

A few minutes later he came down the stairs, eschewing the elevator. He was in his shirt-sleeves. They were closing on deadline. His steps slowed as he came toward me.

"You want something," he analyzed cocking his head and folding his arms. "Something you know is so unreasonable you don't dare even come upstairs for it."

"And here I thought I was protecting you, staying where no one would see me and get curious if you asked questions later."

"Since I'm down here now, I might as well hear it. It's always fun watching you when I turn you down."

"There's a guy named Al. Beale's right-hand boy. I need to know what he looks like."

Jenkins grimaced. "Thought you were going to lay off looking at Beale, Mags."

"Yeah, but some of his boys suckered me and ran me off the road a couple nights ago. I want a straight table."

Jenkins shook his reddish halo. His face had gone somber.

"Jesus, Maggie —"

A woman stopped at the end of the counter nearest us and began to talk to one of the clerks about placing a classified. We stepped out of earshot. Jenkins turned so he could keep an eye peeled for other newshounds who might give us a gander.

"What's Al's last name?" he asked folding his arms.

"Don't know. He's a snappy dresser. Scar on one pinkie."

"Oh, sure! I always make sure to take a few shots of their hands. This one's a shoo-in."

I glared at his sarcasm. He gave me a look that pitied my dimness.

"And just how do you expect me to look someone up in the files if I don't know the last name?"

"Gee, I don't know. Maybe nose out who Beale's associates are? Maybe see if some of the shots of Beale show him with associates? Oh, forgive me. Here I keep thinking you're some kind of newsman. I guess guys who just tag along with a camera don't really qualify, huh?"

It was his turn to glare, except he hadn't had enough practice. "Oh, hell. Ione's away and I'm going to be down here anyway. I might as well do your bidding. Let me see if I can find some shots of Beale."

"I've seen shots of him. Presenting the doorprize at some charity auction, another one at a holiday dance. It's Al I want — his lieutenant."

"A scar on his pinkie, for chrissake." He turned and stomped back toward the elevator.

*   *   *

I spent most of the afternoon driving the routes Peter Stowe had traveled the times Al rode with him. Since Peter used deliveries to spot where the company could improve its services, or filled in if a driver was absent, the trips had taken him in various directions. One went south on Main to Oakwood and Kettering. Another went down Wayne and Wilmington, then looped around and back. One cut southeast to Moraine and Miamisburg. One went east on Third. One ran north on Main across the river and came back down Salem.

At each place that had been broken into I found a place to park while I had a good look, trying to spot any similarity of layout or type of business or how far they were set back from the road. If there was a pattern I couldn't spot it. What did the businesses on that list have in common?

I thought about it all the way back to the office. When I got settled in, I called Flora.

"What sort of things would every one of those businesses need besides office supplies?" I asked.

She was silent a moment gathering her thoughts. "Heat, electricity, phone. Janitors. Furniture. Advertising. An attorney, of course. Insurance...."

I could tell by the pause that she'd hit on the same thought I had not long before.

"Yeah," I said. "Think I'll have a look at that. Thanks."

It was already after four. Less than five hours til I met Muley. The phone rang.

"I'm in the mood for a blue plate special," Jenkins said. "Veal, maybe."

I gritted my teeth. He'd found something. Which meant I'd be buying his dinner since he'd come through for me. The veal part was to torment me, seeing as how it was Friday and I'd be stuck with a fishcake.

"Half past five?" Being polite was the closest I would ever come to martyrdom.

"Make it half past six."

133

TWENTY-THREE

"Ione finally throw you out?" I asked as Jenkins slid in across from me in the booth at Clancy's. He slouched against the hard wood behind him as comfortably as a pasha on a divan.

"She and her mother took the train up to Piqua to visit a cousin who has a new baby. Figured I might as well hang around downtown, catch a few extra pictures, maybe get lucky if the cops catch up with the burglary ring that's put Wurstner's fur up."

"That likely to happen?"

"Not the way I hear it. More likely if the city fathers had coughed up money for the extra cops that FBI report said we needed." His eyes twinkled shrewdly. "This interest you've taken in Beale and his outfit – it wouldn't happen to be connected to the burglaries, would it?"

"It would if I could figure out how to make it fit. Which so far I haven't."

The waitress came. He ordered his blue plate. I decided chowder and crackers appealed to me more than fish cakes.

"So what did you find?" I asked when we were alone again.

Jenkins made a face. "Not enough to make you happy you're buying my dinner." He reached beneath his jacket and produced a manilla envelope which he slid toward me. When I undid the string, four clippings and a photograph peeked out at me. I removed them one at a time, glancing up to make sure no one was watching. I was fairly sure Jenkins could land in hot water for pinching things from the newspaper's files and taking them for a stroll.

Two of the clippings I'd already seen, the ones of Beale at the dance and presenting the doorprize. The others were older. One, taken two years earlier, showed Beale in a group of men who owned fancy cars and were lining up for an amateur race while well-wishers watched in the background. Another, almost five years old now, showed Beale at the opening of one of his clubs as he planted a smooch on the cheek of a singer who held an armful of roses. In that one three unidentified men whose suits didn't quite disguise their line of work stood behind him.

"It's not much," Jenkins said.

I studied the clippings. The one at the car race was all but useless. The camera's focus had been on the drivers. Even though the onlookers weren't far away, their features were blurred, some faces all but blocked by a neighbor's hat. The one of the club opening gave me a good look at two of Beale's men, but given their sturdy builds and the broad nose on one, neither matched the description of Al as 'good looking'. The third man behind Beale looked like he might. He was trim enough and his suit fitted like a glove, but he'd been turning away when the shutter clicked. He was gesturing as if giving an order. All it really left me was a jawline and the shadow from his hat and a cigarette.

With a small sigh I turned to the photo.

"A different one of him presenting that doorprize," I said in surprise.

Jenkins nodded. "Different angle. Showed less of the winner than the one that got used."

It showed more of the space behind Beale, though. A man stood looking on, just far enough away to be out of focus. He might be the same man as at the club opening, or he might not. The blonde clinging to his arm came just to his shoulder, so he might be tall. Or she might be short.

"Shit." I took a better look at the two other goonies, making sure I'd remember their faces, then shoved the whole lot back into the envelope.

"Cops may have a file on him," Jenkins offered. "I waited 'til one of the guys on the crime beat got a snootful after work and chatted him up. He showed off some about who works for Beale. One's a guy named Albert Sikes."

He knew I couldn't ask the cops about it. So did I. But I had other plans for Jenkins, and striking out with the photos would make it easier.

"Since I know your conscience will bother you if you don't earn that veal, then, how about riding along to watch my back tonight while I meet a thug?" I asked when we'd tucked into our food. I'd thought of it as soon as he'd mentioned Ione was away.

He shot me a look. "I'm pretty fond of my neck."

"It's not anyone from Beale's outfit. You just need to sit out in the car while I go into a rooming house, hit the horn if anyone comes in after me. It's only a couple of blocks from downtown."

He chewed some veal. "Any chance of a picture worth using a flashbulb?"

"Probably not – but you might get some background that puts you ahead of the competition. I'm meeting a pal of the guy who threatened me in my office and then wound up dead in the alley."

"Who worked for Beale." Jenkins whistled softly. "Could be you're onto something, Mags."

* * *

By nine-fifteen we were across the street and down a ways from the place Muley stayed, parked in a dark spot where a street lamp was out. If anyone noticed us we'd be dismissed as a couple of lovebirds. Meanwhile I'd get a sense of the street and its rhythm, maybe notice if anything seemed out of order.

The skinny two-storey house we were watching was three times as deep as it was wide, a fact we'd established by driving through the alley beside it before continuing several blocks and meandering back. A hand-painted sign in the left downstairs window advertised ROOMS. Fifteen minutes slipped past with nothing to watch except two guys going into the Ace of Clubs a block and a half away. I pulled my wool tam down over my ears to keep out the chill.

Good conversation made the waiting easier. Jenkins was an honest-to-God college man, a fact he mostly hid from his newsroom cronies though it marginally redeemed him in the eyes of his in-laws, who disapproved of his profession. We were batting around whether war in Europe would mean more jobs and better wages here, when a man strolled into view from a side street. He turned in our direction. He looked like a man who belonged, cap pulled low, hands in his jacket pockets, gait unhurried. Not large enough to be Muley, I thought. At the place we were watching he left the sidewalk and went lightly up the four steps to the stoop. To anyone happening by, he'd seem to be putting his key in. But he took longer than was necessary, and the movements weren't right. Was he forcing the lock?

Uneasiness licked through me. The man on the steps had the door halfway open and was slipping inside.

"If I'm not out in five, call the cops and clear out," I said swinging out of the car.

I sprinted across the street and took the steps two at a time. Even without a porch light I could see the gouges left by a screwdriver in the wood frame. Flattening myself to one side I slid through the door. Steep stairs just ahead led up and hooked left onto a hallway. Keeping an eye on the stairs, I rapped on the door of the room with the sign in the window. A woman peered out so promptly she must have been listening.

"Call the cops. A guy just jimmied your front door," I said under my breath.

Muley had sounded scared, and now someone was breaking into the place where he lived. I drew the .38 from my pocket. In a crouch as low and silent as a cat slinking after a bird I crept up the stairs. Every move had been honed in childhood games with my father.

Before I was halfway up I heard shots above: pow-pow-pow.

Back flattened against the wall, I saw the man in the cap round the short stretch of rail at the top of the stairs. On the verge of racing down them he spotted me. We fired at the same instant. I felt the breath of his bullet as I fired again. There were screams, another shot, maybe two. The man in the cap spun out of view. Hoping he was down I pushed off the stairs behind me. A sharp crack, louder than the others, sounded and I lurched backward.

TWENTY-FOUR

"Mother of *God*!" I opened my eyes to my leg on fire and pandemonium all around me. Men barked words to other men. Shapes sprinted past me. Mingling with the man sounds were those of a baby crying, a woman's shrill hysteria, and somewhere close at hand, a woman's nervous staccato:

"She'd just knocked to warn me when we heard the shots upstairs—"

"Hello, Sunshine. Glad to see that bump on the head didn't do too much damage."

A cop I recognized as one of Billy's pals was kneeling over me. Walker? Waller?

"Don't call Billy or Seamus," I said thickly. "I'm okay."

"– and he fired right at her—"

"Lie still for a minute." Walker/Waller put out a restraining hand as I tried to sit. "Give us a chance to check you, see if we want a stretcher."

My brief disorientation passed. I was lying just to the side of the stairs I'd been creeping up what seemed like only minutes ago. Maybe it *was* only minutes ago. The air still reeked of gunpowder. A shard of wood as long as my forearm dangled from one of the stairs. It bobbled as a pair of feet hurried down them. My left leg burned like sin.

"How many bodies up there?" I couldn't nod to indicate the second story since Walker's fingers were poking firmly but gently at the back of my neck, hunting any hint it might be broken.

"One. Plus some blood in the hall." He sat back on his heels. "Looks like maybe you winged the killer." He glanced up at someone approaching. "Hey, Mick, how about checking her leg?"

"Not me. I've heard what she does to cops who get overfriendly."

"You've got better skills with the ladies than that idiot Fuller. They want me talking to witnesses."

"Gee, I think maybe I can check my own leg," I said. Both of them grabbed to help as I started to sit. I willed my brain back to speed. What the hell was Connelly doing here in uniform this time of night?

"Turn and rest your back against the stairs," he ordered, shifting me as he said it. He looked perversely pleased when I swore at the pain.

Bereft of memory I stared at my leg. It was streaked with blood. Okay, I was supposed to check it. I put two fingertips tentatively to a spot near the worst of the blood.

"Oh, for chrissake. You wouldn't recognize a break or sprain if you found one." Connelly shoved my hand away, his irritation barely contained. He took out a crisp white hanky and scrubbed at his fingers. Holding my ankle and moving it gently he probed and pressed. His hands were strong. Confident. More aware of them now than of pain, I hitched in my breath.

"Hurt?"

"If there's a bullet in there, you're going to shove it in further," I hedged.

"You weren't shot. Though it doesn't appear to be from lack of trying."

Reaching past me he smacked something into my lap with unnecessary force. I looked down at the tam that had kept me warm in the car. Two neat round holes, one in, one out, now punctured the top of it. An inch from where the top of my head had been. Maybe less.

"Your leg got scraped good and proper when the rotten wood in that step gave way under you." Connelly had turned his attention back to my leg. "If you have any sense – which I've yet to see evidence of – you'll have a doctor clean out the splinters and get yourself a lockjaw shot."

Craning my neck I saw the partially missing stair where the shard of wood hung. I remembered the cracking sound.

"Oh." As the full impact of the shootout sank in, it was my spirits that took a bullet. Here I sat with a less than heroic injury. Upstairs a man lay dead, killed even as I arrived. It had to be Muley. Meaning my one and maybe only chance to learn more about Benny Norris – why he'd thought someone was trying to make him a patsy, where he'd gotten money to flash, who might have killed him – was gone. So was my chance to find out what had scared Muley. It all had slipped through my fingers. On top of which I'd ruined a good hat.

"You okay?" Connelly's fingers had paused on the calf of my leg.

"Yeah, spiffy. All I need is a bandage." I pushed his hand away.

"Ambulance boys should be here to patch you up shortly." He sat back on his haunches nailing me with his gaze. I noticed his eyes were blue. "You damn fool girl, what were you doing here?"

"Funny, I was about to ask you the same. Where's Billy? And how's it happen the cops set a speed record showing up?" We'd both lowered our voices.

"Chief has half of us pulling extra duty at night 'til we crack this burglary ring." He hesitated; glanced around. "Also happens Freeze had a car up the street keeping an eye out on this place. Guy who lived here was in gaol with Benny Norris, but he hasn't turned up since Norris was shot. Landlady says he came back last night.

"Your turn. And don't get cute. Freeze'll be here any minute wanting to know same as I did."

I shifted, watching blood ooze from a couple of places on my leg.

"As far as I could see the cops didn't care much who'd killed Norris. I did. I'm the one he warned not to snoop. I'm the one whose office got tossed. I didn't like looking over my shoulder. So I asked around. Learned Norris might have been pals with a guy. I put out the word I was interested and today that guy called. I'm guessing he's the stiff upstairs. I was coming to meet him."

Connelly's hard look had faded. Maybe he'd been expecting some cockamamie story and I'd disappointed him. He was opening his mouth to speak when the force's ambulance crew banged through the door with their kit. At their heels came Freeze with his perfect little nose and his attitude that matched his name. Behind him trailed the same two assistants who looked to be wearing the same cheap suits as the last time we'd met.

"Miss Sullivan. What a coincidence," Freeze said snidely. One assistant continued upstairs like a well-trained puppy.

"Her wound's going to need a good bit of cleaning," Connelly advised the ambulance boys. "No breaks, no sprains."

Freeze sent a reproving look. Beat cops shouldn't speak unless the lieutenant in charge told them to.

"Have you taken her statement?" Freeze's tone was sharp.

"Just about to, sir. Walker called me over to check on her injuries and she seemed somewhat addled at first."

"Take it now. Dobbs, start questioning neighbors. And you, Miss Sullivan, can start by explaining how you happened to be here."

Lt. Freeze struck me as maybe too fond of his status. His other assistant scurried off. Connelly took out a pencil. The nun inside me told me I should be a courteous and conscientious citizen. Instead I smiled.

"A friend of mine wanted advice on his love life. We were riding around and turned on this street and saw a guy jimmy the front door."

Connelly's pencil made an erratic scratch. He stared at me with a dumb-struck fury one step short of the way Moses must have looked when he smashed the tablets. Just then one of the ambulance boys doused my leg with peroxide, or its first cousin. I gritted my teeth to hold back a yelp. Freeze had started to frown, reluctant to buy my tale but still nursing bunions from the last time we'd waltzed. The medical boys were swabbing my cuts now. It took several seconds before I could speak.

"Okay. That's malarky," I managed. "I figure you earned it the last time you questioned me. Here's how it really happened tonight. The dead guy upstairs, his name Muley?"

"Clarence Worth," Freeze said stiffly. "But yes, I'm told he went by that nickname. What's your connection?"

I told him the same thing I'd told Connelly. This time I mentioned the Ace of Clubs and the bartender. With luck they'd lean on the big gorilla. With even better luck they'd learn something. Freeze seemed to recognize I was leveling now and kept his questions on things that mattered.

"I've got a hunch Muley was scared of somebody," I volunteered as the ambulance crewman wound a last lap of bandage around my leg and plastered it with adhesive tape. "He made quite a deal about how the meeting had to be after dark, and right around here."

Someone yelled from upstairs to see if the ambulance crew was finished. I guessed they were needed to bring

Muley down. I no longer was eager to make his acquaintance.

"My landlady locks the door at half past eleven," I told Freeze. "Any chance we could finish this up tomorrow?"

He hesitated. He was a by-the-book sort. One of the cops keeping gawkers away outside stuck his head in.

"Lieutenant, there's a camera hack out here says he heard Miss Sullivan was inside and does she want a ride downtown?"

Jenkins. Bless him, he'd waited. Or maybe it was someone else. I got along okay with a lot of the press corps.

Freeze chuffed out a breath. He gave me a stern look. "I suppose I can trust you not to discuss what happened here?"

I smiled.

Connelly and the ambulance man who'd bandaged me helped me to my feet. My leg hurt like hell, but I could limp okay. The odor of cordite was fading. It no longer masked an underlying smell of dust and lye soap and mops gone sour from scrubbing too many floors. Clutching my tam, which I wouldn't be wearing again, I stepped outside and took a grateful gulp of clean night air.

Jenkins spotted me and hoofed it over to offer an arm when he saw the bandage. He even dropped me at Mrs. Z's although he spent the whole time grousing that the competition would beat him on this. I gave him Muley's name and nickname, enough for him to score a nice little beat on information at least, but not enough for Freeze to know it came from me.

"Once cop cars started arriving and I found out you were okay, I ran up the street to that dump of a bar and called the city desk. At least I'll get a place on page one tomorrow," he told me as he pulled to the curb at Mrs. Z's.

I'd declined his initial offer to drop me at the emergency door of Miami Valley. Further doctoring of my leg could wait until morning. Waving him on his way I went stiff-legged up the walk. At least Mrs. Z's beastly cat wasn't lurking somewhere to add to my misery.

On the porch one of the girls was holding hands with her beau. We said hi and I went on in so they could have another smooch or two. In the front hall I stood for a couple of minutes listening to the orderly tick of the big walnut grandfather clock and savoring the clean smell of my surroundings. Mostly it was an absence of smell – no stale grease, no souring mops, just the faintest hint of lavender from the little china potpourri dish on a sideboard next to the clock. The stairs felt reassuringly solid under my feet as I climbed them.

When I opened the door to my room, I almost stepped on a folded up piece of paper someone had shoved underneath. Grunting some at the effort, I bent to retrieve it. The paper was pale blue. I undid it.

On Main. I have more.

Jolene. She had something on Beale. She'd be at work now, peddling her cigarettes, and I felt too worn and too down in the dumps to wait up. I went down the hall and gave my face a fast wash. Back in my room, I let my clothes fall where I took them off, then crawled into bed with the covers over my head.

TWENTY-FIVE

Crooks and killers set so much store by brawn they overlook gals. Jolene looked smug as a stray cat in a dairy the next time I saw her.

On weekend mornings we had kitchen privileges. Mrs. Z put out a pitcher of coffee cream and let us use her toaster and teakettle. We supplied our own mugs and some of the girls took turns buying coffee. Others brought down tins of tea from their rooms. Everyone pitched in for a couple of loaves of bread and a stick of butter. Every now and then somebody's mother or aunt or sister gave them a jar of jelly to share. Being a farm girl, Jolene was an early riser in spite of working late. She was already at the table, sharing the paper with Esther and Constance and nibbling a slice of toast, when I made my way in.

Her eyes widened at the bandages wrapping my leg.

"Golly! What happened to you?"

"I was following a guy and a rotten board gave way when I stepped on it."

The girls were always pestering for tidbits about my work. For once I could tell them the truth, slightly edited.

"Good thing you weren't following that man who got shot," chirped Constance.

"Because then somebody turned right around and shot at the man who shot him! There must have been bullets everywhere," added Esther. They were sisters and shared a room. Esther waited tables while Constance took a secretarial course. She slid me the front section. "Look –

there's a picture of where it happened right there on the front page!"

Spread across four columns of *The Journal* was the front of Brown's Rooming House with police cars clustered around it. Poor Jenkins, losing out to the competition. Still, the cutline under the photo said the deceased hadn't been identified, and Jenkins had a name to run with his page one picture, so he'd feel some better.

"I need my coffee," I announced to the room in general. Jolene got the hint. She waited until I'd worked my way through half a mug and looked over the first few pages of the front section. Then she made a show of yawning and getting up for more hot water.

At the opposite end of the table from me, Esther and Constance had their heads bent to the society section, which they poured over almost line by line. Jolene freshened her tea and moved to my end, putting her back between me and the others and keeping her voice down.

"The girl I told you about has Wednesdays off, so Thursday was the first chance I had to talk to her, and you weren't around yesterday."

"Yeah, thanks for the note."

"I tried to make it vague – like it could be about a dress shop or something if anyone else saw it."

"You'd make a first-rate spy," I said.

Jolene looked pleased. "Anyway, while we were putting our costumes on I got her talking. Chattering, I should say. I told about some wild things I'd seen at The Mademoiselle. Then I said, 'Hey, I bet you've seen plenty, working at one of Woody Beale's places. I've heard he keeps the desk in his office stacked with moolah and sometimes he invites some of the girls who work for him back and stakes them all to a poker game.'

"Well, she laughed and said that was the wildest thing she'd ever heard, that the manager had sent her back to get a key or something a time or two and she never saw any money, just Mr. Beale and the men who work for him sitting around and talking or maybe playing a few hands themselves. But..." She stretched glancing casually back to make sure Esther and Constance still were occupied. " ... she said way at the back behind the office was this private room where two, three times a week some real high rollers came to play poker. She said that table sure had stacks of cash."

I gave a silent whistle.

"How about that, huh? I make up a story and it's almost like it's halfway true." She plucked a long blonde curl from its overnight tangle and twirled it around her finger.

"This girl say anything else about the place?"

"Just that when there was a poker game a couple of girls from out front would get sent back to take care of the high rollers. Bring them cigs and sandwiches and like. The manager had picked them, used the same three or four. One night one was sick, so the manager picked the girl who was telling me this and sent her back. He told her she needed to be discreet and not tell anyone what she saw and she'd get good tips. Which she did. But one of the so-called gents kept pawing her, and she didn't like it, so after a couple of weeks she started looking around and found another job and she quit.

"Some story, huh? And all while she was straightening her stockings. Can you believe it? I swear, she must talk a mile a minute."

Genevieve came into the kitchen, dressed and groomed like she meant to go shopping.

"Oh, my," she said spotting my leg. "Aren't you a vision of loveliness."

"The face that launched a thousand ships," I said. "Jolene, you are one smart cookie. I owe you a picture show."

Beaming, she got up and bounced on her way. Ginny and I had a cup of coffee together while I gave her the same brief account of my injury I'd told the others. Then I brushed my teeth and got my purse and took my leg for a looksee by old Dr. Hallorhan. He'd been patching me up since I was a kid.

* * *

Waiting to see Doc Hallorhan took most of the morning. When I finally got in he sudsed me and picked out some overlooked splinters and doused me with a punitive amount of antiseptic. After that came a lecture that took almost as long as the treatment. It left me just enough time to get over to Wheeler's Garage, which closed early on Saturdays.

"You got a date tonight, Calvin?" I asked when he and Eli had been reassured that the DeSoto and I were both fine.

Calvin ducked his head bashfully and allowed as how he didn't.

"How'd you and your tin lizzie like to earn a couple of bucks?"

We worked out the details and I said good-by. It was half past one and some good Irish whisky would soothe the stinging in my leg a lot better than a couple of aspirin. Besides, if I didn't stay busy I'd start thinking about how close I'd been to learning something from Muley. So I took a trolley as far as I could and then walked over to Finn's.

On Saturday afternoons it was quiet and cozy, giving no hint how noisy it would be when evening rolled around. I helped myself to a slice of cheese from the wedge on the counter, cut a slice of wholemeal soda bread and took an apple from the bowl next to it. As fine a lunch as a body could ask, particularly after Finn's wife brought me a tumbler of whiskey and water that was stronger on the whiskey.

I savored my meal and listened to a couple of old codgers playing dominoes in the corner. There was time now to look through the rest of the paper I hadn't had time for that morning. I was in hog heaven playing lady of leisure when someone kicked the chair across from me out so forcefully I jumped. Mick Connelly dropped onto it. His eyes were blazing.

"Your da didn't turn you over his knee half enough, you smart-aleck brat. I suppose you were having a grand time spinning Freeze that cockamamie yarn last night and watching me squirm. Let's get the fence straight. You mouth off to him or the other brass, you get yourself dragged down the station, I won't lift a finger to help just because I happen to be Billy's partner."

If I hadn't neared the bottom of my whiskey I'd have thrown it at him.

"You'll be making snowballs in hell before I ask you for help! I'll pick my scraps where I want, and I'll take my licks in them and it's none of your damn business!"

His hand came down, imprisoning my wrist as I started to stand. "Like hell it's not. You listen now, and good. I know you're holding things back – but I don't know what. I don't know your connection to that gobbo got killed last night or why you really were there." Heat from his body smothered me like a blanket. His grip was making my wrist go numb.

"But if you care so little for Billy and Seamus you've got your toe in something crooked I'm not looking the other way. Understand?" He leaned closer. "If you're wheedling information from them or you get mud on their names after all their years of service I will personally – personally – see you locked up for as long as the law will allow. No matter how fond I may be of Billy. Or that

Seamus is the finest man I've ever met. Or how that fallen angel look of yours fogs a man's senses!"

I was flabbergasted. My effort to pull free only made his fingers tighten.

"Let go my arm, you big ox, before I kick you where it counts!"

We were hissing more than speaking, but around us other ears were straining to hear. Finn's wife. The domino players. A guy with a crooked nose who was laboring to write something, scratching out as much as he kept. Connelly's eyes held mine so fiercely that I wondered if he'd even heard me speak. An interval passed before he looked down, blinked at the sight of his hand, and released me. Rattled by his intensity, I sat back rubbing the place where his fingers had been.

"You call yourself a cop? You're acting more like the thugs you're supposed to go after. Now you do the listening: Last time anyone called me dishonest was Maureen Toohey in fifth grade. I knocked her flat. I've got a job to do, same as you. Maybe I don't blab all I know sometimes. Neither do you. Or Freeze. Or Chief Wurstner with his hat full of braid. But I have brains enough not to hold back anything that could get someone killed. Or hurt if they didn't deserve it. So if you want to flex your muscles go flex them at someone else."

With that I got up and marched out, hobbling so much it probably spoiled the effect.

He didn't follow.

Finn's wife, who was something of a romantic, probably thought we were having a lovers' spat.

TWENTY-SIX

"Golly, I've heard of The Owl. It's for fellows with plenty of moolah," Calvin said. Usually he was almost too bashful to speak around me, but nervousness had loosened his tongue. "This old clunker of mine's going to look out of place."

"Not as shined up as you keep it and the way it purrs," I reassured. "And we're just going to drive through the parking lot a couple of times. Remember?"

He nodded.

It was somewhere past ten and we were headed north on Main with downtown and the river retreating behind us. Even though Calvin's car was old and would have been a rattletrap in other hands, he kept it in as fine a shape as I'd let on. In a restless stream of pleasure seekers out for a Saturday night of dancing and booze, we wouldn't rate a second look.

Calvin had picked me up at Mrs. Z's. I'd had two good reasons for hiring him. If any of Beale's boys happened to be hanging around outside the nightclub, they wouldn't recognize Calvin's Plymouth the way they would my car. The twofer was that since I didn't need to keep my hands on the steering wheel, I'd be able to jot down license numbers as we rolled through The Owl's parking lot.

The nightclub sat back from the road and was decked out in stucco with red tile. Arches across the front created an illusion of someplace foreign – Mexico or Cuba, I'd guess. Businesses were getting sparse this far from downtown Except for the club, all the other places around were closed.

"Let's pull in somewhere, watch who goes in and out," I said.

Across from the club, on a side street, we found a darkened restaurant. Calvin pulled up close to the building. It hid us from the traffic on Main but gave a great view.

For a while we just sat and watched. People came. People went. The club had a doorman and a guy in a white jacket who parked cars. I watched one girl practically fall out when her date opened the car door, she was so loaded. None of the cars that came and went looked familiar, although about the only one I'd recognize would be Beale's big green job. Mostly I was after a sense of the place, its rhythm.

"Gonna be chilly tonight," Calvin observed.

I already was noticing it. Even the dandiest mechanic couldn't make a car warm when the engine was off.

"I brought a flask," I grinned pulling it out of my coat pocket.

"I brought a Thermos. Coffee. Warms you right up. Just say if you want some."

"Thanks. Likewise you and the hooch."

He shook his head. "My dad's a real hard Baptist. Made me swear I wouldn't dance or drink tonight."

We fortified ourselves with our respective beverages. I missed the warmth of my tam, but wearing it might have been flirting with bad luck, given the bullet hole in it. I didn't have my .38 either. The cops were entertaining it. I didn't expect to need a gun or I wouldn't have brought Calvin, even if his tall male form did make great window dressing. Just in case, though, the friendly little automatic from my car now nestled in my purse.

Not long before Calvin picked me up that evening, I'd knocked on the door to the Mrs. Z's apartment, which occupied half of the ground floor. While Butterball gave me the evil eye from a chair, I told Mrs. Z I was working that night and might need letting in again. Taking a look at my bandaged leg she gave a disapproving cluck and walked to the little desk where she kept her accounts and paid her bills. She opened a drawer and took something out and handed it to me.

"I can't say I like the business you're in. It worries me, frankly, and it's much too rough for a nice young lady like you. But you've lived here four years without causing a speck of trouble. From now on if you think you might be late, just come and get this. Slide it under my door when you get in."

I stared down at the key to Mrs. Z's back door. You could have knocked me over with a feather.

"And, Margaret," she added. "Don't mention this to the other girls."

Butterball hissed.

Freed of the need to keep an eye on the clock I could afford to let things at Beale's club hit full swing. It was almost eleven when I told Calvin to make his first pass through the parking lot. We left the shadows of the restaurant, went out and over and came up Main again.

"Remember, take it nice and slow," I coached as we turned in. "We've already been to another joint, maybe want a livelier one. Or we're getting a late start, can't decide where we want to light."

Where cars were concerned, you didn't need to tell Calvin anything twice. He glided along like someone hunting a parking spot. A Tommy Dorsey tune spilled out of the club. The sax was weak. A pudgy guy with a cigar and a girl in a white fur shrug came out arguing. If the car park man or the guy on the door so much as noticed us they didn't show it.

Beale's nightclub looked to be popular. Spots for a car were rare in front. Calvin's Plymouth moseyed along the white stucco wall toward the rear. A few cars were parked nose out away from the building, probably brought around by the boy in the white jacket. But it was a handful of cars attached to the building like nursing kittens that drew my attention.

I noticed the building had two back doors. One was faintly illuminated with an awning the size of a doormat, the door a married man entertaining a girl could duck out if an acquaintance who might not understand came in the front way. The door that interested me was maybe five yards to the left and almost faded into the wall. No light. Unmarked. Beale's big green Packard, along with several other cars, sat next to it facing a RESERVED sign painted on the stucco. On the far side of the public door, three other cars waited.

My brain trotted, making assessments. Except for Beale's, the cars by the half-hidden door were nondescript. That probably meant no high rollers were playing poker tonight. My guess was they used the door by Beale's car when they did play, though. Jolene's friend had mentioned a private room. In and out. Unseen.

As Calvin rolled past, I managed to scribble plate numbers from three of the cars next to Beale's. One was the number Evelyn had written down for me.

"What now?" Calvin whispered as we came out into the lights at the front of the club.

"Go on out up the street and we'll make our way back and park where we waited before."

Our brief foray hadn't warmed the car up much. As soon as we were settled back in by the restaurant Calvin filled the lid of his Thermos. I had a nip from my flask.

"Apart from the Packard, which was the best of the cars by the back of the building?"

"That Century." Calvin didn't hesitate for a second. "Not flashy, but those engines are the best Buick's ever built – inline-eight, a hundred sixty-five horses. They do ninety-five miles an hour and better. Eli looked at one in a showroom – just to see. Says they're built solid, too."

It was what I'd guessed, but my eye for cars was nothing compared with Calvin's.

"That Packard's the one I'd like to get my hands on though," he was saying with awe. "Look under its hood."

"If that Packard ever comes into Eli's, you call me fast as you can. Guy that drives it can make people disappear if they get in his way."

I didn't think that would happen, but I wanted to play it safe. I heard Calvin swallow.

TWENTY-SEVEN

Lewis Throckmorton was back to impatient.

"I need this cleared up." He rapped his knuckles on his desk for emphasis. "With Peter away I'm short-handed. And some of the customers may be getting suspicious. One cancelled an order on Friday with no explanation. Another made a comment at church. How much longer?"

"Hard to say." He'd rung before I got my coat off Monday morning, wanting to see me. "Now that I have some idea what's going on, things are starting to move."

"Make them move faster." His bushy mustache bristled. "The purchasing manager at a place we've dealt with for fifteen years has his feathers fussed – it could be there's gossip about these break-ins, or it could be something else. Peter's good at finding out. Smoothing feathers. Now I have to make time to go over and straighten that out on top of everything else. It's no way to run a business, you know–"

"Send Flora. She could probably reel off your whole list of customers and how much every one of them orders each month in her sleep. Send her to see him. Let her take up part of the slack."

He harrumphed and started to speak.

"Just until Pete gets back, of course," I mollified, and changed the subject before he could trot out excuses why she couldn't fill Peter's shoes. "Flora thought you might know who insured a couple of these places, or be able to find out."

He wanted faster, I'd give him faster. I handed him a steno sheet where she'd listed the names of half a dozen places from Peter's delivery list. She'd been on her way to her father's office with it as I was arriving.

"It's not looking awfully encouraging," she'd admitted, giving me a separate page with names of insurance companies for five other places, ones where she was on good enough terms with somebody there to ask. Three had the same insurer but two were different.

"You're barking up the wrong tree looking at insurance." Throckmorton flounced in his chair. "I told Flora as much." He liked pressing other people to hurry; he didn't seem to like the shoe on the other foot. "I can have a word with men at two of these places. Maybe three," he said grudgingly.

He picked up the phone to show me I was dismissed.

*   *   *

I'd parked my DeSoto in its usual spot in a lot just off Third that morning. My leg was feeling almost normal, albeit sore as sin, and walking to Throckmorton's had limbered it up. As I neared Patterson, though, I made sure to gimp along. It gave me more time to check license numbers on parked cars against the list concealed by the newspaper I was pretending to scan. Three doors down from my place and across the street I hit pay dirt: One of the numbers from the parking lot at The Owl. A guy slouched in the driver's seat pretending to read his own paper.

From my office the left window gave a pretty good view of the car. Good enough to tell if it moved, anyway. If Beale's boys were good at tailing, which I figured they were, they'd use various cars to make sure they weren't spotted. They'd take shifts. They'd likely change parking spots when they switched. The guy out there now had probably arrived around the same time I had or a little before. Say half-past eight. Odds were that come eleven, eleven-thirty, someone would turn up to replace him so his bladder didn't burst.

It looked like the plan I'd hatched would work out swell. Somewhere around seven that morning Calvin had parked his jalopy on a gravel lot just north of the produce market. It wouldn't attract attention amid the farm trucks, and I had a key. Fifteen minutes before the guy tailing me was likely to move, I'd go out the back way and get into Calvin's car. Then I'd wait and follow the car that had just spent a couple of hours waiting to follow me.

Meanwhile, I phoned a few places where Peter had made deliveries with Al. I said I was looking to switch insurance coverage at my business and that Peter Stowe had said he thought they were pleased with whoever did theirs. It netted me two names that matched insurance firms on Flora's list, one new one, and two polite refusals to give information. By the time the minute hand on my clock hit twenty 'til eleven I was raring to get into place and follow one of Beale's boys, which would surely be more productive.

Except just then the cops arrived.

"Hell's bells!" I choked as they pulled to the curb. I was at the window taking a final peek at the car I planned to follow. Now I watched in frustration as Billy bounced out and Seamus unfolded his tall, gaunt form from the passenger side. I knew they'd gotten wind of my presence during the fracas at Brown's rooming house and were coming to check on me.

Odds were fifty-fifty I could get out the back way and around to Calvin's car without them spotting me. But the first step in good surveillance was to stop at the powder room, besides which I'd feel like two bits if I gave them the slip. By the time they came down the hall I had my door open and was leaning a shoulder against it.

"Thought I heard the sound of flat feet," I greeted.

Seamus grinned. Billy glowered, a stern gaze assessing my bandage.

"You're in the midst of a shootout, almost get yourself killed, look like you've been over fighting Franco with the Internationals – and we're the last to know."

"I didn't want you to worry." The little girl sound of my voice made me wince.

"See, I told you it'd be that," Seamus said loyally.

I linked my arm through his and gave it a squeeze. "Glad to see you two back together." I flicked a look at Billy. "You get your fill of Rusty's lip?"

"You best not call him that where he can hear. And what have you got against him, anyway? Mick's a fine lad."

I shrugged. Billy decided to come halfway off his high horse.

"Mick had the morning off. He's working extra hours – nights too."

"Him and plenty of others," said Seamus. "Because of these burglaries."

I wondered if the cops had been watching Muley's rooming house because they knew something I didn't. Or because Woody Beale had friends at City Hall. That possibility made me uneasy. Nodding absently, I drifted back to the window and glanced out. The car was still there. Or one that looked a lot like it.

"I'm sorry you worried about me," I said. "I stepped on a rotten board, as you probably heard. I got worse as a kid." My eyes slid to the window again. Still there.

"What's so interesting out there?" asked Billy.

"Kid was looking like he might pinch something from a car. He didn't."

Seamus sighed and shook his head. He hated seeing kids in trouble.

"Funny no one's been nabbed for the break-ins with extra patrols on the street," I said. "Somebody up the ladder on the take?"

"They are not." Billy bristled as I'd known he would. "It's just what the FBI found when they studied us – we're too short on men. City of two hundred thousand and not even two hundred in the department, civilians included."

"Hey, don't you have a birthday next month?" I threw my arm around Seamus. "I'll have to buy you dinner somewhere."

Billy forgave me then, since we both knew perfectly well today was Seamus's birthday. There was a big bash planned for him at Finn's tonight, and if he suspected anything I'd just thrown him off. They said their good-byes. Billy shot me a wink as they went out the door. When they were halfway down the hall I hurried back to my window and looked out.

The car I'd been watching all morning was pulling away.

* * *

At twenty 'til two I launched the plan that I'd had to scrap before lunch. I went out the back way and through Mr. Seferis' place where at lunchtime I'd picked up the tweed cap I'd had made for Seamus. I headed up Fifth with lengthened steps to fit the men's trousers I was wearing. My hair was pinned up beneath a secondhand fedora. The knot in my necktie was perfect since I'd tied a million of them for my dad. All I could say for the cheap suit coat that went with the trousers was that it hid the holster with my automatic.

Entering the produce market on its far side, I made my way between stalls and eventually out to Calvin's jalopy. I slid into the driver's seat. No need to warm it up. The engine would purr like a baby tiger. I opened my paper and waited. My eye was on a gray Ford parked four doors up from my place, a different spot than the car that morning. I'd spotted it on my deliberate jaunt to the Arcade for lunch. The number on the Ford matched one on my list. Too bad all my ventures didn't pay off as well as my night out with Calvin.

Shortly after two o'clock the gray car pulled away from the curb. I slipped out after it, half a dozen cars behind. After a couple of blocks I closed the distance so I wouldn't confuse it with other gray cars. When it started along the very route I'd taken to Throckmorton's house I grew uneasy. Was the driver onto me? A street or two shy of where Throckmorton lived he turned off.

He stopped in front of a nice half-timbered Tudor and turned off the engine. I started past, intending to circle. Before I'd gone ten feet, a car shot out of a cross street, made a sharp turn and stopped on a dime, facing my direction. A Buick Century. *Not flashy but powerful.* I kept rolling.

The driver of the Buick swung out with easy grace and started toward me. He looked like he'd stepped from a magazine cover. Slender. Features many women would find attractive. Clothes so finely tailored they'd easily hide a gun.

I had no doubt at all I was seeing Al.

Another car swept to the curb behind his. Two men jumped out and fell into step with him as if from long practice. Reaching into a pocket of his dove gray topcoat, he removed a pair of brass knuckles.

And looked directly at me.

TWENTY-EIGHT

One of Beale's men behind me, three coming toward me – in the same second I decided to keep my foot steady rather than hit the gas, Al's gaze moved on. At a word from him the two toughs behind him peeled off and made swiftly for the back of the house it appeared was their target. I turned the corner, slowing enough to watch them disappear. Meanwhile Al and the man I'd followed strolled up the front walk.

As soon as I was out of sight I pulled to the curb. I waited for my heart to slow to normal rhythm. What I'd taken as Al's notice of me had been nothing more than a precautionary, probably habitual check of his surroundings.

I hoped.

To my annoyance my palms were sweating. It irked me thinking my night in the ditch could have produced this case of jitters on seeing him. I turned my irritation into a grudge and started the engine. Something was going on at that house back there, and I was going to find out what.

Reversing direction I parked where I had a good view around the corner. My urge to get closer on foot warred with common sense. This time common sense won. The stealth with which the two men had approached the back of the house suggested this wasn't some prearranged meeting. My guess was they'd be strong-arming someone out of the house any minute now. I wanted to see who it was and where they went.

After maybe fifteen minutes, just as I was beginning to worry Calvin's jalopy might stick out too much in this neighborhood, a van appeared that advertised Furniture Removal. It turned into the driveway of the house and two men jumped out and opened the rear of the van. At nearly the same instant the front door to the house opened. One of Beale's men stepped out with a hat in his hand and a dove gray jacket that looked like Al's folded over his arm. He checked left and right then called something over his shoulder.

Out came two more Beale boys carrying a rolled up carpet. It sagged in the middle as if it contained something heavy. They heaved the roll into the back of the van and closed the door. Almost before they'd stepped aside the van began to back away.

When it reached the street Al himself appeared, the last one out of the house. He was rolling down his sleeves, and I caught a good glimpse of the shoulder holster I'd detected earlier. He took out a pocket knife on a chain. The knife sprang open, and he ran the tip beneath his nails as if removing something objectionable. Al closed the knife. The man who'd checked the street held out the jacket and topcoat while Al slipped his arms in. Smoothing his hair, Al settled his hat on his head.

Both men came briskly down the front walk, then turned toward their respective cars. Their other two pals already were pulling away. I was left to face the unsettling likelihood that in less than twenty minutes a murder had been committed and the body whisked away – all while I sat close enough to see everyone but the victim. Ignoring a sour taste, I started my engine to follow Al.

* * *

He led me to a half-dirt-half-cobble street which in not much more than a block petered out into railroad tracks. Figuring he was smarter than the goons who watched my office, I didn't risk following when he turned into it. The seedy factory area without so much as a beer joint seemed an odd destination for Al in his fancy suit. Either he was up to something and didn't want to be spotted or he was meeting someone.

If I wanted to find out what he was up to I'd have to get out of the car. I parked in a coal yard and grabbed the clipboard I carried to make notes during stakeouts. Hoping my cheap tie and gent's suit would let me pass for a salesman I got out and ambled toward the intersection where Al had turned.

His Buick was parked a third of the way up the dead-end street. He was still at the wheel. A guy with a cap shoved back on his head and a cigarette riding his lips lounged against the side of the car. The guy's thumbs were hooked in his pockets as he and Al talked through the rolled-down window, and even at a distance I made him for a thug. It wasn't his clothes, it was the slouch, the way he carried himself.

Al wasn't asking directions. This was some kind of meeting. There was no way to hear, but I wanted to watch. The corner I'd reached held a good-sized warehouse. At mid-afternoon no one was coming or going. I sauntered up close to an L-shaped wall and spread my legs like a gent relieving himself. The thug on the fender appeared to be listening to Al. Then his cigarette flipped up and down a few times as he spoke.

"Old maid at the front desk sees you doin' that, you won't get an order, pal," chucked someone behind me.

My head jerked around. A beefy man had just come out of the door at the opposite end of the warehouse.

"I – uh – didn't see any place–"

"Don't worry. She's yakking away on the phone." He took a couple steps toward me. "What you peddlin'?"

I glanced at the Buick. They were still talking.

"Nuts and bolts," I improvised.

"Nuts and bolts." The man hooted. "You got guts, kid." Still laughing he headed away toward Findlay.

Did whoever owned the warehouse manufacture nuts and bolts, or something that didn't require them like ladies' drawers? I turned attention back to the Buick in time to see Al hand the other man something. The thug on the fender moved lazily, stuffing it under his jacket – but not before I'd caught a flash of green. Anger rose in me as I thought of hungry, honest people – men, women, kids and babies – waiting in endless lines for soup and bread and another slice out of whatever dignity they had left while crooks like these stuffed their pockets with cash at God-only-knew whose expense.

The Buick started. The guy on the fender sauntered clear. The glossy black car edged to one side like it meant to turn back my direction. If I lit out fast I might make it back to Calvin's jalopy in time to follow. Except someone hoofing it double time was likely to attract Al's attention. I waited until he was almost even with me, averted my face and gave my shoulders the up-and-down lift men give after using a wall.

TWENTY-NINE

"Oh, Maggie! You're nothing but skin and bones!" Kate Leary caught my hands so I couldn't escape and planted a kiss on my cheek.

The party for Seamus was already overflowing the back room at Finn's. Most of the time the room was used for storing spare tables, chairs with wobbly legs, and empty crates from the smaller official storeroom across from it. On special occasions, though, the chairs got fixed, the crates went out, and it was used for do's like this.

Of all the cops' wives I'd grown up around I liked Kate best. She was Billy's wife, trim for her age with a wide, kind face. Her eyes assessed me gently. "When are you coming for Sunday dinner, love? It's been too long."

"Soon. Honest." Her invitation was a standing one. Sometimes in the winter, or when I needed reassurance there were still good people in the world, I took her up on it.

"Still no beau?" asked Bridie Molloy.

"You should come to the parish dances. There's a couple of fine new lads been coming," put in Mary Kennedy.

"Is that your angel cake back there looking ready to float away?" I replied.

Mary giggled delight. Giving my hands a quick squeeze Kate let me make my escape.

I drifted through a throng of mostly older cops and their wives, stopping here and there to chat, in the process of which I collected more hugs and handshakes than I wanted. Being back in the circle of people who'd watched me grow up always pulled me in two directions. I felt smothered and overvalued; fretted over by well-meaning people who were sure I'd be happier married and looked after. Yet I somehow felt strengthened by their very predictability. It was especially welcome tonight as I tried to shrug off my growing worry Al knew I was watching him.

"So that donkey's arse Fuller tried to pin a murder on you, eh?" teased a middle-aged cop my Dad had gotten out of a jam once.

"And the good lieutenant's been riding him like a donkey ever since," grinned another.

Laughing along with them I moved on, finally reaching Seamus. There was barely time for me to give him his present and him to unwrap it before other people pressed in to offer good wishes. With a peck on the cheek and a promise to stop back later I bumped along.

I was hungry. A table draped with somebody's good lace cloth held a ham that Kate and Bridie had baked in the parish oven. Surrounding it were mustard and bread and the angelfood cake which was Seamus' favorite. I fixed a sandwich, bypassing a well-provisioned drinks table for a Guinness from Finn. At the foot of the bar I discovered an out-of-sight spot behind a small table stacked with empty crates that Finn had shoved there to make room for the party. Add an empty keg and I had privacy to sit and eat and talk myself out of the growing unease getting close to Al had planted in me.

Okay, so his car had slowed directly beside me as it left the dead-end street that afternoon. Surely he hadn't recognized me standing at that wall in my men's garb. It was just evidence of the same alertness to his surroundings he'd shown heading into a house where unless I missed my guess he'd killed a man – alertness that kept men like him and Woody Beale alive. I was worried for nothing.

Probably. Otherwise he'd have put a bullet in my brain. Instead, I'd heard him move on. When I'd counted to twenty and looked he was disappearing down Findlay.

Taking a swallow of Guinness I nudged my thoughts toward what had happened next. Since I couldn't follow Al, and the thug he'd met was moving toward a wood-slatted pickup, I'd followed him instead, glad I was driving Calvin's jalopy. After a few blocks the thug in the pickup stopped at a house in a scrappy neighborhood. When he honked, two roughly dressed men came out. The three of them drove downtown and on, until after a bit I realized they were following one of Peter's delivery routes.

"Hiding from Bridie's matchmaking, are you?" asked Finn's voice. He was standing at my end of the bar biting into a sandwich. Only a few crumbs remained of mine.

"You're a smart man, Finbar."

He winked. "If she starts talking about her nephew, run like it's the devil himself." He ambled up the bar to wait on a customer.

More time had passed than I realized. The crowd had thinned. Dusting crumbs from my hands I went to have a better chat with Seamus. A couple of well-wishers were just in the process of moving along and no one else was waiting. Seamus sat with the cap from me perched on his head and a handsome green sweater Kate had knitted draped over his shoulders. When he saw me he smiled and pulled over a chair.

"Come and sit. It's not near as mad as it was when you first stopped by. Don't have to shout now. This's an awful fine cap for a head as ugly as mine. You shouldn't have."

"You deserve half a dozen," I said patting his arm.

"Could only wear one at a time though. Anyway, thanks again."

I raised the pint in my hand and we clicked glasses. Seamus was tall and gaunt. Forty-five years and more on

American soil, yet the sound of Sligo still clung to him. His frame and the hollows of his long face called to mind the potato famine two generations before him. He had no family, and since my dad's death a special link had grown between the two of us.

"All the ladies giving you sufficient advice on how to mend your ways?" he asked with a chuckle.

I grinned. Seamus didn't judge, and he didn't butt in. He was easy to be with. We yakked comfortably until a couple of flatfoots came over to razz him and I took my leave.

A few of the younger lads began to put in appearances. To my annoyance Mick Connelly wasn't among them. It would suit me fine if our paths never crossed again, except I needed information and he was the only way I could think of to get it. Even then it would take some doing – not to mention gagging down my pride

Drifting to the edge of a group discussing the Pope's encyclical against Nazis and Communists I turned my thoughts back to the pickup I'd followed that afternoon. When it stopped at a beer joint deep in a factory area the New Deal had brought back to life, I went past and pretended engine trouble, raising the hood to watch. No one got out of the pickup. No one got in. After ten minutes I got into Calvin's jalopy preparing to leave.

The pickup beat me to it.

Lest I attract notice, I sat while they disappeared. I was reaching for the ignition when the truck nosed out of an alley across from where the men had been sitting. It moved slowly at first then picked up speed. Something about that rhythm kept me sitting. A few minutes later it came out of the alley again. The fellows in the pickup were either lost or I'd bet my bottom dollar they were looking over one of the buildings flanking the alley.

Billy interrupted my thoughts by grabbing me and reeling me around the floor while he lilted "The Merry

Blacksmith", having a fine old time on a single pint, which normally lasted him a whole evening. A few people started adding their lilt to his. I glimpsed Finn's wife and Mavis Casey, who'd gotten around a few pints of cider. They'd linked arms and were doing some high steps. The art had been lost in my generation but it broke out among the older crowd at occasions like this.

My face was damp and I was getting my breath back when I looked up and saw Mick Connelly watching across the room. None of his buttons were undone, so he was working an extra shift again. That meant I didn't have time to waste. I lifted my hair to cool the nape of my neck and sauntered toward him. He watched with nothing readable beyond alertness.

"Figured I'd save you having to walk over to me to make your apology," I said extending my arm so he could see the bruise on my wrist. "I've been asked about it three times tonight."

All color, as well as his habitual composure, drained from his face. He swallowed.

"I ... Jesus. I don't know what to say. 'I'm sorry' isn't near adequate. I was.... May God strike me now if I've ever done anything like that to a woman before!"

I felt guiltier than I had in a good long time. No one had even noticed the bruise and I'd had to bang the back of my wrist on a bedpost a couple of times to produce the purple mark where he'd grabbed me during our angry exchange here on Saturday. To set it off, I'd worn my best blouse, delicate silk with lace at the cuff. I let the sleeve glide into place and shrugged.

"I've been told I get hot headed too. What you said that afternoon about Billy and Seamus, I know you meant well. So maybe we should bury the hatchet. There's something I forgot to tell Freeze about Muley – the guy that got shot. Maybe I chose to forget, to tell you the truth.

May not amount to a hill of beans, but sometimes when you pull at a thread...."

He was silent, recovering his balance. "And you want a favor back," he said after a minute. His voice had hardened.

"An address. And not if it bothers your conscience."

He glanced at the door. "I'm on duty. Just ducked in to wish Seamus the best."

"I'll get to it, then. You might want to check whether Benny Norris bought an insurance policy shortly before he got killed."

Connelly's interest sharpened. "Insurance? Why?"

"When Muley called me he said Norris mentioned insurance last time they met. Norris let on like he'd just gotten it; said it would help him if he ever got in a tight spot."

He crossed his arms. I could see his mind working.

"A small time crook like Norris?"

"Yeah. That's what I thought too. Could be it's not that kind of insurance. Could be it's something he had on someone, or thought he had. Anyway, he was bragging about it."

Connelly glanced at the door again. "I better get going." He sent Seamus a farewell lift of the chin and the two of us walked toward the front. "What's the address? What's it got to do with any of this?"

I shook my head. "Only thing I know the address is connected to is the case I told you and Billy about the morning I found my office turned upside down. And that case is starting to look like sour grapes by a jilted lover." Mentally, I crossed my fingers, even though in a manner of speaking Peter Stowe had jilted Al once he wised up to Al's phony bait about being in pictures. "Address is for a guy named Al, maybe christened Albert Sikes. He's rumored to work for Woody Beale."

"That's not someone to get mixed up with."

"Clients don't hire me to play social secretary."

"I'll think about it."

He stopped, just short of the front door at Finn's. His face had regained its discipline but one corner of his mouth twitched.

"For the record," he said, "did I just hear the sound of snowballs melting?"

THIRTY

My nose was buried in *The Journal* and I was eating my oatmeal when I felt someone slide onto the seat next to mine at McCrory's next morning. Someone whose presence hummed like an engine and who smelled of shaving soap.

"Maybe there's some true Irish girl left in you after all, eating porridge," Connelly observed. "I'd have guessed you for toast and coffee." He was wearing regular clothes, a sweater and jacket. He couldn't have had much sleep but he looked chipper.

Izzy was right there to fill his cup and take his order for sausage and beans. Her eyes slid from him to me and she sent me a shy smile as she turned away.

"The name was right," Connelly said quietly. He slid a folded scrap of paper toward me.

I opened it, glanced at the address, and nodded. "Thanks."

"Fellow's bad news," he said in the same muted tone.

"I guessed as much by the man he works for."

Our conversation was strangely private, lost in the sounds of clattering crockery, shoes clicking over the wooden floor behind us, rustling papers, the back and forth of louder voices. I ate some oatmeal. Connelly drank some coffee. The stool on the other side of me cleared and the woman who claimed it lighted a cigarette. I swivelled away from the smoke.

"Let's switch," said Connelly sliding my bowl across and leaving his stool before I could protest. When we were settled he leaned on one elbow blocking part of the smoke. "Figure it's what killed your dad, do you?"

"Yeah." I figured Billy had told him. "Go ahead, though, if you've a mind." I was almost finished and one more addition to the cloud at the lunch counter wouldn't make much difference.

"Gave it up." Cutting an inch from the sausage Izzy had just delivered he chewed efficiently. "Saw I'd have more in my pocket to send back to Ma every month."

I had my address. There was no reason for me to stick around. Safer not to. I could start to like Connelly, and that would lead to too many complications.

I took a final spoonful of oatmeal, left money for Izzy and scooted off. Now was my chance to keep an eye on Al, and I didn't want Connelly or Beale's boys either one keeping an eye on me.

* * *

Before Connelly sat down next to me at McCrory's I'd been following crumbs like Hansel and Gretel. The address he gave me that morning led straight to the witch's house.

From time to time a neighbor let me use his car for a couple of bucks. It was a blue Ford like a million others and my backside was going to sleep from sitting in it when Al, resplendent in his dove gray topcoat and custom-made Uhrig hat came lightly down the steps of his small brick house an hour shy of noon. I couldn't judge his cufflinks or gun or brass knuckles. Ten minutes later his Buick Century was headed north on Main with me trailing. When it looked more and more like The Owl was his destination, I took my own route and was settled cozily behind a delivery van across from the club by the time he turned into the parking lot.

He spent under twenty minutes at Beale's place, which by day seemed unlikely to offer much enticement beyond conferring with Beale himself. When he came out he went all the way down to Kettering and spent a full hour parked in front of an office building. Then he went to the Biltmore where he probably had some lunch and where I couldn't risk trying to see if he met anyone. Then he got a haircut at Ollie's, or at least was inside long enough. Then he went home.

I was brooding some over whether he'd spotted me and was leading me on a goose chase, and wondering if I should give up for the day, when he came out again. If he headed north he'd likely be bound for The Owl, in which case I'd give it up for the day, but instead he went south.

By now it was after five, getting on toward quitting time. Traffic made my tango down Main with him tricky, and I almost lost him once when the light at Third changed against me. The reward came when he pulled to the curb in front of the same building where he'd sat for an hour at noontime. Was Al watching the place? Was this a stop I'd forgotten from Peter's list of deliveries? Or could Al be waiting for someone?

Whichever it might be, he wasn't using the paved parking lot in front of the building. That suggested he didn't want to be noticed. So I sailed into the lot and parked near the door, just another good little wife picking hubby up at the end of the day.

The building in front of me didn't look like a candidate for the sort of break-ins that had been in the news. It was an office building, not a factory or warehouse whose inventory could be shoved quickly into trucks. It was modern, three stories, wide more than tall with a skinny portico tacked across the tan brick to gussy it up. Al had to be watching for someone. Maybe somebody who was avoiding him. Or maybe they just didn't want to be seen together inside.

People started to trickle out, swelling quickly into a steady stream. Girls from the typing pool made for the street and the trolley line a few blocks away. Bosses savored stogies as they strolled toward cars with big fenders and polished chrome. Managers got into lesser models where the little missus waited behind the wheel. Those a little lower joined the parade of clerks and such whose paychecks didn't yet cover an automobile. I watched movement rather than individuals, hoping I'd spot it if someone noted Al and gave it away.

Someone did.

He was in his late thirties, medium build. Straw colored hair deepened to brown at his temples and the brown won entirely on his mustache. He was walking with an older man. By their suits and their confident gaits I placed them as bosses. The older guy offered the towhead a stogie. They were just lighting up when the towhead glanced toward the street and saw Al's Buick. He froze for a second before snapping his lighter shut and resuming the conversation at hand. Another minute elapsed. He said something that made the other man laugh. The towhead turned and began to saunter back toward the building. The older man got in his glossy car. As soon as it rolled clear of the parking lot, the man I was watching turned and made for the street.

In my side mirror I could see Al lowering the curbside window. The towhead leaned down and they talked. A periodic gesture and toss of his head suggested anger. He crossed his arms and kept on talking, stabbing his finger once for emphasis. He acted more belligerent than afraid. I wondered if that was smart.

Bits of information had started popping inside my brain. Something Mae had said about Benny ... Kettering.... A fancy building. That was it: *"He wasn't going to be a patsy just because some muckety-muck in a fancy building in Kettering got cold feet."*

And the manicurist from Ollie's– .

My chain of thought broke as the Buick door opened and the towhead got in. Was he going voluntarily? My hand hovered at the ignition. But I'd followed Al all day. I was on the edge of making sense of things now. If he spotted me he'd close down and out wait me. Or worse. Peter would still be in danger, and I'd bear the black mark of not delivering for my client.

Instead I scooted into the building. They'd be locking the door soon, and I wanted a peek at the building directory.

It didn't dish out the big plate of help I was hoping to get. None of the business names on the board suggested they peddled insurance. A third gave no hint at all what they did. From the floor above I heard the sound of the elevator descending. Since I meant to come back tomorrow, I didn't want to be seen. I hurried out.

* * *

Back at the office I propped my legs on the desk and picked up the phone.

"Officer Connelly there?" I asked when the desk sarge at H.Q. answered.

"Think so – about to head out."

I could hear curiosity.

"Tell him Eve needs a fast word."

Finding another place as nice as Mrs. Z's for what I could afford would be hard, if not impossible. I didn't want to abuse the new arrangement she'd made with the key, and I'd had all the sitting I wanted for one day. Besides, the place the thugs in the pickup had been eyeing yesterday was one which Flora Throckmorton had marked "big" on her list of customers Peter had visited with Al. If I repaid Connelly's favor, I might coax another one out of him somewhere down the line.

I heard a scrape as the phone on the other end was picked up.

"Calling to offer an apple, are you?" Connelly asked wryly.

Had he guessed it was me, or did enough girls call that he shrugged them off?

"I just came across something – long shot – could have to do with those burglaries."

"I'm listening."

"That guy I've been following? Yesterday he went slumming. Rough neighborhood. Met a guy with a pickup truck. Money changed hands." I sketched details, how I'd followed the pickup and watched its occupants stop to study a building. "On my way back to the office just now, I saw the truck again and tagged along. They made another pass. Same place," I concluded. One white lie didn't alter the gist of the story.

Connelly was silent a minute. Then he took down the address.

"You'd have to be mad to look a place over one day and break in the next," he said.

"Yeah. You would."

"Still."

"Still."

THIRTY-ONE

I missed my oatmeal the next morning. I missed my coffee even more. It was just after eight and I was in the passenger seat of my own car at the far end of the parking lot where I'd watched people leaving work yesterday. The building was called The Wellington and the earlybirds were arriving. From time to time I darted a pencil at a fistful of papers, trying to look like a private secretary madly correcting some important document for her boss who had stopped off en route to a meeting.

After the guy with the brown mustache had left with Al last evening, I'd noted the cars remaining in the parking lot. Around eight I'd checked back and only one was still there, a tan Cadillac roadster, maybe not quite as fine as Woody Beale's car, but sporty and guaranteed to turn girls' heads. Today it wasn't around, but after half an hour or so it turned in. Sure enough, the towhead got out. As far as I could see he hadn't been roughed up any and the way he walked didn't indicate nervousness. Maybe he and Al were just pals. I dumped the papers I'd been shuffling and hurried after him into the building.

"Hold it, Sam," he barked at a colored elevator attendant who already had the doors half closed.

The attendant obeyed. I quickened my pace intending to get in too and see where the towhead got off. A kid with a mail cart appeared out of nowhere and I had to dodge. I looked up just in time to see the elevator departing.

With time to kill I checked the building directory again. It still didn't show any insurance companies. A woman in horn rimmed glasses and a mousy man with thinning hair came in. A group of girls from the typing pool ran up the stairs, young and fearful of being late. Half a dozen more pulled up breathless to wait for the elevator. Fishing in my pocket I rehearsed my next move.

The empty elevator clattered back into view. The attendant pulled back the gate. He wasn't very tall, and had a smooth face scrubbed of all expression. I started in with the other passengers.

"Hey, I think this belongs to a gentleman you took up on your last trip," I said as I flashed a cigarette lighter from the second hand store. "Blond guy but with a brown mustache. Seemed in a hurry?"

More people were waiting to get in, except I was blocking their way. I was counting on that to help me, thinking he'd want to move things along.

"Lost 'n found's that way." He pointed.

"Houseman. I think his name is Houseman," offered a girl in the elevator. She turned to her friend. "The one with that spanking car?" They shared a laugh, information exhausted.

"If you tell me which office he's in I can stop by and give it to him," I said.

"Can't help. You going up or staying, Miss?"

Outmaneuvered, I let the people waiting for the elevator jostle me in and rode to the top floor. A stroll past the closed doors of the three tenants there told me nothing. I took a flight of stairs down a level, but no miracles happened there either. Going into offices with my story about the lighter risked drawing too much attention so I headed back to my own.

* * *

Before ambling past Beale's watchdog and indoors for the rest of the morning I picked up a muffin and cup of coffee at Joe's. The muffin sack hung from my teeth, the morning paper I'd bought was under my arm, and my free hand held the mug of hot coffee as I unlocked my door.

"That lock you have wouldn't challenge a choirboy," Mick Connelly said lounging against one corner of my desk.

I startled just enough to almost spill some coffee. Which I didn't.

"I thought that uniform you're wearing meant you were supposed to uphold the law, not break it," I snapped snatching the sack from my mouth and dumping it on the desk with my keys. "What the hell are you doing breaking into my office?"

"Waiting to see if you might have any more details."

"Details about what?"

Leaning forward he snagged the paper from under my arm and flipped it onto my desk with a thump of his finger.

"That."

It was near the bottom, a small boxed item squeezed in after the main press run but in time for the late edition. I sank into my chair, unbuttoning my coat as I scanned the single paragraph.

"Jesus, Mary and Joseph." Police had thwarted a burglary in progress at a factory on Springfield Street. "One day after they checked out the lay of the place?"

I looked up wondering if someone, somewhere, was having a laugh at my expense. Connelly's gaze was narrow.

"Oh, for Pete's sake. You don't think I'd hand you this on a plate if I was setting you up, do you?" I asked irritably. "It felt to me like something was going to go down there, but I've had more than enough hours sitting in cars on surveillance these last few days. I didn't see why I should add more callouses to my backside playing a hunch just to be a good citizen. Those break-ins are your dog fight, not mine."

"Why don't you have some coffee?" Connelly suggested. "You sound like you need it."

If he was trying to get on my nerves he was doing a fine job. To prove that he wasn't I took my sweet time sipping some coffee. Then I ripped open the sack and pinched off a wee bit of muffin, exploring it with the tip of my tongue before I popped it into my mouth.

"It was too flat easy for anything you'd concoct," Connelly said hoarsely. He seemed to have run short of breath and shifted uncomfortably as he watched my act with the muffin. "Team that relieved us had just gone to have a look at that address when they spotted a truck in the alley."

Arms crossed he got up and began to circle my office. It was harder to ignore him in motion than when he was still. Curiosity trumped my peevishness at his presence.

"Anybody talking?"

"Not much."

"They look like the crew behind the rest of the break-ins?"

"Ah, now there's the problem."

He paused to survey the skeleton of my long dead philodendron which, like several before it, had succumbed to lack of water. Why waste money on a replacement doomed to suffer the same fate? With this specimen on display, clients could think I made an attempt at spiffing things up but had been preoccupied with my cases. At least the flowerpot was pretty.

"The one who was giving orders last night has alibis for the last two break-ins," Connelly said. "When tobacco warehouse got hit he was unloading vegetables over at a soup kitchen. Salvation Army captain vouched for him. Time before that he was in St. E's giving up an appendix."

I leaned back, baffled by this blind alley. "Doesn't make sense."

"Nope." He hooked a leg across the corner of my desk again, undermining my concentration. "As you said a minute ago, I've got my dogfights, you've got yours. But some of the dogs are the same. So long as your clients aren't guilty of anything that should concern the police, and so long as you don't expect more than I can give with conscience clear, there'd be no harm if we showed a few cards."

I considered it for a minute. Breaking the muffin in half I offered him some.

"Where's Billy?" I asked to buy time.

"Told him I had a contact might have an idea or two about what happened but that I needed to go alone." He broke a chunk from the muffin and put it into his mouth, watching me all the time. "You still peddling your interest in Albert Sikes as a lovers' spat?"

"First tell me what you meant about Woody Beale having friends at City Hall."

He frowned. "One of the councilmen and some other bigwig down there race cars in the same bunch Beale does, is what I heard. Something to do with racing. Why?"

"Are they pals enough for the cops to back off?"

Connelly planted a hand in front of me and leaned forward

"Do I look like I'm backing off?"

"Freeze reacted when I mentioned the name."

"So? Man's got a mind like a trap. And near as I can tell, Chief Wurstner would sell his own mother to solve these burglaries."

I exhaled in decision. "Okay, there was no jilted lover. Al turned nasty when a fellow he'd been flim-flamming started to suspect something smelled and gave him the brush off."

"I don't suppose you're inclined to tell me what the flim-flam entailed?"

"Just letting Al ride around with him."

"Casing places?"

"That would be my guess. The guy who got snookered is young. Decent. Saw no harm in having company. Al spun him a yarn about being a writer at work on a project."

"Jesus."

I drained the last of my coffee and tapped a fingernail against the mug a couple of times as I thought aloud.

"It doesn't make sense using a different gang. As much attention as this is getting, you'd want men who knew what they were doing – had worked togther, proved themselves."

"Could be somebody liked what they'd been reading about. Decided to try the same thing."

I shook my head. "I saw Al hand cash to a yokel involved in this one, remember? A guy who then made a beeline to check out the place that got hit. When that young fellow Al was riding with put an end to the rides, Beale's boys started roughing the poor sap up. Smells to me like Al has been pulling strings on all these burglaries. Which means Woody Beale is behind them."

"No proof, though. And it's penny ante stuff for Beale."

"True," I agreed reluctantly. "These break-ins haven't been slap-dash though. Until last night no one had been caught."

"Nor like as not then if we hadn't been watching."

I couldn't argue.

"Benny Norris came into it somewhere," I mused. "That's where this whole mess started. For me anyway. And Benny was an errand boy for Beale. I thought I might turn something up with the insurance angle, but I haven't. You?"

"No." Connelly rubbed his chin. "Maybe Benny was the go-between, Beale's contact with the gang doing the actual burglaries. Say something went wrong. Whatever it was put Benny on the hook. Got him iced – most likely by Al or someone else working for Beale. After that, for some reason, Beale switched crews."

"Trust, maybe?"

"Or with Benny dead they just needed another go-between. One with different contacts."

"The one I saw Al meet up north? That slipped him the money?" I frowned. "Like you said, it seems like penny ante stuff for Beale."

We lapsed into silence.   Too much didn't make sense.

"I don't see how they manage to get the night watchmen out of the way at these places." I twiddled my empty mug. "They get paid off? Drugged?" Beale was dandy at drugging people, I thought.

"These days lots of places as big as these just have an electric alarm," Connelly said. "At the one place that still had a watchman as well, the poor old fellow got knocked in the head."

I squeezed back the impulse to shoot up straight as a Catholic school girl.

"More muffin?" I offered.

Connelly looked at me oddly. "Thanks, but I better be going."

I waited until he'd had time to get to the end of the hall. I went to the window and watched until he came out. Then I went to the phone. Perching on the desk beside it and stretching happily, I called Abner Simms, head of security at Rike's department store.

THIRTY-TWO

"Getting skinny with another floor to keep track of?" I asked. Rike's had just added a seventh story, proof to some the Depression might truly come to an end.

Abner chuckled with the satisfaction of one who knew his workplace was as comfy as they came. "Elevators so I don't wear myself out, chilled air so I don't even sweat – it's a wonder I'm not fat as Oliver Hardy. Fine job on that background check you ran for us last month. What do you need?"

"Where do big outfits like yours go for burglar alarms?"

He didn't even need to think.

"Caldwell-Carter."

"After that?"

"Montgomery Security. Maybe Gem City Guardian. A one-person office like yours doesn't need one, surely. You're not closing shop, are you? Hunting a job?"

He sounded hopeful, but I knew it wasn't because he harbored me any ill will. Abner hadn't liked me much when I started at Rike's as a part-time floorwalker, a high school kid who wasn't half as docile as people expected. Partly he thought I was green and partly he thought work should go to a man with a family to feed in those worst-of-bad times eight years ago. Then I stopped a nicely dressed gent who was about to walk out the door with a watch and two pairs of new leather gloves in his pocket that he hadn't purchased. I held him while one of the clerks called a house dick, who happened that day to be Abner.

Thereafter Abner started to thaw. Two years later he moved up to assistant head of security, and I was reassigned to loss prevention – though I still got floorwalker's pay.

"If I ever have to put my tail between my legs, you'll be the first place I come for a job," I promised. "This is for something I'm working. You happen to have any names at those places you mentioned?"

He gave me a couple and we chatted some more about this and that. When we'd said our good-byes I sat for a minute swinging my legs while I surveyed the short list he'd given me.

The girls on the elevator in Kettering had thought the gent with the dark mustache was named Houseman. There was no Houseman on Abner's list. I got out my phone book and looked up listings for security alarms. Caldwell-Carter and Montgomery Security both had offices downtown. Gem City Guardian was at the building I'd visited that morning. The building where Al had waited yesterday and argued with a man who was back today looking unscathed. Time to find out if the man's name was Houseman.

The unsharpened pencil next to my phone had been a key piece of my office equipment from the day I opened. I used it to save my manicure while I swept the digits of Gem City Guardian's number around the dial. A precise voice answered, the kind that made you think the burglar alarms they sold would be equally reliable.

"This is Lydia Vandevier," I said twirling my strand of imaginary pearls since I'd borrowed Lydia's name from the society pages. "Please connect me with Mr. Houseman."

"I'm sorry, Mr. Houseman is with a client. Is there a message?"

"Tell him I hope she's not a terribly attractive client." I laughed merrily and hung up.

Progress.

With one exception all the businesses burglarized used alarm systems rather than night watchmen. Al had visited them all in the course of deliveries with Peter. Al knew a man who sold burglar alarms, a man who judging from his clothes and car was near the top of the heap where he worked. Now I knew that man's name was Houseman.

The next thing I wanted to find out was whether Houseman was the same man the manicurist from Ollie's barber shop had described. She'd called him a "rich guy". The way Houseman dressed and carried himself, he'd probably qualify, but I needed to be sure.

* * *

I waited until the wiseacre kid who sold papers was clear of other customers before I handed him three cents for the afternoon edition.

"How'd you like to sell the rest of those and have the afternoon clear, make a little extra to boot?" I asked.

He grinned at me shrewdly. "What do I gotta do?"

"Meet me over at the Good Neighbors Shop in forty-five minutes. Know where it is?"

He nodded as another customer approached. I tossed him an apple and left.

At a quarter of two, so accurate I wondered if he owned a watch, he sauntered into view with an eagerness to his step he couldn't quite hide. I watched from the small front window of the Good Neighbors second-hand shop. It was down on the tip of Van Buren, run by some ladies' charity group. The clothing it sold was in better condition than it was at most places like it. I left the shop's warmth and went out on its stoop. The newsie's ink-smudged face split in a grin.

"Fifteen papers left, sis. Two bits 'n two dimes."

I handed it to him.

"What's the deal?"

"The deal is I need someone to tag along and play like he's my assistant for a couple of hours tomorrow morning. You'll get a new pair of pants, a quarter in pay, and I'll buy all the papers you'd normally sell. You interested?"

He crossed his arms and narrowed his eyes.

"This something I could get pinched for?"

"No. Strictly legal. Worst that could happen is we'd get the bum's rush."

His expression grew cocky. "I put up as good a fight as the next guy. What's the job, then?"

"Go into an office with me and act like my assistant. Pretend to scribble notes on a pad I'll give you. You can write, I guess?"

"'Course." I'd miffed him and he rubbed his chin, trying to bluff. "A quarter and a pair of pants, huh?"

"From this place. Plus a pair of shoes if you want 'em." Cardboard showed through the bottoms of his.

In answer he stuck out his hand.

"What's your name?" I asked as we shook.

"Heebs. That's a corker, ain't it?"

"Don't say 'ain't' so you sound right tomorrow. Heebs your last name?

"Nah. When I was a kid I always got spooked going down this one alley. Guys I pal with started calling me Heebs – like heebie-jeebies." His grin resurfaced. "I already know who you are, sis."

All at once I felt a flutter of worry. It forced me to ask another question. "You ever work for Woody Beale?"

It startled him so he forgot to be cocky. His tousled head shook. "Now and then I sell him a paper. Reckon if he give me a dime to run in a store and ask a question I would. Other than that I mean to steer clear of him. Ain– I'm not fixing to get shut up in jail, and it don't take a genius to look at the guys who hang around him and know Woody Beale's hands are dirtier'n a ditch digger's."

THIRTY-THREE

As arranged, I let Heebs into my building by the alley door the next morning. He'd been disappointed that I kept the clothes he'd picked out, but I didn't know where he slept and didn't want to risk them getting dirty before he showed up. When we got to my office I sent him down the hall to the gents' to change. I'd brought soap and a washrag, but he'd scrubbed up pretty well before he arrived, so I didn't insult him by offering. When he returned he looked like a stranger with a passing family resemblance to the kid who'd left. Until he grinned.

"Look like I'm ready to work in a bank, don't I?"

"Or chase after the news instead of peddling it after it's printed, at least. Put these on."

He willingly took the vest I'd borrowed for him, but scowled at the wire-rimmed glasses. "Don't need those."

In answer I settled a pair with thick maroon frames on my own nose. They were what passed for fashion if you had money enough to be a clothes horse but had to wear cheaters. Heebs' scowl turned into a snicker as he surveyed me. I struck a pose in my peplum jacket, which I'd dolled up with a neck scarf and a fussy hat sporting a feather the length of a bayonet. Heebs peered at his own specs, saw the lenses were plain glass, and put them on, trying a pose of his own. The transformation from a kid who didn't yet need to shave was impressive. I gave him a hand mirror.

"Guess I don't look too bad," he said casually, standing as tall as he could. He eyed me while he decided if he should speak. "You know that get-up doesn't do much for you, don't you, sis?"

"Good." I smiled and handed him a steno pad and pencil. "Oh, and you'll be carrying my camera for me, Clemmy dear."

"Clemmy!" he sputtered. "That ain't – isn't my name!"

"It is for the morning, dear," I said in a supercilious voice. "You're quite free to show that you hate it, but of course you'd be very rash to actually *say* anything, as I might fire you."

He caught on immediately and plunged in.

"Yes, boss."

"Miss Cox, Clemmy. How many times must I tell you to call me Miss Cox?"

"Cox? Reckon I can remember that name," he chortled.

James Cox had served three terms as governor. He'd also run for vice president on a losing ticket. The kid most likely knew him as the press baron whose holdings included *The Dayton Daily News*. The name would come to his tongue when he needed it, and if somebody where we were going thought I might be a Cox relative, all the better.

Since there were two of us and my current outfit was worlds removed from the drab skirt and tam I'd arrived in that morning, we went out the front door. We sashayed along with Heebs lugging my Kodak while I held my purse in front of me in a fussy two-handed grip unlike my own. Beale's surveillance glanced up as we passed, then returned to his paper, or maybe his girlie magazine. We reached the parking lot, got into my car, and pulled out with no indication he'd wised up. Even if he followed, I could pull off what I needed to.

"So now I'm a Peeping Tommy like you, huh?" Heebs folded his arms behind his head and lounged in the passenger seat of the DeSoto. "Maybe you better give me the dope on what's cooking."

"You call me Miss Cox. You scribble when I tell you to. You rush to open the door and jump when I snap my fingers. Most important, if I say something that sounds crazy, you don't let on."

"That ain't saying what's cooking."

"No, but it's all I'm telling you. Don't say 'ain't'."

"What kind of assistant?"

"What?" I navigated around a truck.

"What kind of assistant? Are you supposed to be one of those efficiency experts, or what?"

The kid had brains even to wonder about it.

"A decorator," I said. "An interior decorator."

He frowned, none too pleased to find himself stumped. "What are they?"

"People who tell rich people what kind of furniture to buy for this room or that. What paintings or do-dads they ought to put with it. What color the walls ought to be and so on."

"Don't make fun of me, sis." The frown was deepening into a scowl.

I laughed and raised my right hand from the steering wheel. "Honest Injun. People get paid for it."

He turned in his seat. "You're telling me people with money enough to buy whatever chair they want don't have sense enough to pick it out for themselves?"

Put like that it was hard to explain.

"I think it has to do with fashion," I said. "Like a woman who can buy new dresses any time she wants doesn't pick one because she likes it but because someone somewhere lets on like everything else is old fashioned."

Heebs snorted, as mystified as most of us would be by such doings. He kept peppering questions at me all the way to The Wellington.

* * *

"Three, please," I intoned as we traipsed onto the elevator.

The Negro attendant who'd been unhelpful yesterday didn't give me a first glance, let alone a second. Heebs and I were the only passengers. We rode up in silence with me using the time to double check the extra flashbulbs in my pocket. When we got out we hunted the number the directory downstairs listed for Miami Valley Guardian. Heebs looked around, taking in as much as his eyes could hold. At a frosted glass door marked 306 I paused and gave him a wink.

"Okay, 'Clemmy'," I whispered. "Open the door."

Heebs complied, all but genuflecting as I swept past.

"Please inform Mr. Houseman that Madeline Cox is here," I told an efficient-looking receptionist as I stripped off my gloves. "Oh, my. This *does* need a bit of spiffing up, doesn't it? That stretch of wall there simply begs for decoration – perhaps a nice bas relief. Are you getting this down, Clemmy? Don't just stand there!"

As instructed, Heebs gave me the camera, then scrambled for his note pad and pencil.

"I'm sorry. I'm afraid there's no mention of you on Mr. Houseman's list of appointments," the receptionist interjected.

I waved a hand, grandly unoffended. "Quite possibly it's just listed as 'decorator'. He was a bit sozzled when we exchanged names. Oh dear, though, I *did* assure him this first little visit wouldn't take long – Some sculpture there, I think, Clemmy–" I brought the camera up and snapped a picture, washing the place with light. "Make a note. Nefertiti on a pedestal, or–"

"Excuse me!" The receptionist was getting upset. "Mr. Houseman hasn't mentioned anything about a decorator."

"Why don't you just tell him I'm here, dear? I assume that's what that box on your desk is about.

"And color, Clemmy. It needs color. Plum, perhaps; that's madly fashionable just now." I directed the last part more or less toward the receptionist, who hunched over her intercom speaking urgently. A younger woman slaving away at a desk in the corner had looked up. Ears on the other side of a wood partition had probably pricked up as well. "We could set it off nicely with a pale, pale mauve. Mauve with a nice hint of gray."

As I spoke I removed the spent flashbulb, which was just cool enough to handle. Unclasping my purse I dropped it in and took out a measuring tape which I handed to Heebs.

"Jot down the measure on that wall. We'll wait for Jimmy to take the others."

The receptionist looked up, unsure whether she should try to stop Heebs as he pulled out the tape. I fitted one of the bulbs from my jacket pocket into the Kodak and dithered this way and that, pretending to decide my next angle. In the wall behind the reception area, maybe six feet right of the desk, was a closed door. At the sound of it opening, I centered it in the viewfinder, drew a steadying breath the way Jenkins had taught me, and pressed the shutter.

The flashbulb gave its satisfying pop. Momentarily blinded, the towhead with the darker mustache stood blinking.

"What's this about?" Off balance from his temporary blindness, he batted at the air in front of his eyes. "I don't know anything about–"

"Madeline Cox." I grabbed his hand and pumped it warmly. "We met at Kitty Dixon's little do last week. You were so keen to have decor that's more *moderne* that I promised to pop 'round the first chance I had to squeeze you in." While I talked I whisked the lace-trimmed hanky from my breast pocket. Its folds protected my fingers as I hurried the still-hot bulb from its socket. "Your assessment of what your customers see was very, very accurate, too. A rare perceptiveness in a man, if I may say. But never fear. The space itself allows great scope–"

"I don't know what you're talking about," Houseman managed to interrupt. "I don't know anyone–"

"That wall in particular," I gestured as if I hadn't heard. Houseman's head turned automatically. Having fitted a new bulb in, I clicked the shutter again, getting him in the edge of the scene, illuminated.

"I don't know anybody named Kitty Dixon." He'd reddened and was growing impatient. "I certainly didn't go to her party. And I haven't talked to anyone about decorating. You've made a mistake."

"Shall I call Mr. Gaynor? Perhaps he spoke to someone," the receptionist offered.

Houseman's glare sent her quickly back to her work. I drew myself up indignantly and thrust the camera toward Heebs, who hastened to take it.

"Let me see that address, Clemmy." I flipped to a page in the notepad. I stabbed at it with my finger. "Archibald Houseman. It is *not* a mistake."

"Well my name's Lyle. And we don't need a decorator," Houseman said through his teeth.

"The address is right," I insisted. "Isn't that this address, Clemmy?"

He edged closer. Eyed the pad. Looked at me nervously.

"Actually, Miss Cox, I think that might be an 8 instead of a 3."

Letter perfect.

"Well–"

"And I think that last name is supposed to be Hanneran."

"Well!" I almost choked at the sound of him speaking again, going off on his own. It undermined the force of my pretended indignation, which maybe wasn't bad. "That's twice that girl has mixed things up with her dreadful penmanship. She'll be looking for another job the *minute* we get back. You did look a teensy bit unfamiliar," I conceded to Houseman. "But Kitty's do's have that effect.

"I am sorry to inconvenience you," I apologized to the office in general.

Houseman had already stalked out. I turned to make my departure with Heebs tripping over himself to open the door. Halfway through it, I leaned back toward the receptionist.

"But really, dear, do consider plum. It would make you terribly *au courant*."

THIRTY-FOUR

It was time to make Beale's lookout think he was keeping his eye on me. Heebs had wanted to leave his new duds at my office and stop by whenever he needed them, but I couldn't be responsible for a kid. I gave him the name of a place that would let him store his things in a basket for a nickel a month and saw him out the alley door in his new shoes. Then I changed into the everyday clothes I'd arrived in that morning and went out the front.

A block and a half away was a place that developed film. Usually it took three or four days, but I had an arrangement with the owner. For double the price, Ernie would give me prints from this morning by quitting time. As I swung along I was pleased to see the car with Beale's boy creep out to follow.

"Ah, Miss Sullivan. Always a ray of sunshine," Ernie greeted. A well-girdled matron went out shuffling happily through a handful of snapshots she'd just picked up.

"I'm guessing she's not one of the girls in nighties who pose for you back there." I tilted my head at the heavy black curtains behind the counter. Ernie snorted. "End of the day?" I slid him my roll of film.

He nodded, scribbling on a scrap of paper. He wrapped it around the film and added a rubber band. "You picking them up?"

"Drop them off at the hat place again." A few times, when I wasn't sure how my schedule would go, I'd asked him to leave them with Mr. Seferis. "You have some throw-away prints I can put in an envelope to carry out?"

199

His eyebrows raised but he didn't ask, just as I never told anyone about his sideline in the back room. He rummaged through a wastebasket, finally coming up with a handful of snapshots. People. A couple of mutts.

"Somebody doesn't pick 'em up in a year, I toss 'em." He slid them into an unmarked envelope.

"Thanks. In case anyone asks, I just came in to pick up some pictures."

Ernie winked.

Outside the shop I paused and made a show of flipping eagerly through the abandoned pictures. The car that had watched my building all morning was parked across the street now. I looked around furtively, took a folded manilla envelope from my purse and slipped the photos into it. Then I bounced off toward the main post office. My knee felt fine.

Inside the post office I dumped the pictures back into my purse so I could burn them at Mrs. Z's. I refolded the envelope since it was still perfectly good and hid it too. After treating myself to a well-deserved tongue sandwich at the Arcade, I walked back to my office and picked up my car. I drove across the river to the Art Institute.

With its grand hilltop perch and elegant arches the museum looked the way I imagined temples had in ancient Greece, or maybe Rome. Wandering its vast, silent rooms made a fine change from sitting in a car all day waiting for lowlifes like Al to make a move. My trip here, like waving useless snapshots around and the trip to the post office, would give Beale plenty to wonder about. And worry some. Meanwhile I could enjoy myself. Being here always felt like visiting a foreign country, and I could think here as well as I could in my office.

I went to the medieval cloister, which as usual was deserted and peaceful. This time of year the chill crept in quickly, but I sat down anyway.

Beale had to be behind these burglaries. All had occurred where or when burglar alarms weren't working, which wasn't a likely coincidence. Beale's henchman Al knew Houseman, who worked for an outfit that sold burglar alarms – who in fact appeared to be a big-wig in the company. What did it all tell me?

I was fairly sure the manicurist from Ollie's would identify Houseman as the "rich guy" who had argued with Beale. I was only a shade less certain that Houseman was the "muckety-muck in a fancy building" Benny Norris had been angry about.

Houseman was the linchpin. I needed to find out more about Houseman.

* * *

My office looked drab after the museum. Maybe I needed a fancier pot for the dead plant. An urn that looked a million years old.

The phone rang.

"Miss Sullivan, I am paying you quite well and I've had no report from you in some time. Are you making any progress at all?"

"Yes, and I'm trying to follow up on it – which I can't if I'm talking to you."

I hung up. Something about Throckmorton rubbed me the wrong way.

Since he'd interrupted my thoughts about redecorating, I picked up my pencil and called the other two burglar alarm places Abner had mentioned.

"This is Lula Thompson," I said when someone answered at Caldwell-Carter. "Is Mr. Houseman in, please?"

"Who?"

"Lyle Houseman."

"I'm sorry, there's no one here by that name." The voice sounded young.

"Dear me. Could I possibly speak to someone who's been there, oh, five or six years and might possibly know where he's gone? It's about his cousin."

"I've been with the company twelve years. No one by that name has worked here."

Sometimes how a voice sounds is about as reliable as a Ouija board.

Things looked up when I tried Montgomery Security.

"Is Lyle Houseman there, please?" I asked.

A hiccup of silence alerted me. "There's no one here by that name. Could someone else help you?"

"Oh, my. I'm a friend of his aunt's. She asked me to look him up when we got to town. I'm sure she said this was where he worked; I wrote it down–"

"Just a minute please," the voice at the other end said hastily.

I heard her lay the receiver down. Somewhere in the background there was a murmur. Maybe just conversation in progress. Or maybe not. The phone was picked up again. A different voice spoke, this one lowered and uncomfortable.

"The person you asked about hasn't worked here for some time. Three or four years I should say. I'm afraid that's all I can tell you. Thank you for calling."

The line buzzed in my ear. That was okay. I'd learned something. Lyle Houseman had worked there, and the reaction his name produced told me he hadn't left under good circumstances. I leaned back and used my emery board on a bothersome spot while I thought.

Houseman had worked for one alarm system company. Now he worked for another. Why had he switched? What did the place he worked now have to do with the robberies? Or Al? Or Beale? All of which brought me back to the central question that kept bothering me: Why would a big-time crook like Beale be involved in a rash of what by his standards had to be small time burglaries?

The thought of taking the pieces I had to the cops and letting them finish the puzzle skipped invitingly through my mind. I resisted temptation. Connelly had eased my concerns that Beale's "friends" might include someone in the police. What held me back was my lack of hard proof, along with the chance of Peter's name getting dragged in. Throckmorton was a pain of a client, but he'd get his money's worth and more.

I gave the clock on the wall an irritated look. It was still too early to check with Mr. Seferis to see if my photos were there. In any case, I needed to find some other pictures to put with them. That meant sorting through some of the files that had gotten dumped when my office was ransacked. I'd been avoiding it. With a sigh for the peaceful elegance of the museum I set to work.

Forty-five minutes later I had one file drawer more or less back in order and three useful photos. Two were crooks I'd watched in the course of old investigations. Both were in prison. The third was a smooth talker who'd slunk out of town in disgrace after I'd given his well-to-do wife a more interesting photo that confirmed her fears of his infidelity. I tapped the photos into an envelope and called Mr. Seferis, but this morning's pictures hadn't arrived yet. Ten minutes later he called back to tell me they had.

I raised my window and leaned out to take a big breath of air, hoping it was movement enough to catch the eye of Beale's lookout. In case it wasn't, I stretched my arms and spread them to take another big breath, then propped my chin on the sill for a minute trying to look bored. When I'd closed the window I put on my coat and crab-walked out the narrow space that led to the alley.

It was time to surprise Ollie's manicurist.

THIRTY-FIVE

The manicurist's avarice the day we'd talked in the back of the hat shop had left me somewhat skeptical of the information she'd given me. Two days after that, I'd watched when she left work for the day so I'd know what trolley she took in case I needed to shake her. The more I'd learned, however, the more my skepticism had receded. Now what I wanted was confirmation my two plus two came out four.

I waited in a doorway next to her trolley stop until I saw her trotting along. She quickened her steps as the trolley approached, a terrier of a girl eager to get what she wanted. Keeping back I stepped into the knot of people getting on. By the time I boarded she was busy fluffing her hair and peering into her compact to check the fellow across the aisle. She didn't notice me until I sat down next to her.

"What a swell chance to catch up on gossip," I said.

She looked up and gasped. I crossed my legs, expertly blocking her as she looked toward the aisle.

"Hey! You can't follow me! I'll tell the cops!"

"Fine by me. Half of them either dandled me on their knees or went to school with me. They'd be pretty interested in the little chat we're going to have, but I thought you might like it better if we kept it girl talk."

Her eyes darted desperately, but the trolley already was pulling away. She lapsed into sullen silence.

"See? I knew you'd like that better," I said cheerfully. "All I want is for you to look at some pictures; tell me if you recognize anyone."

She crossed her arms defiantly. "What's in it for me?"

"You have me out of your hair in two more stops. If you tell me the truth. If you don't, I tell the cops to pay you a visit, ask you what you know about Woody Beale and his button boy Al. Maybe have them do it at Ollie's so Ollie can call Beale and tell him about it."

Her face had paled. Her tongue ran nervously around her lips.

"Yeah. Okay. But you're sure some bitch. A nice girl wouldn't put another girl on the spot."

I smiled and took out my four photos. She flipped past the first, paused briefly on the second, but only because the man in the photo was handsome and she was predatory. When she came to the third she gave a flick with the back of her fingernail.

"Yeah. I recognize him." She took a look at four and shook her head. "Just the one. You can get off now."

"Which one did you recognize again?"

She flipped back to three and stabbed at the picture impatiently. "Him. He's the one argued with Mr. Beale. Now let me alone."

She turned her face to the window. I pulled the cord to get off.

The man she'd identified was Lyle Houseman.

* * *

Genevieve and I had the blue plate at a cafeteria and sat through half of a free lecture comparing Pearl Buck's novels to Edna Ferber's.

"By a man," sniffed Ginny. "You'd think they could have a woman discuss woman writers. Wouldn't you like to see China, though?   Kimonos and pearls and those exquisite jade carvings."

"And nationalists fighting communists and both of them fighting the Japs and all three armies burning down cities while the people who manage not to get killed starve by the millions? No thanks."

She sighed. "I guess it is just about the bloodiest place on earth, isn't it?"

"And to get the pearls you might have to be a concubine."

"Which has lots to recommend it over being a wife," she said archly.

We laughed and talked about it all the way home. Then we sat in what she called her 'suite' because it was the only room at Mrs. Z's that had a second room adjoining it. Ginny used the second one, which wasn't much more than an alcove, as her bedroom. The bigger one had a couch and drop-front secretary and a hotplate where she made some tea to give us a Chinese feeling while we yakked some more. We weren't allowed to cook in our rooms, but Ginny was older and dependable as a clock and Mrs. Z had said it was okay as long as she kept it where the other girls didn't see it.

After that I washed my hair and wound strands around my fingers in nickel-sized coils to make pin curls, crisscrossing each with a couple of bobby pins to keep them in place. As soon as my head hit the pillow, in spite of the pins digging into my head, I floated off in a sea of dreams.   There were gardens where women in silk kimonos sat drinking tea and admiring peonies while people fanned them. Those had somehow flowed into an even nicer dream involving strong male fingers on my leg when I was roused by soft yet urgent knocking at my door.

My eyes blinked open on darkness. Through a gap in the curtains I saw the moon was still out. As I swung my bare feet into slippers I sniffed the air for smoke, wondering what else would cause this nighttime rousing. The Big Ben next to my bed said three a.m. I was still struggling into my robe when I opened the door and saw Mrs. Z.

"Someone just phoned," she whispered. "Said tell you there's a fire at your client's place and you should get down there."

"Did they give a name?"

"No. They hung up before I could ask."

"And that's what they called it? My client's place?"

"Yes."

I already was snatching out the bobby pins as I thanked her. Three minutes later, in girl trousers and with my hand gripping the .38 in my pocket I ran for my car.

The client the caller referred to had to be Throckmorton. Was the fire at his home or his business? I could check the business first since it was on the way. As soon as I turned onto Zeigler I saw traces of light cast into the surrounding blackness by fire engine lanterns. A minute later I spotted the trucks. The office buildings and wholesale places next to Throckmorton's were still closed tight at this pre-dawn hour. It was easy to park up close to the scene, right behind a car that belonged to a flash bulb boy for the *Journal*.

We passed each other as I walked toward the scene, him leaving with camera in hand, me arriving.

"No injuries," he volunteered. He sounded disappointed. I nodded, continuing.

The fire crew lights showed more here. I could see sparks flying out of Throckmorton Stationery and Office Supplies. Embers. Smoke. Lots and lots of smoke. But I didn't see flames. Not a big fire then. Just outside the fire line, as close as officials allowed, hovered several figures. One oversize shape with shoulders broad enough to lift a train turned and I caught a glimpse of a slimmer shape standing beside him. Flora Throckmorton made me out seconds before I recognized her.

"I'm so sorry to wake you and make you come down here," she said coming toward me. "I panicked – told Kimmel to call you as we dashed out. There's nothing you can do, of course, but I didn't know–"

"It's okay. What happened?"

She gestured helplessly. "We got a call. From the fire department. There doesn't appear to be a great deal of damage, thank heavens. It may have ruined our engraving machine, but that's insured. If the fire had been in the other side, where we store our paper, the whole place might have gone up."

The bruiser towering beside her was giving me a sharp-eyed assessment. Flora seemed to become aware of it.

"Oh, this is Paolo."

"Your bodyguard." I ducked my head in greeting. "Sure he's not too small?"

Flora looked puzzled. Paolo's gruff expression eased.

"I meet tough guys, I yell for my big brother." He jerked a thumb and I grinned. The shape he indicated matched his size and bulk and stood next to someone I took to be Lou Throckmorton.

"You're sure it was the fire department who called you?" I asked.

"You think it might not have been?" Flora sounded startled. "The person who called gave his name, though. Sergeant something." She pressed the heel of her hand to her forehead, the first time I'd seen her composure waver. "Do you think – could the fire have been set? Could it be a warning?"

"Money on it."

She drew breath, digesting the thought. The protective alertness with which Paolo watched her while still noting everything happening around her assured me anyone who tried to get at Flora would have a hard go. I wondered if her father inspired equal loyalty.

"There's something you probably should know about," she said. "Though I can't see what help it is. Last night – not this one we should still be in bed from; the one before that – anyway, on the way home from work a car pulled up almost on my bumper and nearly ran me off the road."

"Nearly?"

"Since Dad and I have been riding to and from work with Tony and Paolo, we decided it would be simpler to have them stay at our place. There's a little apartment above the garage. In my grandfather's day it ... well, the gardener lived there." She looked embarrassed. "But one of our better customers had asked Dad and me to lunch with him at the country club to talk about some upcoming needs of theirs. So we'd taken two vehicles in to work, my car and the truck."

"Usually we all go in our truck," said Paolo. "Miss Flora, Mr. Throckmorton, Tony and me. But our gas tank maybe leaks, so we borrow a cousin's truck. Big bull, lots of dents."

"Tony was driving the truck, just a space or two behind us," Flora continued. "He saw the car start trying to run me off so he pulled up and whammed it just enough to make it skid off on the opposite side. It was quite artistic."

"Artistic." Paolo nearly strangled restraining his laugh.

"Did you call the police when you got home?" I asked.

Flora shook her head. "We were too afraid we'd wind up having to explain about Peter. Besides, the Fazios weren't very keen to."

"Can't trust cops," said Paolo. "They might have tried to take my shotgun. Then how am I protect Miss Flora?"

"I want to find out if there's anything else your father can add, and what the firemen have told him so far," I said.

Flora put a quick hand on my arm to discourage movement.

"This isn't a very good time for talking to Father. He's awfully upset. I'm afraid he's not the nicest person when he's all worked up."

The next day turned out not to be so good for talking either.

THIRTY-SIX

I got to the office early, but not early enough. The phone was ringing as I unlocked the door. When I managed to snatch the receiver up, I was greeted by the voice of Throckmorton's secretary. Only it wasn't exactly a greeting.

"This is Helène in Lewis Throckmorton's office," she announced in clipped tones. "Mr. Throckmorton wants you to see you immediately."

Click.

Helène didn't seem to be warming up to me.

I thought about cooling my heels for twenty minutes or so. Maybe reading the paper. Letting Throckmorton expect me to jump as soon as he snapped his fingers would be a mistake. Then again, the man's business had almost burned down, so I maybe I shouldn't get sore that he didn't trot out his best manners. I turned around and went back to the elevator without so much as removing my coat.

As far as I could see, no one was sitting in a car outside my building. It put me on guard. My guess was that Beale had arranged the fire at Throckmorton's business to scare him off. If so, maybe Beale didn't think he needed to sit on me any more. Shortly after I turned onto Patterson, a pug nosed guy like the ones who'd been catching up on their newspaper reading outside my office stepped out of a shop and sauntered along a good ways behind me. Beale hadn't given up on me; he was getting smarter.

A residual sharpness of ash met my nose as I neared my destination. Just before I turned onto Zeigler my shadow melted into an office building. That probably meant Beale now had someone keeping tabs on Throckmorton's building. Someone who knew what I looked like and could pick me up there if I happened along. My pulse thumped harder a couple of times. Changing tactics usually meant someone was upping the ante. Sometimes they were desperate. Sometimes they had something up their sleeve. Either way, I needed to stay on my toes.

At the site of the fire broken windows and a scorched patch of wall were attracting some gawkers. I went inside. On the second floor I nearly collided with Thelma, who was marching down the hall with an armful of ledgers.

"Oh – hello," she managed as we both sidestepped.

"Hi," I said. "How are you?"

"Fine. Perfectly fine." She whisked out a hanky and rubbed her nose savagely. "P– that man I was worried about was less interested in me that I thought. But I'm perfectly fine." Her eyes were moist. "It's - it's a relief, actually. Not having to worry. I need to get going." She marched on before I could caution her she still ought to watch her back.

*　*　*

Throckmorton's secretary tapped a stack of envelopes into alignment and gave me the fish eye. She took her sweet time placing the envelopes in her OUT box before announcing me to her boss.

He was at his desk, one index finger tapping angrily on its surface. Everything about him looked drained. Same suit, same glasses and mustache, but someone had forgotten to starch him. He didn't get up. He didn't invite me to sit.

"I have paid a substantial amount for your services, and all I have to show for it is nearly having my business burn down," he began without niceties.

I opened my mouth to object. He held up a hand.

"Peter's no safer now than he was before. You've done nothing to stop the thugs who are after him. Nor have you done anything to keep his stupidity from ruining this company." His voice was hoarse and angry and oddly flat. "All you've managed to do is stir things up and jeopardize a business three generations of my family struggled to build. You've endangered everyone involved in its running.

"I am terminating your employment with me, effective immediately. Please don't bother sending an invoice for this week's services as it won't be paid. In view of the dismal results, I'm sure you'll agree you've been paid quite enough already. That will be all." He turned his attention to some papers before him.

I'd been insulted plenty of times. I'd even had my competence questioned. But until this moment I'd never been fired.

"Now just a minute–"

"That's *all*, Miss Sullivan!" Something wobbled on the tightrope of his voice along with the anger. Desperation, maybe.

Still stunned and with my own anger rising, I was dimly aware that if I said anything I'd probably regret it. My best move was to turn and leave. So I did.

Of all the arrogant, overbearing, thankless.... My hand gripped my purse so hard it shook as I thought about waking up drugged in a ditch. About the connections I'd painstakingly been drawing together.

"Miss Sullivan."

Here I was, on the brink of getting the goods on Woody Beale, of tying him to the robberies, of ridding the city of an out-and-out crime boss whose power grew daily. All I needed was – what? One more day? Maybe two?

"Miss Sullivan!"

The sound of my name finally registered as I went out the front door of Throckmorton Stationery and Business Supplies. I wasn't sure whether I wanted to look back, but I did. Flora Throckmorton hurried after me, her face concerned.

"I heard," she said awkwardly. "He was in such a lather this morning that I called down to check, and Helène said he was with you. By the time I got downstairs you'd left and she told me–"

"It's okay." I tried not to think about the chunk of money I'd be out for my efforts these last few days. Unpaid hours sitting in cars. Clothes and payment for Heebs.

"No, it's not. Not after all the work you've done–"

"It's okay." All I wanted right now was to wash my hands of the Throckmortons.

"It's unfair. And dammit I know he's only going to make things worse giving into their threats. But they've scared him! There's no reasoning with–"

"Threats?" Something in what she was saying pierced my anger. "The fire department says the fire was set, then?"

Confusion creased the space between her brows. "They say they can't be sure. But the phone call–" The piece that had eluded her fell into place. "He didn't tell you."

I shook my head.

"First thing this morning. Just as we were leaving the house. When he answered the phone, someone told him, 'Dump the detective or it'll be a bigger fire next time.' Verbatim, I should think. Father doesn't use slang."

Attempting a smile Flora hugged the sleeves of the thin silk blouse she was wearing. She'd doubtless removed her suit jacket when she sat down at her desk, and hadn't grabbed it when she raced out. Her words made puffs in the air. "I'm so awfully sorry."

I nodded. "I think Beale has somebody watching this place now. Keep Paolo and Tony close."

She went inside. I went back to my office.

* * *

It was 10 a.m., too early for gin, so I tried to read the paper. Chamberlain and Daladier had signed an agreement with Hitler in Munich. It said he could have the Sudentenland if he promised not to take anything else. I wondered how the Czechs liked losing their territory. About as much as I liked losing a client, probably. Tossing the paper aside I sat with my chin in my hands.

Woody Beale was a son-of-a-bitch. Since he wasn't in jail, he knew I didn't have evidence yet linking him to the burglaries. He also knew I couldn't afford to keep digging for it with no client paying me. He'd scared Throckmorton off to stop me, which had to mean I was getting close.

I got up and aimed a kick at the trash can, which obligingly slid halfway to the door. My grudge against Beale was doubly personal now. First the ditch. Now getting me thrown off a case. Throckmorton was just the sort who once he got over being scared would start to believe his accusations about me – if he didn't already. Six months or a year from now if someone mentioned me in a conversation he'd twitch his mustache and say he had it on good authority I wasn't worth the price.

Yanking open a drawer I looked through the bills I was facing this month. I could manage without the last payment from Throckmorton. But only barely. The phone leered at me urging me to pick it up and say I'd changed my mind about the extra insurance work I'd been offered or to ask Abner Simms if he needed any help on background checks. Why not find out for once what it felt like to have more than five bucks in my savings account?

One day, or maybe two. That was all I needed. The certainty of it stung like salt in a wound. I picked up the trash can and was halfway back to the desk with it when I had an idea who might be willing to pay my fee for the two days I needed.

If.

If-if-if.

If only I could find a scrap of compelling evidence for what I suspected.

Fast.

Sometimes desperation gives rise to wild ideas. Sometimes they turn out to be not so wild. I slow-waltzed the much abused trash can back to where it belonged as those ideas began to cut in fast and furious. I'd been looking at too many trails and thinking they crossed in the wrong places. If that was right, I had a hunch where I could find some answers.

Grabbing my coat I set out for Mae's – and hoped she wasn't home.

THIRTY-SEVEN

As I drove I examined what I'd been missing, trying to evaluate my emerging theory. Benny Norris had seen or heard something that got him killed. But following that trail had led me too far out of the way. Woody Beale and his golden boy Al were searching for something. That's where I needed to focus. What if Benny's so-called insurance policy was what they were after but it had never occurred to them Benny might have it?

That could make sense.

Benny had been a company man when he came to my office. He'd threatened me and tried to pry out the name of the client who'd hired me. He'd never said anything like *'Where is it?'* His only question had been *'Who?'*

In the argument overheard by the manicurist from Ollie's, Houseman had referred to an errand boy. Even Mae said Benny's role for his boss had been a minor one. What if Benny had been too far outside Beale's inner circle to know about their lather over the missing item? His room hadn't been searched the night he was killed. Nor had Mae's place. Or Muley's.

Instead, it was my office someone had ripped apart. Because they believed Peter had whatever they wanted and – because of my inquiries in his behalf and my line of work – that he'd maybe turned it over to me.

"It fits," I said aloud, so satisfied I had to hit the brakes hard for a red light in front of me.

Caught up in thoughts, I hadn't been as aware as I should. Now I checked the rearview mirror but didn't see anything that looked like a tail. To play it safe I zig-zagged awhile and parked four blocks from my real destination. I went into a little grocery where I watched for a few minutes, then moved my car to another spot half a block from where Mae lived.

Decked out in the glasses I'd worn with Heebs and toting a shopping bag that contained an old sweater, I walked up the street. Pretending to collect for a rummage sale had gotten me out of several tight spots when I'd been caught in a place I shouldn't be.

It wasn't the kind of neighborhood where you needed to lock the front door. I let myself in and paused to let my eyes adjust and to listen for signs I'd been noticed. The hall wasn't fancy, but there was a clean smell miles removed from Muley's down-at-heels rooming house. Behind the door to my left someone was ironing. Chatter from a radio mostly muffled the thump of the iron, the sort of domesticity that people for some reason always thought I should share.

No sound at all filtered down from upstairs. I tiptoed to Mae's door. When laughter from the radio across the hall seemed likely to keep other occupants of the house from hearing, I tapped lightly. No sound of movement. I waited for another burst of laughter and tried again.

I carry a couple of crochet hooks in my purse. I couldn't use them to make loops in thread if life depended. Locks seldom resist them, though, and Mae's was no exception. Thirty seconds later I was inside, calling softly.

"Mae? Hey, Mae, it was unlocked."

Mae wasn't at home.

Leaning against the closed door I surveyed the living room. Where would Benny have stashed whatever he meant by his "insurance policy"? I doubted it was cash since he'd need both guts and opportunity to steal from his boss. Besides, Al wouldn't carry a wad of cash when he'd made rounds with Peter. Yet Al had believed whatever he was after had been lost in the delivery truck. Most likely I was looking for some sort of paper. A document. Or photo. I hoped.

Mae was a tidy housekeeper. Surely Benny must have seen he couldn't shove something into a vase or under a stack of magazines and expect it not to be found. I tried to recall every detail Mae had told me about their last meeting. He'd been angry. Mae hadn't liked him in that sort of mood. She'd told him to leave; come back when he'd cooled off. He'd maybe been standing right here, just inside the door. He'd asked for a drink of water.

Closing my eyes, then opening them again, I saw afresh what Benny would have seen that night. And could have reached in the short time Mae was in the kitchen. Stepping forward I began to time myself. The couch had probably been Benny's spot when he visited. It offered more room for a man to sprawl than the doily trimmed arm chair. A quick check under its cushions revealed nothing hidden there, though. Neither did the arm chair. Getting down on my side I checked the steel springs, in fine position to look as though I'd fainted if the door began to open.

Nothing.

If Benny Norris had hidden anything here, either Mae had found it or he was smarter than I was. I was fairly sure it wasn't the latter. On the other hand, I could think of only one other place to check, and the thought of it curdled my stomach.

* * *

No one had cleaned in the Ace of Clubs since I'd been there. Or since Lincoln was assassinated, by the looks of it. I'd waited for its noontime clientele to empty their glasses and go back to plastering walls and pushing papers. As I'd hoped, it was as empty as on my first visit.

The two guys leaning on opposite ends of the bar looked like same pair who'd been there last time, but the place was so dim it was hard to tell. The rouged woman wasn't at the table today. Three rickety booths on the back wall also were empty.

The hulking bartender shot me the curious look any unknown woman alone would produce if she came through the door. Then a scowl appeared.

"You're the one left the message for Muley."

"Great memory for a big guy."

"Soon as I give it to him I had cops crawling all over me."

"Nice to see you're so sentimental over Muley meeting his maker. Two customers dead in what, ten days? Two weeks?"

"Get outa here before I throw you out." He started around the bar.

"Lay a finger on me and you'll have half the cops in the city working you over in shifts until you pee blood. And I'll see to it the city closes this dump as a health hazard."

He paused uncertainly. One of the barflies had looked up, too glazed to understand what was happening but aware of drama.

"On the other hand, if some high-priced musclemen have come around trying to wring information out of you, I can maybe keep you from winding up dead like Muley and Benny."

He turned his head and spit contemptuously. On the bar. Nice touch, as it would have been lost on the floor. "Don't need no help with musclemen. You some kinda cop?"

"Nope. Private."

"A dame?"

"Yeah. We can vote, too."

"Why are you in here? What d'you want?"

"Love letters." I tossed him a nickel. "Buy yourself a beer and show me where Benny usually sat. Quickest way to get me out of your hair."

Hercules kept a glare on to show he didn't like me, but he reached for a glass. It had a residue in it. He upended it so the dregs dribbled into a tub. He squinted as if assessing its cleanliness. When he'd filled it with beer he finally answered.

"Anyplace he could find at the bar, mostly. If him and Muley got together it was that corner booth."

I moved briskly hoping it wouldn't occur to him to come and watch. Sliding into one side of the booth I eyed every surface. Table, seat, wall – even the ceiling which was scarcely visible in the dimness. I peered in the crack between seat and wall and poked my fingertips in for good measure. When that produced nothing, I did it all over again on the other side. Across the room my pal sipped his beer and watched me.

Desperate now, I steeled myself for a final effort. Getting down on my knees on the filthy floor, I turned my face up to the even filthier underside of the table. Held in place by two thumb tacks amid wads of discarded chewing gum there was an envelope.

My maneuver roused curiosity in the bartender, who started to move. Shoving my fingers into crusty remains that harbored God only knew what kind of diseases I pulled the envelope loose. Rocking onto my feet I waved it gaily.

"See – a love letter. And to think that son-of-a-bitch left his last words to my mother in a place like this!"

I sailed past the bartender, well out of reach and prepared to run if he lunged. Just short of the door I shoved the envelope into my pocket and wrapped my hand around my .38.

THIRTY-EIGHT

I was jittery as an old maid on a picket fence all the way back to my office. Dumping my coat I took the envelope and draped a sweater over my arm to hide the .38. My eyes and ears confirmed the hallway was empty, so I scooted down it around the corner and up the back stairs. The fourth floor housed a real estate firm and a place that peddled advertising doodads. This time of day the salesmen were usually out. If anyone started up to where I was, sounds from the elevator or the echoing stairwell would alert me. I sat down at the top of the stairs by the ladies restroom and opened the envelope.

Inside was a single sheet of paper folded in thirds. Tiny holes pierced it where the thumbtacks had been. I smoothed it flat on my lap and tried to make sense of Benny's "insurance policy", for which Beale and Al would gladly kill.

It was a florist's receipt. For two dozen long stems. The clerk who sold them had dutifully noted "Mr. Beale's account".

Above the florist's letterhead were several lines of cramped, tidy handwriting. What drew my attention, though, were two drawings on the unused bottom half of the page. Squiggles. Circles. Short lines connecting things. I didn't know what they meant, but I surmised they were some sort of electrical or mechanical diagrams. Burglar alarms? Next to one, in the same cramped hand as at the top, was more writing:

Your boy must have bumped the white wire.
That triggers it. Come in from here and crimp
the red lead.

Two arrows pointing into the diagram showed the locations specified.

Beneath the drawings a different, sloppier hand had noted: *He says forget the 618's. They take a special instrument.*

I leaned back on my elbows as satisfaction spread through me. Someone – probably Houseman – had drawn up diagrams of burglar alarms and slipped Beale info on how to disarm them. The writing at the top of the sheet proved to be addresses. A three digit number followed each group. One of those numbers was 618.

It was all making sense now. Some of the addresses looked familiar. Dimes to donuts I'd find them all on the lists Flora Throckmorton had typed.

I had proof.

Footsteps rose in the stairwell. I went on full alert. Sticking the paper and envelope into my pocket I reached beneath the sweater folded beside me and wrapped my hand around the .38. Without a sound I eased onto my feet and backed up the stairs and around the corner. An instant later I recognized the light tap of a woman's shoes.

"Oh! You gave me a start!" exclaimed the woman from the employment firm next to my office.

"It's too quiet up here this time of afternoon," I said smoothing the draped sweater with my free hand so it didn't slip and give her a worse start. She chuckled agreement and turned into the ladies. I headed down.

In my office I locked the door and sat at my desk while my head whirled with what I now knew. What I had. My fingers edged toward the blotter and the list of Peter's deliveries hidden beneath it. I was eager to compare those addressed to the ones on the page with the diagrams. First, though, I had to make sure this single, irreplacable bit of proof wasn't stolen or destroyed.

The phone rang.

"Hey," said Jenkins. "Ione and I just decided to take in some jazz tonight. Want to come?"

"Gee, I can't," I said.

Even before I heard his voice, I'd discarded the thought of asking him for help. From our paling around I felt sure he could take a photograph of the paper Benny had hidden and somehow make prints. Problem was, Stutzweiler or somebody else might come in, and was sure to ask questions if they noticed he wasn't developing a picture of people or buildings.

"You on the trail of something?" Jenkins knew it wasn't like me to say no to jazz.

"Bad tooth. Got to see a dentist."

He commiserated. I hung up and steepled my fingers. Assuming Ernie knew how, he'd be willing to take a picture and make some prints in his backroom porn studio. But he'd charge me an arm and a leg for the rush job and still wouldn't have it done by the end of the day. Plus I wasn't sure how much I could trust Ernie if a higher bidder showed up. Especially one with a gun.

With either of those choices, the document also would be, however briefly, out of my possession. And Woody Beale was willing to kill for it. I puffed my cheeks and tilted my knees side to side to swivel my chair. After several minutes it occurred to me there was a better way to get what I needed – if whoever I talked to wasn't fussy.

* * *

The abstract office was up toward Miami-Jacobs. I'd been there a year, maybe eighteen months, earlier. A teacher at the theological seminary suspected his elderly aunt was being snookered in a land transaction. Some digging on my part lent weight to his suspicions. The chain of ownership on the property suggested there might be a problem. Since he'd come to me late, we'd had to scramble to get proof in front of her and a lawyer who could dissuade her from signing. The lawyer had told me about the place I was now headed.

"They can make you three copies in twenty, thirty minutes," he'd promised. "Like pictures." He'd been right. But I hadn't had reason to think of them since.

It was half an hour before quitting time, maybe the best time for my purposes since people were less inclined to argue if it meant staying late to do what you asked. I bounced up the steps to my destination and gave the woman at the counter my best smile.

"Oh, hi. Mr. Shaw needs three copies of this for a meeting first thing in the morning. He called about it."

The woman eyed me without encouragement. "I didn't hear about any phone call."

"Oh, gee – he said he'd call. And he's already gone to meet some lawyer buddies for cocktails...." I took the page with the diagrams out of the fresh envelope I'd provided and slid it to her as I talked.

"It's only one page. It won't even make you late getting off – I've seen what a whiz you are with that big machine." I wasn't at all sure she was the one who'd run the machine, called a Photostat, when I'd come here before. Nonetheless she looked up, weakening at the compliment.

"I guess I'm caught up on everything else...."

"I could talk to your boss–"

"I'll do it. Next time call ahead though, okay?"

I nodded a vigorous promise and kept her busy with questions while she ran the machine. Most people like it when you take an interest in their job. It also distracted her from taking a good look at the document she was copying for me.

While I watched I wondered whether Jenkins had ever seen one of these machines in action. Two minutes to make what the woman called a blackprint of the florist's receipt with its incriminating additions. Then, using the blackprint and sheets of special paper, maybe fifteen seconds for every white copy. A little more time to set up and finish, but still a whiz. Some day would Jenkins and his fellow shutterbugs use a gadget like this to print pictures?

In under twenty minutes I had three copies on unwieldy oversized sheets. It didn't come cheap. But the woman who'd waited on me had warmed up. When I asked to use scissors, she told a younger girl who worked there to trim my copies on their paper cutter. I slid the end product into the manilla envelope I'd brought and scooted.

Whatever happened now, the evidence against Beale would be safe.

Provided I made it to Finn's in one piece.

THIRTY-NINE

It was quitting time, so there were people on the street. Mostly good, but it made it harder to keep an eye on who was around me, too. I was ready to jump ten feet by the time I walked through the door at Finn's and slid onto a stool. My thin leather gloves were okay for gripping the Smith & Wesson in my pocket but lousy at keeping out cold.

"Fancy a black?" Finn asked with a wink as I blew through my hands.

"Yes, but I'll have to start a tab."

It was rare that I ran one, though plenty did. Unconcerned, Finn moved off to put the perfect top on a Guinness. By the time he returned I'd unfolded another manilla envelope and dropped one copy of my evidence against Woody Beale inside.

"Mind hanging onto this for a couple of days?" I asked licking the flap and sealing it with the edge of my fist. "Someplace safe where it won't get lost? I might make a buck if I'm right about something."

Finn grinned, thinking this involved some kind of bet between friends, which is what I meant him to think. If anything happened to me, he'd give it to Seamus or Billy or one of the other cops, who'd be smart enough to figure out what it was. I enjoyed my beverage and feeling my nerves uncoil while the pub filled up. I kidded some with a grammar school classmate who took the stool on my right. After a time I made my way back to the "convenience".

My preparations for getting and safeguarding the magical prints had included a regular envelope, stamped and addressed to a post office box I keep. Much as I hated to crease the stiff photostat paper, I folded another copy and shoved it inside. On my way out of Finn's I'd drop the envelope into a mail box half a block up. That left the original, which went into a pocket a seamstress had made for me under the shoulder pad of my coat; plus one copy which I'd work with, comparing it to the list from Flora Throckmorton. The blackprint I'd give to Jenkins once things played out a little bit more. He could read a negative as easily as a real image, and he'd have a scoop.

Back at the bar I ate some stew and bet one of the regulars two bits I could spot more Plymouths between Finn's and my office than he could. He wasn't about to pass up a bet like that with a dame. Half a dozen others trotted along beside us, enjoying the free entertainment and shouting encouragement. The regular won, but meantime I'd had a chance to shove my envelope through a mail slot, not to mention getting a dandy escort back to my office.

"Double or nothing from here to the parking lot," I challenged. "You can pick the kind of car."

He took the bait again and didn't object when I said I needed to run upstairs first and pick up some papers. While I retrieved Flora's list, he had a chance to crow like a rooster. It didn't last long. By the time the boy-os from Finn's delivered me to my car, I'd spotted six Dodges to his three.

* * *

I spent Friday night on my bed cross-checking lists: the one of businesses Al had visited with Peter; the one I'd made of places burglarized; the addresses on the sheet Benny Norris had hidden.

On Saturday I fidgeted.

On Sunday I went to dinner at Kate and Billy's. I'd promised, and it meant a lot to Kate and it kept my mind off work.

By nine-fifteen Monday morning I was fidgeting again, this time in a coffee shop on South Ludlow. Across from me stood a serious looking office building whose occupants included Montgomery Security. Fifteen minutes more and I'd exhausted my patience. By now the man I needed to see should be at his desk. I entered the building with the sort of satisfaction an actor probably feels stepping onto stage for the final scene of a long drama. Except I wasn't completely sure how this particular play was going to end.

Montgomery Security occupied the whole top floor of the building. A door with a polished brass handle let me into a reception area with cornice molding. A receptionist raised her head with a courteous smile. Two younger girls worked away to her left, one typing and the other answering the phone, possibly the same girl whose hesitation had helped me pick up the scent when I called pretending to hunt Cal Houseman.

"Maggie Sullivan, " I said. "I'm here to see Ed Viner."

Beyond the filing cabinets lined side-to-side behind the receptionist a well-lit hallway led in three directions.

"Is he expecting you?"

She was cordial, unlike the woman at Houseman's firm. Leaning closer I lowered my voice.

"No, but I can maybe put a tourniquet on the cash he's bleeding from this rash of break-ins."

Her eyes swung to the younger girls. They were lost in their own work. She pushed uneasily to her feet, drawing back as I held out a business card. With a couple of glances over her shoulder she disappeared into the hallway. Before I'd drawn more than a couple of breaths she was back.

"If you'll follow me, please." The sweep of her hand betrayed tension.

I followed her past the file cabinets. We turned left down the hall and stopped at a half-open door.

"Miss Sullivan," she announced, withdrawing even as she spoke.

A man with ruddy cheeks and a keen gaze surveyed me from behind a desk stacked with paperwork.

"Before your Girl Friday calls the cops, talk to Abner Simms up at Rike's. He'll vouch for me." I kept my eyes on his.

His gaze never wavered. I waited. His finger raised. Still watching me he jiggled the hook of his telephone.

"Never mind that call. Get Rike's Security instead. Abner Simms."

The regulator ticking on his wall was the only sound. Then a bubble of voice seeped from inside the telephone.

"Ab? Ed Viner. There's a woman named Maggie Sullivan in my office–" Some comment by Ab made Viner almost grin. His wariness eased a fraction. "You know her, then? Okay. Good. I appreciate that."

He hung up and regarded me without much evidence of a thaw.

"Why don't you sit down," he said at last.

I took the chair in front of his desk and crossed my ankles.

"I'm not looking to shake you down," I said. "I needed to get your attention. Fast."

"You did that all right."

"An investigation for a client turned something up. I don't have quite enough proof yet, but if you'll hear me out, I think I will have. And maybe we can help each other. I figure you're getting a ton of mud you don't deserve from these burglaries."

"Go on."

"I need to know about Lyle Houseman."

"Spoiled. Cocky. Cuts corners. Stoops pretty low to get what he wants."

I liked Viner. No beating the bush.

"Low enough to set up burglaries at businesses using your alarm systems?"

He sat back slowly. "You think that could be happening?"

I took out a photostat and slid it to him. For a minute he studied the diagrams and handwritten notations, too intent to breathe. His eyes sucked in every dot and letter. Finally he let the sheet fall to his desk. His expression was grim.

"It's his handwriting. I recognize the hook in the L's. Among other things."

"Those drawings are your gadgets? Alarms?"

"Yes. Where did you get this?"

"From a dead man. A small-time hustler who got his head blown off, most likely for seeing something Houseman didn't like. Maybe a meeting Houseman thought could link him to this."

"He's underhanded, but it's hard to imagine he'd kill anyone," Viner said frowning.

"He has friends who would. Who do." I slid him a list I'd hand-copied of the places Peter had stopped when Al was riding with him, addresses plus business names. It held at least twice the number of businesses burglarized so far. "How many of these places use your burglar alarms?"

Viner scanned it. He set it on top of the photostat.

"About forty percent. We're just about neck and neck with Caldwell-Carter when it comes to installations at businesses. But this other list..." He tapped the groups with numbers after them at the top of the photostat. "...I don't keep all the addresses stored in my head, but some I recognize as belonging to our customers. And those numbers after each batch – they match model numbers for some of our alarms."

Confirmation. But not enough to take to the cops yet.

"We keep a list by street numbers. For servicing, mostly, and checking when an alarm goes off." Viner picked up his phone. "Edith, bring me the street list."

While he waited he steepled his fingers and tapped them against his lips.

"Lyle." He let out a breath of frustration. "The little bastard worked for me. I trained him – promoted him." The ruddiness of his cheeks had condensed into angry patches of red.

"You said he was spoiled." I wanted to fill in some gaps, and Viner looked ready to talk.

"His family had money," he said grimly. "Not money like the Pattersons and Ketterings, but some. Enough for good schools, a fancy car, expensive tastes. He apparently had some sort of falling out with his father. Got cut off. That's the version from people who knew the family, anyway. Lyle had some sort of trust from a relative – aunt or grandmother – but apparently not enough to live on, at least in the style he liked."

"How'd you come to hire him?"

"Mutual acquaintance. Said he knew a bright young fellow looking for work, did I have any openings. Happened I did. When times got bad and the streets filled up with people who'd lost everything, more and more businesses started wanting alarm systems."

"They could have hired night watchmen. Taken a few of those people off the streets."

Viner looked away. "The trouble is, people can go soft when a cousin or brother-in-law's out of work and has kids to feed. They can turn blind while a few things are pinched here and there, even let themselves be tied up and gagged so more can be taken and it looks like a robbery."

A knock at the door announced the secretary who had shown me in. She placed a folder on Viner's desk and withdrew. I sat in silence, watching him run the finger of one hand methodically along the groups on the photostat. With his other hand he flipped back and forth through the typewritten file he'd requested. His steel-jawed focus, unlike Throckmorton's indignation, was likely to accomplish things.

When he finished he sat back and regarded me for some time.

"Every address on this page with the schematics has one of our alarms." He tapped it. "Curious math, don't you think? A hundred percent when – as I said – the number of local businesses using our systems adds up to less than half of the market?"

"Curious," I agreed.

"Now let me show you something." Opening the lower right drawer of his desk he took out a phone book. Bending again he took out a sheet of lined paper. I surmised it was something he'd hidden. "We guarantee our alarm systems. When two in a row failed I couldn't believe it. When it happened again, I was numb with shock. Our alarms don't fail. They have excellent engineering. Excellent parts.

"These are places hit in these recent break-ins. Ones large enough to use an alarm and large enough to get written up in the press anyway.

"All ours but one. My senior installer and I have gone crazy every time there's another one – analyzing what could have gone wrong, trying experiments. I've been placing long distance calls to the manufacturer twice a week, sometimes more, hoping their engineers have been able to find something.

"But the units haven't been failing, have they? That bastard Lyle's been disabling them. Or telling someone else how to, by the looks of it."

I gave a nod. "That would be my guess."

Viner had been pacing. He sat down now. He steepled his fingers again and blew between them.

"I believe you said something about us helping each other, Miss Sullivan? Let's talk."

FORTY

Three hours after we met, Ed Viner and I said good-by with a hearty handshake. He'd hired me for as long as it took to nail Lyle Houseman. In addition to writing a check up front, he'd offered me a handsome bonus if my carpentry took place before another business using one of his alarms had a break-in.

If Viner was anything but a straight shooter he was a swell actor. He'd recognized Woody Beale's name from the papers. My description of Al hadn't rung any bells. The acquaintance who'd recommended Lyle Houseman turned out to be a respectable businessman who'd served on a parish board with my dad. What was I missing that linked Houseman first to Viner and now to Beale?

"I'll call as soon as we've checked every damn alarm we've installed since Eve ate the apple," Viner promised walking me to the door.

He was itching to get rid of me. Freed from the nightmare he'd been stumbling through in recent weeks, he could scarcely contain his impatience to act. Well before I'd finished my questions, he'd begun laying plans to visit half his customers while his chief installer called on the others. Between them they'd ensure every alarm they'd sold was functioning properly.

"Stop by my office instead," I said. "I'll get some work done."

"It may be after six before I get there. Small talk's going to take more time than making sure the equipment's working."

"Don't worry if it takes 'til midnight. I've slept at my desk before. I'll tell the night watchman downstairs to keep an eye out for you."

* * *

It was well past noon, so I swung by McCrory's and let Izzy serve me one of my favorites which also happened to be the Friday special, tuna salad on toast. This time of year when the fresh tomatoes were gone it came with an extra slice of pickle. Dad always had lectured me not to eat tuna salad at lunch counters where it might have sat too long and turned. It was one of the rare issues where I ignored him, and I hadn't died yet.

While I savored the sharp, sweet taste of my sandwich, I sifted through my new information about Lyle Houseman. He'd been hired as a salesman and according to Viner he was a natural. Charm. Polish. A quick mind. In less than a month he'd learned the workings of the various alarm systems well enough to dazzle would-be customers by reeling off advantages and drawbacks of different models and exuding assurance.

Needless to say, the other salesmen hadn't liked him. Neither had the other men at Montgomery Security – installers, repairmen, clerks. A couple of the young women developed crushes on him, but he ignored them.

"Lyle was better educated and he didn't bother to hide it," Viner had told me. *"Didn't mingle. It was hard to escape the feeling he thought he was better than everyone else."*

His work was excellent, though. Within a year it netted him a small promotion. His new responsibilities included coordinating schedules for half the installers. It wasn't surprising Houseman had the skills to draw those diagrams on the back of the florist's receipt, but Viner didn't think he'd acquired them because he was contemplating something underhanded down the pike. Neither did I. So why was he mixed up with Beale and the burglaries?

"More coffee?" asked Izzy. An easier question to answer.

"No, but you can bring me a vanilla malted." It would get me through a long afternoon of waiting, and in case I had to hang around past suppertime for Viner's phone call.

Back in my office and sufficiently fortified, I doodled on a tablet and sorted the nuggets of new information I'd gotten from Viner. I couldn't see Houseman's current employer risking involvement in burglaries to put a competitor out of business. When I'd asked whether Houseman himself might have grudge enough, Viner had given a mirthless laugh and ticked off three: Viner's choice of an employee with twenty years' experience for a new supervisory position which Houseman had eyed. Nixing things when Houseman asked out Viner's daughter. Last of all, reading the riot act when he forgot something and returned to his office to find Houseman bent over his desk reading financial sheets.

"You fired him," I'd guessed.

"Damn right. He was good, but not irreplaceable. He wanted to be the golden boy without the drudgery of crossing t's and dotting i's. He worked at what came easily to him and sloughed off the rest."

If Houseman was as stuck on himself as Viner had made him out to be, I reasoned swiveling in my chair, he might have drawn those diagrams to get revenge. But that didn't explain Beale's involvement. I groaned. Some of the burglaries connected to this had resulted in substantial losses, but they still were peanuts by Beale's standards.

I got up and paced to crank my brain. I sat down again. I paced some more. I sat some more. A good part of the afternoon slid by with me grabbing for connections as successfully as a dog snaps at fireflies.

By four o'clock I was fidgeting so I could hardly sit still. If I walked to the bank it might clear my head, and I could deposit Viner's check so I'd stay solvent. But if Viner finished earlier than he'd thought, I'd miss him. I gave his receptionist a jingle.

"Mr. Viner back yet?" I asked when I'd introduced myself.

"No, nor Matthew either. Is there a message?"

"Just tell him I've stepped out to the bank. I'll be back in ten minutes."

I scribbled a note to the same effect and hurried out. It was payday for a lot of folks, but it was early yet so only four or five people were in line ahead of me. I made my deposit and kept a few bucks for the weekend, then headed back. As I stepped outside, the blustery autumn wind bit into me with an equally chilling thought why Beale was mixed up with Houseman. I all but ran back toward my office, slowing at the end enough to spot what might be one of Beale's lookout cars across the way.

Upstairs I dumped my coat on the rack and blew between my fingers so I could dial Viner's office again. Before the receptionist finished saying I'd reached Montgomery Security I cut her off.

"It's Maggie Sullivan. Is he back?"

"No. I thought–"

"He said to ask you if I needed anything. Do you happen to know if your company does alarms for any banks?"

"Yes, I think so. I think.... Oh!"

"If he calls or comes there before he comes here, tell him to double check them."

"Yes. I will. Oh, dear!"

"It's just a hunch. Keep it under your hat."

The more I thought about it, the more it made sense. The haul from warehouse burglaries and such wouldn't be great by Beale's standards, but if he could get into a bank without an alarm going off, and he had a good safecracker.... Since I hadn't sat down I was already in position for pacing again. Maybe the earlier burglaries were test runs, or meant to have the cops chasing their tails before Beale hit the big target. Or maybe banks used a different kind of alarm. Viner had pointed out to me this morning that he installed several other models besides the ones on the page I'd found, and one of the comments scribbled on that page had mentioned a model that needed a key.

I crossed my arms and pinned my hands under my elbows so I wouldn't be tempted to dial his office again. His girl Edith would let me know if she heard from her boss. The minute hand on my clock crawled to five, and then half past, and then toward six.

I'd just given in and perched on the edge of my chair with my pencil ready to dial when my door burst open.

But it wasn't Edward Viner who stood there.

It was Flora Throckmorton. Wild eyed. Holding a gun.

Pointed directly at me.

FORTY-ONE

"Where's Peter?"

It was a dinky little excuse for a gun, but at this close range and keyed up as she was, it could still cause damage. Her question made no sense. I shook my head.

"I thought–"

"They're not here, are they?"

Her eyes had scoured the room. She slumped. The gun hung limply at her side.

I didn't know what she was talking about, but it sounded like trouble.

"Sit down before you keel over." I pushed a chair toward her.

She blinked and seemed to realize she still blocked my doorway. With a grimace she dropped the gun into her pocket, closed the door and came to sit in the offered chair. The abruptness with which she sank down made me wonder if her knees had gone wobbly.

"What's going on? I thought Peter was in St. Louis."

She shook her head. "He called yesterday. Father told him about the fire."

I took out my bottle of gin and poured a finger into an extra glass which I slid across to her. She knocked back half of it, hitching her breath in ever so slightly. By the time I'd splashed some gin into my own glass, a trace of color was returning to her cheeks.

"Look, I'm awfully sorry about – I've never threatened anyone–"

"It's okay. Catch your breath a minute and then tell me what's going on. Is Peter back?"

She nodded and took a very small sip of her gin. It wasn't going down as easily now so I brought out my bottle of tonic and raised my eyebrows. Seeing her nod I gave us both a splash.

"He called and Father told him about the fire. Did I already say? The idiot must have walked right out and caught the next train back. He came in just before lunch today, straight from the station. Hadn't shaved, didn't even have a bag. He was crazy with worry. Insists the fire's his fault."

Seeing a smart dame like her so undone made me want to give her cousin a good shaking. In a way he was to blame for the fire. But only because he'd been helpless as a rabbit destined for a hawk's dinner when Al swept down on him. Now I had a bad feeling he'd mucked things up even worse.

"Has somebody snatched Peter?"

"I think – I think so–"

"What made you think they'd come here?"

"Because...." She tried futilely to organize thoughts.

"Start with Peter coming back. Right before lunch, you said?"

She nodded and took a healthy swig from the glass in her hand.

*   *   *

It was the ripple that alerted her something was up. That undefinable office ripple you sense rather than see. Something that spreads, though you seldom glimpse anyone raising their head from their work or leaning to the person the next desk over. One girl sprang up and ran to the ladies room dabbing at tears.

And then, with no warning, there was Peter coming grimly up the stairs. He looked ghastly. Exhausted. Miserable.

"What are you doing here!" She caught his arm.

"Putting an end to this disaster. Where's Uncle Lou?"

"At the insurance agent's. Don't let's stand out here."

He hadn't resisted when she led him into her office.

"Pete, you've got to get out of town until this is over—"

"No! I'm done hiding. If I hadn't been such a coward there wouldn't have been any fire." He paced. He refused to sit down. "I'm going to the cops. I'll tell them everything. I'll tell them I was the only one involved, that you and Uncle Lou were in the dark. I'll make them promise to keep the business out of it if I testify against Al."

"You'll make a hash of it if you go like this. You're barely coherent."

That brought him up short.

"For God's sake, Pete, you're on the verge of collapse. You look like you belong in a strait jacket. Stretch out on the cot in the sick room 'til Father gets back."

"Like a girl with female complaint? That's about what I am, I suppose." He drove the side of his fist against the wall.

Flora jumped. She'd never seen her cousin slug anything.

"That's a rotten thing to say about women. It's beneath you, Pete. Do you want to make a fool of yourself with the police or do you want to rest and have a shave so they'll take you seriously?"

He reddened at her censure. Sheepish, he let her take his sleeve and steer him to a tiny room with a cot. When

Hèlene called Flora to say her father was back, she collected Peter and waited while he washed his face. The shave could wait.

* * *

"Then what?" I asked.

"He went down to see Father. So did I. This whole mess affects me too, and I decided if Father didn't like me being there it was too damn bad." Flora's chin went up but she blushed.

"It was already half past two by then, and I felt rather sorry for both of them, actually. They both looked frazzled. The insurance man had told Father it could be months before we'll see a penny for repairs because the fire looked suspicious. He'd come back despondent. But when he saw Peter his spirits rose and he started saying they'd find a way out of this, but then Peter said the only way out was going to the police, which was where he was headed.

"They argued forever, with Father saying Peter couldn't throw away his whole future, and Pete saying he'd go somewhere else and start over. Finally he practically shouted that he didn't want to spend the rest of his life selling office products. It's the first time he's ever stood up to Father. After badgering him some more and then coaxing, Father sort of deflated. He said if Peter was determined to throw himself on the mercy of the police, at least would he wait while Father called our lawyer to accompany him." Flora sighed. "Father's a terrible stinker at times, but he truly cares about Peter – more than he does protecting the business."

At least this was passing the time while I waited for Ed Viner. What I still didn't understand was why Flora thought her cousin might have come here.

"Did the lawyer spook him?" I asked.

She shook her head.

* * *

She and Peter were on their way back to the third floor to wait for the lawyer. Their shoulders bumped in mutual reassurance just as in childhood when one or both were in trouble. The secretary she and Peter shared came racing down the stairs toward them.

"Mr. Stowe has a phone call! Someone from California. He said Mr. Stowe wouldn't want to miss it."

Peter leaped the stairs two at a time. Hampered by her skirt, Flora lagged behind. By the time she reached his office he was shouting.

"She has nothing to do with this!" His face was ashen. "Leave her out of this, you bastard – No! You son-of-a-bitch!"

She'd never heard him like that. Not just the profanity. He was hoarse. Beside himself. It frightened her. He banged down the phone.

As he charged out she made a futile attempt to grab his sleeve. He shoved her aside. She tried again, conscious of curious faces turning to watch. There was no stopping him.

"Peter!"

He was at the stairs again, skidding down so precipitously she was sure he'd break his neck.

"Peter! Slow down! What's going on?"

"Go back, dammit! I've got to put an end to this!"

But she'd known from the moment she'd heard his tight, strained voice on the phone that the call was from the men who were after him. As she knew without being told he was going to meet them. Icy fear drove her after him, her pace almost as reckless as his own. Nevertheless, by the time she reached the street he'd disappeared.

* * *

"I thought when he said 'leave her out of this' that it must be you he was talking about," Flora concluded. "Since you were helping."

So she'd charged over here with her dinky gun knowing those goons could be waiting. The lapse in her usual level-headedness could have gotten her killed. But she had spunk.

Where the hell was Ed Viner?

"You know how to use that popgun?" I asked while I thought what to do.

"Oh yes." She sounded embarrassed. "Paolo insisted I have it. Made me promise to keep it beside my bed. He had me shoot at bottles out in a field until I could hit them rather well. I feel awfully foolish–"

I waved away what I was sure would be an apology. She brushed despairing fingertips across her forehead.

"I know I shouldn't ask it after Father sacked you, but please – will you help? I'll pay, of course."

I nodded. "I've got no beef with you."

Peter Stowe had charged off into a trap and probably knew it and probably also knew his rashness had a good chance of getting him killed. Adding that up gave me an unpleasant hunch who they'd used as bait.

"There's a girl works on your floor. Her name's Thelma. Pretty and about as innocent as a baby."

"Thelma Taylor. One of my best account clerks."

"She at work today?"

Flora frowned. "As a matter of fact she's the girl I mentioned who burst into tears."

"What about when you came up to wait for the lawyer – when Peter got the phone call? Was she there then?"

Her puzzlement deepened. "I - I'm not sure–"

"Would someone else know? She and your cousin are sweethearts. Head over heels. He broke things off right before he left for St. Louis out of some hair-brained notion it would protect her."

Her fingers had flown to her mouth but she wasted no time. "Let me call–"

I whipped the phone around. She grabbed it and dialed without the least regard to her manicure.

"Dad? No time to explain. Peter's in danger. So is one of the girls from the office. I need the number for Thelma Taylor. And the name of the girl at the next desk – the one who sniffles. Yes. That's it. Yes...."

She didn't hang up. She was waiting for something. I looked at the clock. Half past six. Throckmorton had gone somewhere to hunt for the numbers.

A minute later Flora thanked him. She jiggled the hook and dialed again. When she looked up I saw the bad news in her face.

"She hasn't come home yet. Her mother's worried." Another quick call and she looked up again, confirming the worst. "Thelma got a call right after lunch. They told her it was the bank, that there was a problem with her account and she needed to come right down. She told her supervisor and left. She never came back."

FORTY-TWO

We split up the tasks at hand. Flora paced while I called the police. No agitated young man had come in wanting to talk to them. That meant Peter hadn't gone there.

We switched roles. Flora called the cops while I wore out the linoleum. In a businesslike tone which discouraged a run-around, she told who she was and said that one of the girls who worked for her had gone missing. She mentioned the hinky phone call and that someone had seen the girl being pushed roughly into a dark green Packard. The last part was an embellishment I'd suggested. We both thought it justified since it might spur them to take a look at Beale and his boys.

"Now what?" asked Flora, her face tense with worry.

"Is Paolo still at your building?"

"Yes. I was too set on catching Peter to get–"

"Let me make some quick calls. Then you have Paolo come over and meet you downstairs."

Nobody answered at Montgomery Security. I looked up Viner's number at home, but his wife said he hadn't come in yet. While Flora called Paolo I got out the blackprint of the page that Benny Norris had hidden. I stuffed it into an envelope and used a wax pencil to write Matt Jenkins' name on the front in big letters. I was sealing the envelope just as Flora finished.

"You and Paolo take this over to the *Daily News*. Give it to the night clerk."

247

She nodded. For several seconds I contemplated telling her to go from there to the police station and talk to Connelly, who should be coming on soon if he'd pulled extra duty tonight. But my new evidence on the robberies took some explaining. On top of which we had no proof except our own certainty that Thelma and Peter were in danger. Even if Connelly believed what she told him, convincing the powers that be to do anything would be another story.

While I was weighing those facts, I took out my .38. I checked the cylinder even though I knew it was ready. I tossed extra rounds in my pocket. Flora watched somberly.

"What are you going to do?"

"Find Pete and Thelma." My words held more conviction than I felt.

I watched at the front door with Flora until Paolo's formidable bulk arrived and they were safe in his truck. After a run to the ladies, I made one more futile attempt to reach Viner. I wasn't worried he was in any sort of jam; his rounds were just taking as long as he'd warned me. Finding Thelma and Peter was a matter of life and death. Waiting for Viner wasn't. I'd leave him a note, but I couldn't say too much in case the wrong eyes saw it. After thinking a minute I licked my pencil and wrote:

> *Sorry–*
> *A girl who's 40% a friend needs help.*

My fingers were crossed that Viner would remember telling me his company installed about forty percent of the local alarm systems. Maybe he'd make the leap that I'd left for some reason having to do with the burglaries. In any case, it was the best I could do.

I shrugged into my coat and took a blue hat with a stiff spot at the edge of the brim from the coat rack. Not a stylish number, but maybe a good choice tonight.

* * *

I didn't have time to play games with Beale's goons so I went out the front door. No one followed me to my car, and after a dozen blocks or so plus a couple of loops I felt confident I didn't have a tail. Now the question was where to look for the pair that Beale or someone working for him had snatched. Thelma would have been easy to hustle into a car while she was too startled to scream. Snatching Peter off the street would have been harder. He'd have made a stink, and Beale was too slick for that. So was Al.

Okay, then. Whoever called Peter that afternoon had suggested a meeting place. Or Peter had blundered off to hunt for Al at some spot where they'd met in the past.

Doubling back downtown I tried Ollie's Barber Shop. From the street it looked closed and dark on a Monday night just like its neighbors. I pulled in the alley and parked a few trash bins away but the back looked as dark as the front. When I crept close and listened and waited and finally used my crochet hook, the inside proved as empty as the outside promised.

I tried Al's place with no better luck. No Buick outside, and when I got in there was nothing that hinted the kidnaped pair might have been there. All I saw was a closet full of hand-tailored suits, furniture that made me envious and a three-foot marble nude whose arm held a discarded necktie.

"Crime pays fine for some," I grumbled to the DeSoto as I slid back under the wheel. When I turned the key her six cylinders purred commiseration.

Next I tried Beale's clubs, first the glossy ones I'd watched with Calvin, then the one across the river in the Negro section, where I leaned out the window and got directions from a smartly-dressed couple. There was no sign of Al's car there, or Beale's or any matching the license numbers I'd copied. All three nightspots were busy, with people coming and going, but I'd have as much chance getting inside and snooping around for prisoners as a mouse would of leaving a cat convention.

It was after ten now. Had Ed Viner been to my office? Had he understood my message? Were Thelma and her well-meaning hero still alive?

Indifferent to my questions the city around me kept its routine. The Art Institute stretched golden and temple-like on its hill. Near the downtown end of the Third Street Bridge, men with no other place to go were lining up at a shelter. What looked like a family with plenty of kids curled together under blankets by the steps of Sacred Heart.

Time was running out. Once Beale snatched somebody he wouldn't dawdle. He'd get them out of the way for keeps tonight. Meanwhile, where would he stash them? Someplace he knew of that wasn't connected to him. Someplace where they wouldn't be noticed. But where? Where else could I look?

It came to me in a flash.

* * *

The bumpy dead-end lane where the thug with the wood-slatted pickup had gotten a wad of cash from Al looked even less inviting at night than it had by day. A place with only one way in and out, easy to watch and fine for trapping someone. A place where, inside any of the hulking industrial buildings, sound could be muffled. I rolled past the lane without pausing, drumming my thumbs on the steering wheel and trying to think. The gate of the nearby coal yard was locked for the night, but traffic on Findlay was scarce, so I did a U-turn and went past again. Hard to tell without turning in so my headlights could show me, but the short scrap of thoroughfare looked deserted.

If I was right about this location, chances were Beale had a lookout. Driving past a third time would be too risky. Parking close enough for a quick escape was also out of the question. I'd have to take my chances on foot. The corner warehouse where I'd pretended to relieve myself my first time here had a strip of concrete next to a loading dock on the Findlay Street side, out of view of anyone in the lane and good for a quick getaway. I parked and sat for a minute letting my eyes adjust. I watched for movement at the mouth of the lane, the glint of a light, anything. Pulling my hat snug I got out, .38 in hand.

Again I waited, mostly listening now while my vision continued to sharpen. A freight train wailed in the night on the tracks several blocks behind me. From my day visit I remembered that some sort of rail spur was partly responsible for the dead end at the foot of the lane. That meant I'd be keeping my eye out for hobos as well as Beale's men. Slowly I began to move. When I reached the mouth of the lane, it looked to be empty of cars.

Half an hour or so later I'd crossed the lane and worked my way down to the place where I wanted to be. A train whistle sounded, this one distant. A dog barked. I was standing a few feet away from where the cocky guy with the truck had leaned against Al's car smoking and talking. At the time I hadn't paid much attention to the building behind them. Now I did.

It looked like any other mid-sized two-story warehouse. Brick. High ceiling on the ground floor. Hard to tell in the dark, but it looked like it might be empty, or little used. There was a small door in front, but one of the two windows in what had probably been the office was boarded up.

Given the size of the lane, it could be the meeting I'd witnessed hadn't been set for any particular spot. But I was guessing the one I was looking at was a place Al knew. Or more likely one Beale knew from his bootlegging days. With lives at stake it was worth a try.

I inched my way to the side of the warehouse. There was a loading door midway and a regular door toward the rear. A wide dirt area, long enough for trucks to load and pull around and leave, separated the building from its neighbor. The area was empty of vehicles and I didn't hear anything, so I made a slow circuit of the building watching and listening. My arm was tired from holding the .38. When I got back to where I'd started, I decided to have a look inside.

Since no one had unlocked the door for me, I shifted the gun to my left hand to use my trusty #2 Boye. I'm an indifferent shot with my left hand, but I'm strictly a right handed lock pick. After a couple of minutes I felt tumblers fall into place. A minute later I was in.

It took some more adjusting to the darkness in here. Outside there'd been light from stars at least. Meanwhile I breathed softly, checking for smells. Cigarette. Men's cologne. Not very strong. Hard to tell if someone was in here, but someone had been, and recently. Straining my ears I hugged the perimeter of the warehouse, moving toward what from the outside looked like an office. At every step I was glad I'd put on matronly lace-up shoes with noiseless soles.

The office had the look of disuse about it. No shape suggesting a lunchpail or cup on the single desk. I went out silently and made my way around the opposite wall. By now I could see well enough to make out shapes. There were a few barrels lined up in one corner; some crates stacked in another. That was it except for what looked like a bucket or paint can in the middle of the floor at the end where I'd entered.

Crouching behind the barrels I took my flashlight out of my coat pocket, made an arc with its beam and snapped it off waiting for shots. When I'd tried it in other directions with no ill results I made another circuit around the inside. The stairs leading up were covered with cobwebs, but some primal instinct told me others were here.

I bent down and ran my light along the floor and picked out my own footprints in the thick dust. I saw other prints, too. One had the small heel of a woman's shoe. They led to the paint can I'd noticed. The can looked brand new and there was a brush beside it and a canvas drop cloth spread underneath. What would you paint in a warehouse that hadn't been used in months, maybe years?

I moved the canvas aside and saw the trapdoor. Dousing my light I lifted the panel as quietly as I could and felt for the stairs. Thanking the Holy Mother there were treads instead of rungs, I made sure my footing was firm and started down, gun at the ready and darkened flashlight ready to use as a club. When I thought my lungs would burst from holding my breath, I heard a whimper. Someone was here, left in pitch darkness, hurt or terrified.

Shifting the flashlight and holding it half against me to keep it from blinding, I switched it on. Ahead of me on the floor, hands and feet bound and a gag in her mouth, Thelma stared up in fear.

Something crashed against my head and I heard a faraway voice.

"Sweet dreams, princess."

FORTY-THREE

Someone was shaking my shoulder, only it felt odd. I heard a thread of sound like a tire leaking air.

"Miss Sullivan!" The thread firmed into a whisper. I opened my eyes. It was mostly dark but a faint glow showed somewhere. Enough for me to make out a shape and gather in the memory of where I'd been.

"Miss Sullivan! It's me – Thelma. From Throckmorton Stationery," said the shape.

I nodded and squinted my eyes and when I opened them again I could see her. The gag that had covered her mouth bunched on her lower lip.

"I'm going to work your gag loose so we can talk. If somebody comes, push your tongue out hard to hook the cloth and pull it back up." She wiggled around and worked at my gag with her bound hands. Within a matter of minutes she'd moved it down. "Try the thing with your tongue a time or two so you can do it fast," she said.

My wits were returning enough now to see she was plenty scared. If she could soldier ahead, so could I. After I tried the business with the gag a few times I turned my head, which repaid me by pulsing irritably, and looked for Peter. He wasn't far away. His eyes were open and glassy. I was pretty sure it wasn't the glassiness of death. His gag was in place and from what I could see in the dimness, he'd taken one hell of a beating. Dark patches that were either blood or bruises covered most of his features.

"He – they hit him so hard!" Thelma whispered. "And he kept telling them to let me go or he wouldn't tell them anything. I couldn't even get him to open his eyes until I was trying to bring you around. Is he – will he–?" Her voice caught.

"Don't fall apart on me, Thelma. He's probably got a concussion, but he'll be okay." I could be lying, but it was what she needed to hear. "Peter – are you awake? Do you know where you are?"

The glassy eyes moved fractionally.

"Where's the guy who clobbered me?" I asked Thelma.

"I – I don't know. He tied you up and called you terrible names and said somebody named Al might want to see to you personally. Then he left. He – he took your gun. But he must've forgotten your flashlight. He had one too."

That explained the glow, then. And maybe we had a weapon.

"Okay, listen fast, in case he comes back. You and Peter are going to be okay. The cops know you're missing and they know who has you. So does Flora Throckmorton. There's a razor blade inside the brim of my hat. It feels like a dent. The two layers come apart easy. If we get split up before we get out of here, make like the hat is yours and hang onto it. Understand?"

"Yes. Does–"

"Is the guy who was down here with you the only one?"

Thelma's head shook. "There's two. Watching us now, I mean. There were others at first, when they beat Peter. Then they stuffed us in the trunk of a car and brought us here. Since then I've only seen two. One went somewhere close where there's a phone. I think - I think maybe from what I heard they killed the night watchman in some building."

It made sense. I'd been bothered not seeing a car. If they were somewhere close it wouldn't be long before at least one of them returned. As long as it took to make sure no one saw him moving stealthily to one of the nearby buildings; make sure whoever was waiting there didn't shoot him; call Al or maybe somebody who'd reach Al. Maybe wait for a call with instructions. After that it would be a fast trip back. And both goons would probably come.

I'd had harder cracks on the head but it hurt anyway as I tried to think.

"How'd you get your gag down in the first place?" I asked to get my mental wheels going faster. "Not with your tongue."

"No, I sort of scraped it off. I couldn't reach my own shoulder so I scooted over and rubbed my chin against Peter's shoulder. I was awfully scared I'd hurt him more, but–"

"You think fast on your feet, Thelma."

She was making her way toward Peter again by flexing her haunches, walking on her backside like an animal with very short legs. Peter was the weak link in an attempt to escape. He was in bad shape. I saw his eyes had fallen closed again.

"Peter!" I whispered sharply. They fluttered open. "Did you hear what I said before? About people looking for you? Your cousin Flora nearly blew my head off with a gun, she's so determined to find you."

As I'd hoped, that part proved as effective as smelling salts. His eyes snapped wide. I knew he was listening now.

"No more heroics. We've got to outsmart them. I'm pretty sure I've found what Al's been after. I can get them to bargain, or at least think they're bargaining. The important thing is for you to do whatever I tell you to, or what Thelma tells you. Don't do anything to get yourself punched again or you won't be able to move, and Thelma won't leave without–"

Thelma's feet kicked my leg. She was watching the stairs. I saw her gag flip up just as I heard the trapdoor. It took me two tries to get my own gag back into place. I glanced at Peter just in time to catch a small nod as his eyes snapped shut.

"Not so feisty now, are you?" A voice I suspected was Al's lashed at me and I was blinded by a light in my face. He laughed at my muffled growl. "What happened to that smart mouth of yours?"

Two pairs of hands yanked me to my feet. Somehow Thelma had managed to douse my flashlight in time. Was she sitting on it?

"This one still alive?" Al asked from in front of me. Still blinded by the light in my face I could make out little more than smudgy movement as his leg reached out to nudge Peter. "Not that it matters," he assured the men with him. "Go to the club. Make sure you're seen. At half past one come back and torch this place. It'll take care of these two."

I heard Thelma whimper. I tried to look in her direction, but Al seized my shoulder.

"And you, you meddlesome bitch, have a special invitation from Mr. Beale."

* * *

I didn't get to ride up front. Al stuffed me in the trunk of his car just as the boys who worked under him had done with Peter and Thelma. When he hauled me out again, the silence and the feel of the air told me I was somewhere out in the country. In a matter of seconds my eyes, already accustomed to the dark of the trunk, confirmed it. Amid landscaped grounds big enough for a couple of football fields sat a swank modern house. A chill climbed my spine as Al began to muscle me toward it.

With every step I was assessing my situation. I didn't have a weapon. No one knew where I was. I doubted there were any neighbors close enough to hear. Beale's property probably had a fence and at least a couple of guards. And unless Thelma somehow managed to get herself and Peter out of their prison – or I could get back to them – they'd burn to death when Beale's boys torched the warehouse.

A sinewy fellow whose shoulders were rounding with age beneath his white jacket opened the door.

"Where the hell's Jimmy?" snapped Al as we stepped in.

"Maybe watching from the bushes, sir. The boss told him be extra careful tonight."

The butler or valet or whatever he was had an accent. Italian, Spanish. He took no notice of me. Guests probably showed up here bound and gagged all the time.

"Boss in his office?"

"Yes, sir." The rounding shoulders bowed as he took Al's hat.

Al marched me past gleaming blocks of wood supporting a staircase. We were heading toward the back of the house. We turned down a hall that led to the left and marched some more. Al rested the hand with the gun lazily on my shoulder, ready to spin in an instant toward my head. At the end of the hall an open door gave a glimpse of a sitting room on one side. We turned the opposite way toward a thick paneled door.

Al reached around with his free hand and yanked the gag down.

"Scream all you want. Nobody will hear." He rapped on the door. "Boss. Brought you a present."

"Come in," a voice invited calmly.

Al nudged me once with the gun, then rested it on my shoulder again as he pushed me ahead, using me and his elbow to shove the door wide.

I had just enough time to register a man with wavy dark hair at a desk and another man standing beside him before a shot rang and a force I couldn't fight plunged me to the ground.

Disbelief filled my parched throat as I fell. I hadn't expected Beale to kill me the instant he saw me. The floor hurt as I hit it, which sparked the flashing thought that maybe I wasn't dead. But when I tried to move I couldn't. Was I paralyzed or was this how dying felt? I tried to feel my fingers and thought I could. I tried to wiggle my toes. Fighting the weight that seemed to hold me motionless I turned my head.

And looked into the unseeing eyes of Al.

Just inches from me.

With a bullet hole in his forehead.

FORTY-FOUR

"Who are you?" demanded a voice. A voice that teetered between authority and panic. "Don't move, or I'll kill you too!"

The door I'd come through slammed shut. I closed my eyes so I didn't have to stare into Al's. I tried to swallow but only managed a dry heave, not because I'd never looked at violent death before, but because it had so nearly been my own.

"Her name is Maggie Sullivan," said the calmer voice that had bid us enter. "She's a private detective. She's been throwing sand in this whole operation and she's sweethearts with the cops."

On the other side of the door a quick knock sounded.

"Boss?" inquired the voice of the round shouldered servant.

"Everything's fine. Just a business matter."

I had the barest inkling I might be sliding into shock. Succumbing to it would seal my doom. The only chance I had of surviving – however slender it might be – was to show some moxie and keep my wits.

"How about letting me sit up so I'm not kissing a corpse?" I managed to say. Why had Beale had one of his goons pop his own lieutenant?

"Her hands are tied," the voice I figured was Beale's reassured. "She knows some things it would be to both our advantage to hear."

"She knows.... Sit up! Sit up, dammit!"

Slowly it dawned on me Beale might not be calling the shots.

Using my feet and the heels of my bound hands I eased backwards from under the weight of Al's body, put a little more distance between us and sat up. I didn't look at Al from my new position. I knew the back of his head would be worse than the front. Instead I turned my attention toward the desk, and the man behind it whom I recognized from the newspaper photos as Woody Beale. Standing at his left shoulder was the guy with the agitated voice, the guy whose marksmanship had put a clean hole between Al's eyes.

It was Lyle Houseman.

He stood with his legs spread holding a pair of revolvers like some movie cowboy. One pressed the back of Beale's head. The other pointed at me.

"I'm nearly as good with my left hand as my right," he warned. "Don't risk the percentage."

His words were tight with nervous excitement, but the guns remained steady. I nodded.

"Which hand you shoot Al with?"

"The right. No taking chances after the mess the bastard made."

"I'd give you a medal if I had one and wasn't tied up. Where'd you learn to shoot like that?"

"Ten years of summer camp with the cream of the East."

His smirk of superiority confirmed Ed Viner's assessment of him being stuck on himself.

I was getting my bearings now. Another body lay half visible to the right of Beale's desk and a little behind it. His bodyguard, probably, sprawled face down. Houseman must be as fast as he was accurate.

"I think Lyle's acquiring a taste for killing." Beale's silken tone held a mocking note. "It's more exciting than hitting a target, isn't it, Lyle? Makes you feel powerful."

"Shut up."

"But it's made you jittery, too, that rush."

"I said shut up!"

Tense as Houseman was, he'd go off as easily as nitroglycerine. I tried to figure out what I'd walked in on. Why were he and Beale on the outs? Beale's eyes, which were almost as dark as his hair, told me nothing. Their lack of expression signaled more danger than anger would have, for it suggested calm calculation.

"You're a smart dame, figuring out where I'd stashed those two nuisances," he said studying me. "You've been nothing but trouble since we crossed paths. Sticking your nose in. Figuring things out. It would be a waste getting rid of someone with your skills when you could put them to work for me instead. Earn three, four times what you make in that rathole office of yours. What do you say?"

"Doesn't look to me like you're in any position to hire right now, Beale."

He chuckled.

"Lyle and I have no differences now, do we, Lyle?" He redirected his smoothness to the man with the gun. "In fact you may have been right, telling me Al was losing his edge. Otherwise you'd be the one with a hole in you, wouldn't you, Lyle? Oh, his gun moved the second he saw you, but it was too late. But Al's out of the way now. Benny's out of the way. That gullible chump who drove Al around will be out of the way as soon as the fire that should be starting soon hits the cellar. There's no one wise now but us, Lyle – and Miss Sullivan, sitting here gift wrapped."

He was good. The words. The soothing tone. Houseman for all his cockiness was starting to waver.

"Too bad there's an envelope I'm supposed to pick up tomorrow," I said. "If I don't, the guy I left it with will open it." Actually Jenkins would open the envelope I'd sent by Flora the minute he saw it. "He'll see those drawings Houseman made for disabling the burglar alarms and he'll have a good idea what those model numbers and addresses where they're installed all mean."

It broke the spell.

Houseman's gaze swivelled back and forth between us.

"She's bluffing," Beale said flatly.

"The drawings are on a florist's receipt for roses Beale ordered. I put a note in saying someone could decipher them at Montgomery Security."

Beale's eyes narrowed. He sat very still.

"You've ruined me, you bastard!" Houseman's rage made him hoarse. "The Keystone Cops could have pulled this off better than you and your outfit!"

I began to take inventory. If what Mrs. Salmon had told me there in her kitchen still held, Beale kept a gun in an ankle holster. Probably one in his desk as well. The bodyguard's automatic lay only inches away from his splayed, nerveless fingers. But I'd be dead before I reached it, even if my hands were free.

The gun which Houseman had trained on me waved erratically. He rammed the nose of its mate into Beale's ear.

"You told me this would be easy–"

"Shut up and calm down." For the first time Beale spoke sharply. "Shoot me and how are you going to get any money?"

While they snarled I chanced a look and spotted the gun apparently forgotten by both of them. Al's. It lay almost under his body, his left shoulder hiding it from the men at the desk. He'd fallen with the arm he'd swung up to fire angled under him. The gun had slipped from his hand. *But my hands were tied.*

"That's what you stormed in here demanding, isn't it? Money?" Beale was saying. "Fine. I'll give you enough to get out of the country. Live in style for a couple of years. Buy a business somewhere."

My racing mind retrieved a memory: Al cleaning his nails. With a knife that sprang open. I swayed woozily and inched back closer to him.

Houseman laughed, nervous but cocky. "Think I can't put a couple of holes through the dial in that safe and open it?" He jerked his head toward the back wall where two large paintings showed flashy racing cars on country roads. "If you're smart you're going to shut up and give me every dollar that's in there."

He thought he was in charge. I had a feeling he was wrong. I swayed again, repositioning slightly. Beale had glanced at me from time to time, but his attention was mostly on Houseman.

"Better hope it's a lot of loot," I said. "Bank robbery brings the federal boys in. You'll need to go pretty far to outrun them."

"Bank robbery?" Houseman's voice veered to soprano. "What the hell are you talking about?"

My fingers found the chain that led to the knife in Al's pocket. I slid it out slowly ... slowly ... praying my body hid it from view. I wasn't entirely sure yet what I meant to do.

"Didn't he tell you, Lyle? I didn't think so." If I caused Houseman to panic, there was no predicting consequences but I needed time. The rope that bound my wrists had made my fingers half numb. "That's his real plan. The reason he wanted dope on working those burglar alarms." My exploring fingers found the spot and pressed and there was a click. I ducked my head pretending a cough. "The others—" I coughed again, arching my back and forcing my wrists apart enough to ease the knife beneath the rope and began to saw. "A bank's his real target. The break-ins at the other places have been—"

"Is she telling the truth? She is, isn't she? Get up and open the safe you son-of-a-bitch!"

I saw the danger. "No! Don't let–"

Too late.

Under guise of complying, Beale rammed his rolling chair back into Houseman. There was a cry of rage, a shot. The two men spun like dancers with arms locked overhead. Another shot. A yelp so filled with agony my hair stood up. One figure crumpled. I scarcely had time to recognize that it was Beale turning toward me. I flinched, anticipating the shot that marked my own demise.

FORTY-FIVE

Beale waggled the gun in his hand.

"Don't even think of it, Miss Sullivan."

His eyes flicked to the weapon by the dead bodyguard. With his heel he hitched it back and kicked it into the room's far corner. Stepping behind his chair he did the same to the other gun Houseman had held, the one not currently in his own hand.

"And you might as well give up trying to work your hands free. I'm sure Al took extra care when he tied you up."

I thanked several saints he didn't know why I really was wiggling. An animal keening issued from Houseman. He lay on his back a few feet beyond the bodyguard. He was clutching his belly, his hands oozing red.

"A girl's got to do what a girl's got to do," I said dry mouthed.

Beale chuckled. "Suit yourself."

With vicious swiftness he turned and planted a kick in Houseman's ribs. I closed my eyes. But I resumed sawing away at the rope.

"And you, you gutless sissy." He kicked Houseman's leg this time. "Did you really think I'd let you walk out of here after you killed three of my men? How'd you get the one outside without anybody hearing?"

"Drugged. Just drugged," Houseman whimpered. "You ... tricked me...."

"You tricked yourself thinking I'd take the chances I have for the piddling amount you paid me to settle a score with a boss who didn't think you farted gold."

Beale kicked him a third time, this one close to his injured belly. The howl was excruciating. I thought I felt an easing of the rope at my wrists.

"Think you're smart, don't you? Smarter than everyone."

Apart from the door Al had pushed me through, the only way out of the room was through two windows high in the wall on the side where Beale was standing. His guarantee no one could shoot him from outside. Too high to jump through, even if I could outrun a bullet and didn't mind hurling myself through glass.

"Those places we've been knocking over aren't worth peanuts," Beale was saying. "But you didn't even have spine enough for that – for your own plan – once it got started."

Beale was circling Houseman now, the gun hanging casually at his side. Its barrel jeered at the man on the floor.

"There I am dealing with real problems. A Cincinnati outfit trying to muscle in on my territory. And right in the midst of it you come bellyaching how Al sent Benny Norris to give you a message and now he can recognize you – a two-bit sad sack I kept on the payroll because he didn't ask questions and couldn't add two and two on his fingers!"

Houseman writhed, probably terrified he'd be shot again. Which he would.

"When that page you'd scribbled on for Al went missing, you panicked. Whined like the spoiled little mama's boy you are. Started telling me how I should run things. How Al had botched things with the paperclip salesman and I put up with too many mistakes. I got news for you, pal. The only mistake I made was thinking you had guts enough to see this through."

"You made another one, Beale." His head jerked up and we locked gazes. "Benny Norris wasn't as dumb as you thought." The rope around my wrists was down to a thread. I needed a breather to let blood return to my fingers and figure out how to keep the ends of the rope from flopping into view when I severed it. "It was Benny who found the page with the drawings on it – or took it – when it went missing. All the time you were roughing up Peter Stowe and sending Benny to threaten me trying to find it, the sleazy jerk didn't even know that's what you were hunting. Because he was just your errand boy and occasional bruiser, not privy to anything.

"Thing is, Beale, he liked his job. It made him feel important. He probably had no idea why Houseman was making a stink over him, just that he was. He was worried you'd fire him to pacify Houseman. Didn't even know Houseman's name, just that he had dough, and that guys with dough usually get their way. However he came by the list, he kept it as insurance you wouldn't give him the sack." I sat stock still severing the final threads of the rope and catching them before they could fall. "Guess Benny didn't figure on getting a slug in the back of the head for all those years of not asking questions. Not that the world isn't better without him."

"He got a slug in the head for not getting anything out of you," Beale snapped. "Benny knew how to throw a scare into people. Dames especially. He claimed you wouldn't talk. I thought he was holding out." He aimed another kick at Houseman, ever careful his shoe didn't get so much as a speck of blood. "Because of you. Because you kept whining he knew too much and pissing yourself thinking he was a risk."

This time Houseman's cry was barely a whimper. His breath had begun to sound raspy. I swayed, pretending dizziness. It allowed me to tuck the cut rope under my fanny and inch a bit closer to Al's gun. But not close enough.

"Where was it?" Beale asked, eyes glittering at me. "Where had he stashed that damned list of addresses?"

"Doesn't matter." I needed to get closer to the gun. Spin it so the grip was toward me.

Beale lifted his own gun demanding my answer.

"If you – oh, Jesus!" I played my other tidbit from Mrs. Salmon the madam. "What are you doing with a rat in here? That your idea of a pet?" I stared fixedly at the floor beneath a stand that held a fancy radio.

Flesh contracted around Beale's eyes, but he didn't fall for it.

"Go on and shoot me before that thing gets me!"

I pushed myself back, cringing. My voice went higher. "Come on, Beale. Shoot me and let's get it over. I had a rat bite me once when I was a kid."

His gaze jigged. I swiveled and scooted.

"There aren't any rats in this house." All the silk had gone from his voice. A muscle in his top lip twitched. "You're right, though, I am going to shoot you. Between Lyle's rashness and your tale of having that list, I'll have to speed up the bank job. Tonight's too late, but tomorrow should still work fine. Better than originally planned, in fact. Lyle doesn't show up for work. His car's abandoned down in Cincinnati near the train station. What a pity you're found in the trunk, tied up and killed by the gun they find in his car.

"All the pieces will fall into place. How he planned everything and took off with the loot. You started to figure it out but got too close." He laughed. "Even if that list gets to your cop pals and they work out what it means, there's nothing on it that will alert them to a bank robbery. When the bank gets hit I'll make sure to have a good alibi.

Didn't Benny warn you going up against me was no game for a dame?"

The carpet around where Houseman lay was soaked now. One way or the other, he wasn't going to make it.

My fingertips brushed Al's gun. The wrong end. It shifted away. Then I felt the merest nudge of the butt. Keeping my eyes on the nonexistent rat I sucked in breath and drew up my knees. Beale's eyes flicked just long enough for the first joint of my middle finger to snag the gun and give it a small tug.

"You won't get away with it, Beale."

"Oh no?"

Almost lazily the gun in his hand began to rise. There was no time left for stealth. I dove and yanked Al's pistol grip into still-clumsy fingers. My shot went wide as I rolled and fired. Beale's own shot hit air where I'd sat a second earlier. Clamping both hands on the gun I held, I fired at his heart.

His arms jerked out. He went back like someone who'd slipped on the ice. The door to the hall burst open as a figure in blue somersaulted in low, his shotgun delivering a blast that would have torn Beale half in two if he'd still been standing.

For several long seconds the shotgun's echo blotted out all other sound. Images swirled. I remained crouched, too drained to rise. Aware of cops rushing in. Aware of one hunting a pulse in Houseman, then shaking his head. Aware of Connelly, still on his knees and leaning against the shotgun, his breathing visibly ragged as he looked at me.

"Jaysus, lad! Where'd you learn a stunt like that?" someone asked clapping him on the shoulder.

He didn't respond.

Later I would absorb what voices around me were trying to tell me: Ed Viner had found my note on the door and guessed what it meant. Concerned for my safety, he'd gone to the cops. Flora was already there, pressing them to find Peter and Thelma. Their intersecting stories spurred the police to look for my car. The cops who found it also spotted a building on fire, and Thelma and Peter stumbling to safety.

Right then those bits and pieces were lost in the nightmare of what had occurred here tonight. My exhausted mind grasped only two things. One was that I'd killed a man. In his entire career my dad had never killed anyone. The other was that Connelly had just risked his neck to save me.

I met his eyes. They were pinched at the edges.

"You okay?" he asked.

I nodded.

Handing the shotgun to a passing cop he finally rose. His gaze swept the scene: Al dead by the door. The bodyguard. Houseman. Beale. And me – the only one left alive.

He started to speak and cleared his throat and tried again.

"Looks like you were at one hell of a party."

He offered a hand to help me up.

I held on tight.

The End

ABOUT THE AUTHOR

M. Ruth Myers is a former reporter and feature writer for daily papers including *The Journal Herald* (Dayton). Most of her novels have been published in foreign translations as well as in English.

Ruth's time at the typewriter allows her husband to climb on the roof with untied shoelaces and the cat to sprawl on the kitchen table without reprimand.

Her Maggie Sullivan mysteries continue with the novel TOUGH COOKIE.

Readers are welcome to contact Ruth at her website http://www.mruthmyers.com.

37797879R00165

Made in the USA
Middletown, DE
02 March 2019